MURDER IN ABSENCE
A **CRIME CLUB** *Novel*

A Crime Club Detective Story

FIRST, there was a murder in Hembury in the Home Counties, then Desmond and Mavis Merrion went on a cruise—two events with no apparent connection between them. But as the freighter *Ballerina*, with her small complement of passengers, steams between the ports of the Eastern Mediterranean, Beirut, Famagusta, Istanbul, and then remote Fetiyeh, it becomes clear that Merrion is once more faced with a mystery. Tensions rise aboard the *Ballerina* as the odious Mr. Wilberton takes increasingly to drink, the sprightly Mr. Pulham to women, and Mrs. Stewart-Patterson, the formidable Scotswoman, resolutely continues her sketching. Once again Merrion solves a multiple crime in a story of extraordinary ingenuity and suspense.

By the Same Author

HEIR TO MURDER

MURDER ON DUTY   MURDER OUT OF SCHOOL

BEWARE YOUR NEIGHBOUR   A VILLAGE AFRAID

GROUND FOR SUSPICION   LOOK ALIVE

DEATH TAKES THE LIVING   DEVIL'S RECKONING

DEATH IN SHALLOW WATER   A WILL IN THE WAY

HEIR TO LUCIFER   SITUATION VACANT

THE CAT JUMPS   EARLY MORNING MURDER

NOT A LEG TO STAND ON   THREE CORPSE TRICK

FOUR-PLY YARN   MURDER M.D.

DEAD STOP   THIS UNDESIRABLE RESIDENCE

MURDER IN ABSENCE

by
MILES BURTON

Published for
THE CRIME CLUB
by COLLINS 14 ST JAMES'S PLACE
LONDON

PRINTED IN GREAT BRITAIN
COLLINS CLEAR-TYPE PRESS: LONDON AND GLASGOW
1954

CHAPTER I

BESIDE THE entrance of an office in the flourishing market town of Hembury, a brass plate bore the words ' H. Jones and Son, Estate Agents, Auctioneers and Valuers.' On the morning of Tuesday, 15th September, two men sat in one of the rooms within, going through the correspondence which had arrived by the first post.

The business of H. Jones and Son had been started in the early years of the century by Henry Jones, a well-known local character. But Henry had been dead many years, to be succeeded by his son, who, comparatively recently, had taken into partnership Tom White. The business, though not on a large scale, was prosperous, and the time of both partners was usually fully occupied. As indeed was that of their senior clerk, Miss Pauline Chirton, an attractive and extremely capable woman in her early thirties.

Rufus Jones took a letter from the tray, and perused it. He was a man of forty-five or thereabouts, heavily built and inclined to stoutness. His expression was one of professional good humour, and he had the gift of making himself superficially pleasant to his clients. But, behind the wide-framed horn spectacles which he habitually wore, a keen observer, detecting a look of malice in his weakly-coloured eyes, might have doubted his true character. Perhaps his doubts might have been without foundation. Though Rufus was not the popular figure his father had been, no reflection had ever been cast upon his business integrity.

Tom White was of quite a different type. Whereas his cousin was dark, he was fair, with that fairness which gives the impression of extreme youth. At first glance Tom, with his open ingenuous countenance, might well have been taken as little more than a schoolboy. Actually, he was thirty-one, and had been married for over two years. In this again he differed from his cousin, who had remained a bachelor. It should be added that Tom, despite his air of inexperience, had a remarkably shrewd head for business.

Rufus, having finished his perusal of the letter, handed it over to Tom. " Have a look at that," he said.

Tom took the letter and examined it. It was typed on a sheet of business note-paper, which bore the heading ' Podmores Ltd., Wholesale Grocers, Consort Square, Manchester.' It was addressed to ' H. Jones & Son, Estate Agents, Hembury' and ran as follows.

> ' Dear Sirs,
>
> With reference to your advertisement concerning Cherry Trees, Lingmarsh, I shall have occasion to be in Baleminster on Wednesday next, 16th September, and shall be glad of the opportunity of viewing the above property. I shall arrive at Baleminster from London on the 11.10 a.m. train, and shall be glad if your representative will meet me at the station and drive me to Lingmarsh. If the property is suitable to my requirements, I shall be prepared to conclude the matter then and there. Yours faithfully.'

The signature, in ink, was difficult to decipher. Two initials and a surname beginning with what looked like a P. The name of the firm printed at the head of the sheet suggested that it might be Podmore. The names of the directors were also printed at the head of the sheet, R. W. Podmore and A. F. Podmore. Yes, on closer inspection, the signature might be interpreted as R. W. Podmore.

Tom handed the letter back. " Mr. R. W. Podmore, I think," he remarked. " But I don't know what advertisement he can be referring to. We haven't advertised Cherry Trees for months."

" He's got hold of an old copy of some newspaper, I suppose," Rufus replied. " It might have been sold by this time, for all he knows. What he doesn't know is the state it's in. One look at it will be enough for him."

" Oh, it's not as bad as all that," said Tom cheerfully. " I was out that way the other day, and had a look round. The house is in quite good repair, and so is that cottage in the orchard. I'm bound to admit that the garden is hopelessly overgrown and that the paddock looks like a wilderness."

" Which is exactly what strikes a client's eye," Rufus

grumbled. "Mr. Podmore will turn it down as soon as he sees it."

"Oh, I don't know," Tom replied. "I can guess what it is. The two directors are father and son. Father means to retire to a nice little place in the country, leaving son to carry on. The owner's instructions to us are that she will accept any reasonable offer. If Mr. Podmore can get the place cheap, he may make a hobby of putting the property in order."

"When you've been in this business as long as I have, you won't be so optimistic," said Rufus. "You know very well that Cherry Trees has been hanging on our hands for over a year, and that nobody wants the place as a gift. It isn't very likely that even a retiring wholesale grocer will fall in love with it at first sight."

"We shall have to give Mr. Podmore the chance, anyhow," Tom remarked.

"I know that," Rufus replied. "Wednesday, 16th September, he says. That's tomorrow. You can't meet him, for you've got that valuation at Wodeley Manor, and it'll take you all day. I'll go myself."

He laid the letter aside, and took the next from the tray. As he read it, his features relaxed, until at last he laughed aloud. "Here you are, Tom," he said, handing it over. "Here's something to open your eyes."

Tom took the letter. It was written in ink, in a rather shaky but still legible hand, on a sheet of plain note-paper. The address written at the head was 14 Blundell Street, Birmingham, and below this, in bold letters across the page, were the words ' For the personal attention of Mr. Jones.'

The letter went on. ' Dear Sir, you must be aware that long ago I asked my nephew to find me a house in your town. He has so far been too stupid to be able to do this, and I have decided to take the matter into my own hands. I am coming to Hembury next Thurdsay, when I shall expect you to meet me in person. I don't want to be put off by any understrapper. You will then arrange for me to see any houses which are likely to suit me. Yours faithfully.' This time there was no doubt about the bold signature, ' Jasper L. Wilberton.'

Tom laughed in his turn, for Mr. Bewdley's uncle was a long-standing joke in the office. Mr. Horace Bewdley was an inoffensive, if rather fussy person, a director of Joseph Ruilett and Sons, a firm of millers of considerable local importance. It was long ago that he had first approached H. Jones and Son on behalf of his uncle, who now lived in Birmingham but wished to move to Hembury. Particulars of every property which came into the market had been given to Mr. Bewdley, who had viewed each in turn and, presumably, reported to his uncle, whom neither of the partners had ever seen. But in every case there had been some objection. The price was too high, or the position was wrong, or the rooms were too poky, or the garden was too large, or the staircase too steep. It seemed that Mr. Bewdley's uncle must be difficult to please.

" Well, I'm blessed ! " Tom exclaimed when he had run through the letter. " So we're going to see the old boy at last, I was beginning to believe that there was no such person. Dictatorial old chap he seems to be, too."

" Insolent's the word " Rufus replied. " He orders me about as if I were his office boy. He hasn't even the politeness to say what time he's coming. I can't hang about for him all day, for I've got that auction at Nettlebed Farm on Thursday afternoon. I suppose you know Bewdley's away ? Gone abroad somewhere ? "

" I had heard something about it," said Tom. " But I imagine he'll be back by Thursday. One supposes that his uncle will stay with him while he's here ? "

Rufus shook his head. " I know for certain that Bewdley isn't expected back for quite a while yet. And his house is being decorated while he's away. If his uncle means to stay here, he'll have to put up at the Three Crowns."

" By Jove " Tom exclaimed. " I believe I can guess what's in the wind. Bewdley doesn't want his uncle here, sitting on his doorstep. He may be a dutiful nephew, but he'd rather the old boy stayed in Birmingham. That's why he's reported unfavourably to him on every property we've offered him. And now Mr. Wilberton has smelt a rat. He's coming to have a look round for himself while his nephew is out of the way."

" That may be right," Rufus said dryly. " Not having met Mr. Wilberton, I can't say. Any friction there may be between uncle and nephew is no business of ours. We've got to try to satisfy this client of ours. I know what he wants, or at least what Bewdley says he wants. A small house, in the town, or at least within easy walking distance of the shops. I shouldn't wonder if what he really means is within easy distance of the pubs. It's obviously no good taking him out see to places like Cherry Trees. Let's have a look, now."

He opened a drawer and took out a file containing descriptions of various properties, each on a separate sheet, and frowned as he turned them over. " There's nothing here that Bewdley hasn't already seen. Except Mavourneen, which was put in our hands last week. The position's all right, in Silver Street. Three reception, four bed, two bath, conservatory. Probably a bit too big for Uncle Jasper. Besides, the price is a bit stiff. Six thousand seven hundred and fifty. There's nothing else that Bewdley hasn't told him about ? "

" Does that matter ? " Tom asked. " If my guess is right, Mr. Wilberton no longer trusts his nephew's judgment. He practically says so himself. He may take to one of these properties if he sees it for himself."

" We'll have to chance it," Rufus replied. He selected half a dozen of the sheets and handed them to Tom. " That's the best we can do, Ring up the occupiers, and ask them if it would be convenient for us to bring a client to view on Thursday, we're sorry we can't say at what time. If he comes in the morning, I'll take him round. If he doesn't, you'll have to."

" He won't like that " Tom objected. " He's most insistent upon dealing with you in person. He'd probably regard me as an understrapper, as he puts it."

" Confound the fellow ! " Rufus exclaimed violently. " I feel inclined to tell him to go to blazes. He'll probably waste everybody's time for the whole day, then say that he's seen nothing to suit him. However, it's never. been our policy to offend a client, and in this case as he's Bewdley's uncle, we shall have to be particularly nice to him."

He paused for a moment, frowning at the papers on the desk before him. " I'll treat him as a very special case," he went on. " It's Bewdley I'm thinking about. If it wasn't for him, I wouldn't put myself out. If Mr. Wilberton comes in the morning, well and good. If he doesn't, I'll wait for him here and you'll have to take the auction at Nettlebed Farm. It'll be an infernal nuisance, but I don't see how it's to be helped."

There was nothing else in the post of any great interest, and Tom White went to his own room. He was relieved at his

partner's decision to take the responsibility for Mr. Wilberton
upon his own shoulders, for he threatened to be an awkward
client to deal with. Mr. Bewdley had hinted more than once
that he was apt to be difficult. Rufus must be impressed by his
importance, for never before had he consented to abandon an
auction over which he was to preside. But then Mr. Bewdley
had influence locally, and he might be resentful if his uncle
were not treated with all possible deference.

Tom busied himself on the telephone, making the necessary
arrangements to view on Thursday. This done, he allowed his
thoughts to dwell for a few minutes on Cherry Trees. How
often had he driven clients to the place, without eliciting any
response whatever? It was the sort of property nobody seemed
to want, remote, a good mile from the village of Lingmarsh
along a winding country road. No main services whatever,
water to be pumped by hand from a doubtful well. It would
cost almost more than the property was worth to put it into
any sort of decent order. Tom had very little hope that Mr.
Podmore would fall for it.

Other matters occupied his mind for the rest of the day, and
at six o'clock he went home. He and Betty, his wife, lived in a
small flat not very far from the office. During the day Betty
was not idle, for she acted as secretary to the local Red Cross
organisation. She had just come home when Tom arrived at
the flat, and, as usual, he gave her a brief sketch of his day's
work at the office. Betty was the sort of person whose shrewd-
ness and common sense could be relied upon.

She fully shared the old joke about Mr. Bewdley's uncle,
and was immensely intrigued that this mythical person was
actually to appear. " How marvellous ! " she exclaimed. " I
do wonder what he looks like. I must try to catch a glimpse of
him. Do you think he'll be as nice as Mr. Bewdley ? "

Tom smiled. " His letter doesn't suggest that he possesses
any particular charm."

" Well, he won't be your funeral, you say," Betty replied.
" Perhaps he'll turn out to be a disagreeable old curmudgeon.
I rather hope that he does, and that he leads Rufus a dance all
over the town."

" Don't talk like that," Tom said gently. " I know very well
that you don't like Rufus."

" You know too that if he weren't your partner and your

cousin, I should tell him to get away and stay away," Betty replied.

" Oh, it's only his way," said Tom. " You must try to put up with him. He doesn't mean any harm really."

Betty looked at him speculatively. " Are you quite blind ? Or is it merely the instinct which impels one male of the species to support another ? Rufus would mean all the harm in the world if I gave him half a chance. It's lucky for you that I'm a faithful wife, and that I hate him. There, don't let's talk about him any more. Tell me what you've been doing."

Wednesday came, and as Tom reached the office, his cousin drove up in his new, big, resplendent car. This was not used for ordinary work-a-day occasions. It had been bought solely to impress clients who had to be driven about the district. Tom wondered whether its magnificence would serve as an inducement to Mr. Podmore to buy Cherry Trees.

The routine of the office went forward as usual, the partners going through the correspondence together. That morning it contained nothing more than mere matters of routine. This formality over, Rufus announced his intention of setting out. " It won't take me all that time to get to Baleminster station," he said. " But as I've got to go there, I may as well call on one or two of our colleagues in the town."

" I shall be starting for Wodeley Manor very soon," Tom replied. " And I'm not likely to get back till fairly late."

Rufus nodded. " That'll be all right. We can trust our excellent Miss Chirton to hold the fort. Anyway, I expect I shall be in the office myself after lunch. One glance at Cherry Trees will probably be enough for Mr. Podmore. Unless I can persuade him to let me take him round one or two other properties, he'll most likely take the next train back to London. Well, I'll be off."

It was not much later that Tom left the office in his turn, in the small and unpretentious car that was used when clients were not to be conveyed. He and the young clerk he took with him reached Wodeley Manor and set to work without delay. The owner had recently died, and a valuation of effects for probate had become necessary.

The house was full of goods and chattels of every description and of varying worth. Tom and his assistant worked at the

job all the morning, then desisted to eat the sandwiches they
had brought with them. This took no more than a few minutes,
after which they resumed their task. In spite of this assiduity,
it was past four o'clock when the job was finally completed.

As soon as Tom got to the office, he went to his partner's
room, to report the completion of the valuation and to ask
what Mr. Podmore had thought of Cherry Trees. But he found
the room empty. He supposed that Rufus must have been
called out on some other business, for he could surely not be
spending the whole of the afternoon with his client. As Tom
crossed the passage to his own room, Pauline Chirton appeared
from hers. She was a tall, graceful woman, who usually wore a
particularly winning smile. But on this occasion she looked
unusually disapproving. " Hallo, Miss Chirton," Tom greeted
her. " I've just come back from Wodeley Manor. Mr. Jones
has gone out again, I see."

" Mr. Jones has not been back since he left here this morning," she replied meaningly.

" By Jove ! " Tom explained. " He's hanging on to that
client of his like grim death. I expect Mr. Podmore wouldn't
have anything to do with Cherry Trees, and Mr. Jones is
taking him round everything else we've got."

" I don't think that's it, Mr. White," Miss Chirton replied.
" Mr. Jones sent a telegram. I have put it on your table."

Tom went into his room, to find the telegram on his blotter.
He picked it up and read it. It was addressed to the firm's
telegraphic address, Estates, Hembury, and had been sent
from Baleminster at 1.25 p.m. The text was ' Detained here
over tomorrow. Apologise Wilberton pay him special attention, Jones.'

CHAPTER II

TOM FOUND the contents of the telegram so amazing that for a moment he stared at it speechlessly. Miss Chirton had followed him into the room, and stood silently at his elbow. He turned upon her, waving the telegram before her face. "You've read this, of course?" he asked. "What does it mean?"

"I really couldn't say, Mr. White," she replied demurely. "So far as I know, Mr. Jones did not expect to be detained in Baleminster."

"I'm sure he didn't," said Tom. "He'd made up his mind to wait here tomorrow for Mr. Wilberton, all day if necessary. He told me that if he didn't turn up till the afternoon, I should have to take the auction at Nettlebed Farm. He must have something very important indeed on hand to make him change his plans like this."

Miss Chirton made no helpful suggestion, but her expression of disapproval deepened. "I have no doubt that Mr. Jones considered it very important," she replied significantly.

Tom slapped the telegram down on the table. "Why did he send this?" he demanded. "It tells us nothing. Why didn't he ring up and explain? Then we should have known where we were."

"Perhaps Mr. Jones did not wish to explain what had detained him, Mr. White," she remarked icily.

For a moment their eyes met, then each averted their glance in some confusion. The senior partner's private affairs were no concern of theirs. But this was a business matter. He was burking an appointment which he had himself considered to be of the first importance. He still considered it so, as his reference to Mr. Wilberton showed. Never before had he allowed pleasure to come before business. Such private affairs as he might have had he had invariably relegated to his hours of leisure.

It was not a subject to be pursued between them. "We must make the best of the situation," said Tom. "If Mr. Wilberton comes here to-morrow morning, I'll do my best to

13

cope with him. If he doesn't, you'll have to. I must take that
auction, whatever happens. And if Mr. Wilberton goes off
in a huff it won't be our fault."

" How would it be to send Mr. Wilberton a telegram,
asking him to postpone his visit ? " Miss Chirton suggested.

Tom shook his head. " Better not do that. He doesn't
sound the sort of person who would appreciate his plans being
upset. No, let him come, and we'll do our best to tame him.
We've had difficult clients to deal with before now."

As soon as he got home, Tom told Betty of the inexplicable
telegram. " It strikes me all of a heap," he went on. " When
Rufus left this morning he was determined to put everything
else aside in order to meet Mr. Wilberton personally. And then
comes this shattering wire. Detained here over to-morrow.
What the devil does he mean ? "

" It's perfectly plain to me," Betty replied. " Rufus is as
usual chasing some woman."

" That's what Miss Chirton thinks," said Tom. " Though I
hasten to add that she didn't say so."

" Pauline Chirton is an observant woman," Betty replied.
" She's told me, between ourselves, several things about Rufus
which I'm not going to repeat. Don't misunderstand me. She's
perfectly capable of taking care of herself, I assure you. And
we needn't enquire too closely what Rufus is up to. He'll
have some perfectly plausible story about urgent business
when he comes back, you may be sure."

Tom smiled. " You women seem to have made up your
minds. Whatever Rufus's amorous failings may be, he doesn't
discuss them with me. The fact remains that he's gone off
leaving me to hold the baby. He's never done such a thing
before."

" From what you tell me, you'll find Mr. Bewdley's uncle a
pretty fractious baby," said Betty. " Never mind, it will be a
valuable experience for a young house-agent. I should love to
watch you soothing him."

" With any luck, it'll fall to Miss Chirton to deal with him,"
Tom replied. " Beauty and the Beast. By the way, I wonder
if Rufus has let Mrs. Paston know that he won't be back ?
If he hasn't, she'll be in a terrible stew when he doesn't come
home to-night. I'd better run round and see her. She's so
deaf that she never takes in what one tells her on the phone."

Rufus lived in the house which his father had owned, Number Twelve, King Street, the best residential quarter of Hembury. It did not take Tom long to get there. He rang the bell, and Mrs. Paston, Rufus's housekeeper appeared. " Good evening, Mrs. Paston," Tom shouted. " Has Mr. Rufus let you know that he won't be back to-night ? "

Mrs. Paston smiled benignly. " No, Mr. White, I've heard nothing from Master Rufus. I'm not to expect him, then ? "

" That's right," Tom shouted back. " He's been detained in Baleminster over to-morrow. Good-bye."

As he walked back home, Tom reflected that Mrs. Paston had taken the matter very calmly. As though it was nothing new for Rufus to spend a night away without giving her warning. She had known him all her life, had, in fact, been his nurse since his earliest infancy. No doubt he told her that his absences from home were occasioned by business. Knowing him as she must, she probably saw through that pretext clearly enough. But one would expect her to be indulgent to his feelings.

That might be good enough for Mrs. Paston. But Tom found the affair far more serious. It was not that, as he had expressed it to Betty, he had been left to hold the baby. That was all in the day's work. It was the principle which bothered him. If Rufus was going to neglect the business in pursuit of his pleasures, the outlook was not particularly rosy. Tom did not as yet feel competent to take the whole burden of H. Jones & Son on his own shoulders.

He said no more to Betty that evening, feeling that the subject of Rufus was better avoided between them. On his way to the office on Thursday morning he wondered whether there might be a letter from Rufus in the post. But there was no word from him. Miss Chirton, bright and helpful as ever, made no allusion to the senior partner's absence. There was nothing, beyond the impending visit of Mr. Wilberton, which demanded his personal attention.

Tom, settled down in his room, found himself unable to concentrate. Every time his telephone bell rang, he anticipated some message from Rufus. But in every case it was merely some trifling matter which could be dealt with out of hand. That morning there were as usual several callers at the office. Whenever he heard footsteps in the passage, Tom paused and listened. Not for the voice of Rufus, but for the call which would announce to him the arrival of Mr. Bewdley's uncle.

But the morning passed without Mr. Wilberton putting in an appearance. Tom collected what he would need for the auction, then went to Miss Chirton's room. " I shall have to go along now," he said. " I shall snatch a spot of lunch, then I shall have to go straight to Nettlebed Farm. I can't say when I shall be back. It looks as though you'll have to deal with Mr. Wilberton. I'm awfully sorry."

Miss Chirton smiled at him. " Don't worry about that, Mr. White. It's not your fault. I'll do my best. Perhaps he won't turn out to be so very alarming, after all."

It was between two and half-past when the girl in the enquiry office heard what sounded like a hostile raid. Heavy footsteps in the passage, accompanied by the thumping of a stick on the floor. The door of the enquiry office bore the words ' Knock and enter.' The visitor accepted this at its full value. He hammered violently on the door, apparently with the knob of his stick, then flung it wide open. A portentious figure presented itself. To the girl's startled eyes he appeared gigantic, but actually the visitor was no more than average height. He had coarse features, bushy eyebrows and prominent false teeth. His massive body seemed to be as round as a barrel, but in contrast his limbs were long and muscular, like a gorilla's. He carried a walking stick as thick as a young sapling.

So much the girl took in when the visitor spoke, in a harsh disagreeable voice. " My name is Jasper Lawrence Wilberton. I have come here to see Mr. Jones, and I don't expect to be kept waiting."

The girl had been schooled in the part she was to play when Mr. Wilberton called. But this startling appearance unnerved her for the moment. " Mr Jones——" she began, then suddenly recollecting herself, " Will you come this way, please ? "

She led him to Miss Chirton's room, and she opened the door. " Mr. Wilberton to see Mr. Jones," she announced. Then, without waiting for the storm to burst, she ran back to her own place.

Miss Chirton rose from her chair. " Please come in and sit

down, Mr. Wilberton," she said ingratiatingly. But Mr. Wilberton seemed stuck still where he was, glaring at her. " I didn't come here to sit down ! " he exclaimed, emphasising his words with a resounding thump of his stick on the floor. " I came to see Mr. Jones. He must have received my letter, surely ? Where is he ? "

" Mr. Jones has unfortunately been prevented from being here to-day," Miss Chirton replied. " We hoped we should have seen you this morning, when the junior partner, Mr. White, could have attended to you. This afternoon, however, he has had to conduct an auction at an outlying farm."

" How the dickens did you expect me to get here from Birmingham in the morning ? " Mr. Wilberton demanded. " I have never been subjected to such treatment in my life. I write to Mr. Jones, telling him that I wish to see him today, and when I arrive I find that he isn't here, or his partner either. I was a business man myself before my retirement, but I never carried on my business in this fashion."

" It is most unfortunate, Mr. Wilberton," Miss Chirton replied. " Mr. Jones gave instruction that we were to offer you the most profound apologies on his behalf. He was quite unable to put off a prior appointment. But, in the unavoidable absence of the partners, I feel sure that I shall be able to help you."

Tom was fond of saying that Pauline Chirton's smile could melt a stone. It certainly seemed to have its effect upon Mr. Wilberton for at least he took the chair she indicated to him. " I must make the best of it, I suppose," he grumbled ungraciously. " I don't want to have come all this way for nothing. I expected Mr. Jones to find me a house in this town. I told my idiot of a nephew long ago that I wanted one, but he's done nothing about it."

Miss Chirton picked up a sheaf of orders to view. " We have looked out half a dozen or so that might suit you, Mr. Wilberton. Mr. Bewdley has advised us of your requirements. Perhaps now that you are here, you would like to look round these properties yourself ? "

Mr. Wilberton snatched the papers from her and glanced through them. " They don't sound too bad," he muttered after a while. " But then you house-agents always dress up your geese to look like swans. I daresay when I see them I

B

shall find them very different from the particulars you give here. That's why I wanted to see Mr. Jones himself, and make him understand that I wanted the truth and no nonsense." He looked up, with an unpleasant leer. " You'll take me round and show me where these places are, young lady ? "

" I'm very sorry, Mr. Wilberton, but I can't do that," she replied primly. " I couldn't possibly leave the office when both the partners are away. But I will certainly send a clerk with you."

" I don't want a clerk trailing at my heels," Mr. Wilberton exclaimed angrily. " I expected to be treated with far more consideration than this. A firm which treats its clients in such an off-hand way cannot expect to continue in business very much longer. I shall write to Mr. Jones and tell him so."

" I am very sorry, Mr. Wilberton," Miss Chirton replied. " Had you given us longer notice of your visit Mr. Jones would have been able to arrange to meet you. Won't you let me send for a clerk to show you where the properties are ? "

" I don't want a clerk, I tell you," Mr. Wilberton exclaimed. " I'm quite capable of finding my own way round. I've got a tongue in my head to ask, haven't I ? Has my fool of a nephew seen these places ? "

" I believe Mr. Bewdley has seen them all, with one exception, Mavourneen," she replied.

" Silly name," Mr. Wilberton growled. " Fancy having an address like that ! I'm a plain man, and I like a plain number. Number fourteen Blundell Street is a good enough address for me. As for my nephew, I wouldn't trust him to buy me a pennyworth of tintacks. I'll go round and have a look at these shacks of yours for myself."

Miss Chirton rose to show him out, but he completely ignored her. She was left to watch that barrel-like body, with the long swinging limbs, shambling out through the doorway. Its progress down the passage was punctuated by the thumping of the heavy walking stick. The slamming of the outer door was enough to shatter the glass panels.

Left to herself, Miss Chirton gave full vent to her indignation. A piece of waste-paper had fallen to the floor. She picked it up and screwed it violently in her hands, wishing it had been Mr. Wilberton's neck. In common with most other people, she liked Mr. Bewdley. He was always cheerful, and his manners were above reproach. The discovery that he had such an absolutely hateful uncle was a definite shock to her. It seemed somehow unnatural. She had been fully prepared to find Mr. Wilberton inclined to be crotchety. That he should be preposterously rude and overbearing was incredible. The last straw had been the leer with which he had suggested she should take him round. And to address her as young lady! Insolent old brute!

It was some minutes before she could calm herself sufficiently to resume her interrupted work. But she was doomed to further interruptions. That afternoon there were several callers at the office, and, in the absence of both partners, she was compelled to interview them all. During the next couple of hours her thoughts were distracted from her disagreeable visitor. Until the flinging open of the outer door and the savage thumping of the stick on the floor of the passage heralded the return of Mr. Wilberton.

He did not observe the formality of announcing himself at the enquiry office, but walked straight into Miss Chirton's room. He strode up to her desk and pounded it with his fist. " I never saw such a collection of hovels in my life!" he bawled. " Don't you understand that it's a house I want, not a pigsty? If that's the best you people can do, you'd better shut up shop right away and try to earn your living by singing in the streets."

" I'm sorry you weren't able to find anything to suit you, Mr. Wilberton," Miss Chirton replied, curbing her wrath.

" Suit me!" he exclaimed. " Most of the places you sent me to wouldn't suit a superannuated scavenger. There's only one with any possibilities. The Chestnuts. It's a rabbit-hutch, and it'll want a lot doing to it before it's fit for a decent man to live in. And I shouldn't dream of paying anything like the price the fellow wants for it."

" We will approach our client and ask him what is the lowest offer he would accept," said Miss Chirton.

" He'll have to accept my price or leave it," Mr. Wilberton grunted. " By the look of him, he wants any money he can get. Anyhow, I shall have to talk it over with my sister. I can't waste any more time here. It'll be close on midnight before I get back to Birmingham as it is. And you might tell your Mr. Jones that I consider his failure to be here to meet me most insulting. I'm not used to being treated in such a fashion."

With no word of farewell he shambled out of the room, leaving Miss Chirton speechless. His remark about Mr. Haughley, the owner of The Chestnuts, had literally taken her breath away. Looked as if he wanted any money he could get ! Why, Mr. Haughley was the leading builders' merchant in the district, and a personal friend of Mr. Jones. The only reason he wished to sell The Chestnuts was that he had bought a house at Triptown-on-Sea, whence he could drive daily to his business in Hembury. If he met with any impertinence from Mr. Wilberton, he would soon tell him where he got off.

Just before the office was due to close, Tom came in, looking quite pleased with himself. " The auction was a pretty good show," he said. " The stuff fetched more than I expected, and the farmer's full of beans. Any word from Mr. Jones ? "

Miss Chirton shook her head. " Nothing. But Mr. Wilberton has been, and I am thankful to say, gone."

Tom chuckled. " You didn't take to him, I gather ? "

" Take to him ! " she exclaimed in disgust. " I never met such an impossible man in my life. He's horrible to look at, and his behaviour is even worse. I hope to goodness he won't settle here, for I never want to set eyes on him again."

" Is there any likelihood of his settling here ? " Tom asked.

" He's got his eye on The Chestnuts," she replied. " I'll tell you all about that." She told him of her conversation with Mr. Wilberton and described his appearance. " He's positively revolting ! " she went on. " And he doesn't look all that old. Not so old as I should expect Mr. Bewdley's uncle to be, I mean."

" One's uncle needn't be so much older than one is oneself," Tom remarked. " He might be one's mother's very much younger brother. If he's such a Yahoo, that probably explains why Mr. Bewdley wasn't particularly anxious to have him here. I don't think it's very likely to come to anything. I'm pretty sure that Mr. Haughley won't consider any reduction of the price he has set on The Chestnuts. He's in no urgent hurry to sell the property."

" I hope he won't," Miss Chirton replied. " Mr. Wilberton has gone back to Birmingham, and I hope he'll stay there."

" Or in some other place, more remote and murky," said

Tom. " I'm sorry you had this unpleasantness. You seem to have got through it very well. At all events, Mr. Bewdley can't accuse us of not having done all we could for his uncle."

Tom fully expected his partner to turn up at the office on Friday morning. Detained over to-morrow, his telegram had said. That must surely mean that he would put in an appearance next day. But Rufus was not there at his usual hour, and the time passed without any sign from him. Tom had plenty of work to occupy him, and he was engaged on this when his telephone rang. As he reached for the instrument, he felt sure that the caller must be Rufus. But the clerk's voice disappointed him. " Mr. Haughley is on the line, asking for Mr. Jones. Will you take the call, Mr. White ? "

Tom agreed, and spoke. " This is Mr. White, Mr. Jones is not in this morning. Can I do anything for you, Mr. Haughley?"

" Good morning, White," came the reply. " Yes, you can do something for me. Don't send any more bears to my house as you did yesterday. I never met such an offensive brute in my life. I don't know how I refrained from chucking him out of the front door, neck and crop. He told me he was Bewdley's uncle. Next time I see Bewdley I shall tell him he'd better buy his uncle a collar and chain and lead him round the town to show his paces. The fellow's a bear, not a man, I tell you."

" I'm very sorry, Mr. Haughley," said Tom. " I understand there is a possibility that Mr. Wilberton may make an offer for The Chestnuts."

" Then I shall turn it down," Haughley replied firmly. " It would be a crime against Hembury society to sell my house to a creature like that. Try to find a buyer who is at least a human being. All right. Give my kind regards to Jones when he comes in. Good morning."

He rang off, and Tom smiled to himself. It hadn't been all prejudice on Miss Chirton's part, then. Mr. Haughley had taken as violent a dislike to Mr. Bewdley's uncle as she had. No wonder Bewdley had sent him unfavourable reports on all the properties he had viewed on his behalf ! He must regard the prospect of his uncle as a near neighbour with considerable alarm.

Both Tom and Miss Chirton were busy, and though they met at intervals that day for consultation, neither mentioned the continued absence of the senior partner. It seemed that they had tacitly agreed that it would be more tactful to avoid an awkward subject. Friday passed without any word from Rufus.

But Betty's curiosity was not so easily satisfied. As soon as her husband came home she tackled him on the subject. " Well, Rufus has returned from his adventure, I suppose? What tarradiddle did he offer to explain himself ? "

" He hasn't come back," Tom replied. " And there's been no word from him. I'm getting a bit worried."

" He must have found the lady very charming," Betty remarked acidly. " You won't see him till Monday now, for he's sure to spend the week-end in her company. I shouldn't worry my head about him if I were you. Bad pennies always turn up again sooner or later, we're told. You don't think he's absconded or anything like that, do you? "

Tom laughed. " There's nothing for him to abscond from. I don't suppose he owes any debts, and as far as I know the firm's accounts are in perfect order. Rufus is a rich man, I may remind you. His father made a pot of money, and left it to him. He never gave his nephew a thought, I regret to say. I've got an uncomfortable feeling that something may have happened to Rufus. Had a road accident, for instance."

" If anything like that had happened, you'd have heard about it long before now," said Betty reassuringly. " We know our Rufus. He's off on the jaunt somewhere with some enchanting blonde he's picked up. He knows you can carry on quite well till he chooses to come back. Anyhow, it's his affair, not ours."

CHAPTER III

BETTY'S PREDICTION proved to be correct, for Rufus did not return on Saturday. But Tom's anxieties increased when Monday morning came, without any word from him. So much so, that he was driven to consult Miss Chirton. " It's most extraordinary," he said. " Do you think we ought to do anything about Mr. Jones ? "

" I don't see what we can do, Mr. White," she replied. If Mr. Jones doesn't choose to let us know where he is and what he is doing, he would hardly welcome a search being made for him."

Tom was bound to agree that was true enough. On his way to the office he had called at Number Twelve, King Street, only to find that Mrs. Paston had no news of her master. But this seemed to cause her little concern. " I expect Master Rufus is taking a holiday," was her explanation. " It's about time he did, for he hasn't been away for so long for months. He'll be back again before long, I daresay."

So Tom decided to take no active steps. After all, what could he do ? Rufus's telegram had said that he had been detained. ' Over to-morrow ' might be interpreted as a vague and indefinite period. And if feminine intuition were correct, he wouldn't be likely to reveal his whereabouts. All the same, Tom found it rather disturbing.

He had barely settled down to work in his room, when he was informed that Mr. Draycott had called to see him. Mr. Draycott was an elderly man, living with his wife in a small house in the centre of the town. He had modest means and devoted his time to study, the fruits of which were displayed in occasional contributions to the learned journals. He and Mrs. Draycott had taken a fancy to Tom and Betty, who were not infrequent visitors to their house. But this was the first time either of them had called at the office. " Show Mr. Draycott into my room at once," Tom replied.

Mr. Draycott came in, briskly enough. He had the expression and bowed shoulders of a scholar, but was active

enough for his age. " Good morning, White," he said cheerfully. " Are you desperately busy this morning ? I'd like a
chat with you."

" I'm never too busy to see you, Mr. Draycott," Tom
replied. " My time is entirely at your disposal. Do sit down.
What do you want to talk to me about ? "

" Myself, mostly," Draycott said, taking the chair which
Tom offered him. " I'll put my case as briefly as possible.
I've been having trouble with my chest, and last week Dr.
Eleigh sent me up to London to see a specialist. You know
what those chaps are, and I won't trouble you by repeating all
he said. The long and short of it is that he told me I was
leading too sedentary a life. Spending too much of my time
indoors. He wants me to give that up, and be out of doors as
much as possible in future. Mild exercise and plenty of fresh
air. That's his prescription."

" I'm very sorry to hear about this trouble of yours, Mr.
Draycott," Tom said sincerely.

" Oh, it's nothing really," Draycott replied. " The specialist
told me I was good for many years yet, if I followed his advice.
My wife and I have been talking it over during the week-end,
and we're agreed that it would be great fun to start afresh at
our time of life. To find a little place in the country, with a
garden and a few fruit trees. That ought to provide me with
the open-air exercise I'm supposed to need. But it would
have to be cheap, for I haven't much capital to spare. That's
why I came to you this morning. You've got a ruin somewhere out Lingmarsh way, haven't you ? "

" Cherry Trees ? " Tom suggested. " It's not exactly a ruin,
but it's been sadly neglected. And I think it might be considered cheap. The owner's asking two thousand five hundred
for the property, which is quite reasonable. But, between
ourselves, she would accept any reasonable offer for a quick
sale. The place has been vacant for a long while, and I know
that she is anxious to have it taken off her hands. If you'll
excuse me for a moment, I'll get the particulars for you to
look at."

He went out, and returned with a sheet of paper, which he
handed to Draycott. " I think that's a fair description," he
said. " But I must warn you that time and a certain amount
of money would be required to put it in order. The house wants

interior decoration, and the garden and orchard are in a shocking state."

Draycott read through the particulars. "The accommodation seems to be just about what we should want," he remarked. "And there are two acres of ground, I see. Of course, it has its disadvantages. Main electricity not available. Well, a few oil lamps would get over that, I suppose. Good supply of water from well, with semi-rotary pump in scullery. H'm. More healthful exercise for me. But there seem to be two houses. What's this about a substantial two-roomed cottage in the orchard?"

"It's not inhabited," Tom replied. "It was, I believe, built some years ago for a gardener, a single man living alone. While she was in occupation, the present owner used it as an apple store. It isn't an eyesore, and it's substantially built of brick, with a tiled roof."

Draycott nodded, and read through the particulars again. "Cherry Trees might suit us old folk," he said. "I daresay we could get the place straight gradually. Look here, White, do you think I could go and have a look over it? I'd like to be able to give my wife my personal impressions."

"Of course you can see it, Mr. Draycott," Tom replied. "Cherry Trees isn't much more than ten miles from here. I'll run you out there now, and we can look over it together. How would that suit you?"

"Perfectly," Draycott replied. "It's very good of you. But are you sure you can spare the time?"

"Our time is our clients'," said Tom cheerfully. "If you don't mind waiting a minute or two, I'll run and fetch the car."

He went to Miss Chirton's room, and told her where he was going and why. The car was kept in a garage at the back of the office, and while he was getting it out he reflected rapidly. It was to be supposed that Rufus had taken Mr. Podmore to see Cherry Trees on the previous Wednesday. But, since nothing had been heard from either of them, it might be assumed that no sale had been effected. The property could be regarded as still in the market.

Then Tom remembered the matter of the key. This, for the sake of convenience, had been deposited in the village. There was a paragraph on the sheet of particulars of Cherry Trees. 'The property is vacant, and Mr. George Grudge's shop,

opposite Lingmarsh church, has the key.' Rufus would have
called for it and, having shown his client round, would surely
have returned it to Mr. Grudge. There would be no difficulty
about that.

Tom and Draycott set out, and chatted amicably on the
way. The elderly scholar seemed quite excited at the prospect
of house-hunting. " We've lived where we are now for a
number of years," he remarked. " And neither of us ever
supposed that we should move again. Well, I daresay that
both my wife and I shall enjoy the experience. Oh, by the
way, something has just occurred to me. I hope Jones won't
be offended at my applying to you, instead of to him, the
senior partner ? "

" Not in the least," Tom replied. " As it happens, he's away
from the office for a few days, just now."

" Then he can't possibly take offence," said Draycott. " I
much preferred to deal with you, even at the risk of a breach
of etiquette."

Draycott's tone implied that he didn't like Rufus. He wasn't
alone in his dislike, as Tom very well knew. But that had
nothing to do with the present matter. Rufus would be glad
enough to leave this client in his partner's hands. And further
business might result. If Mr. Draycott found a country
property to suit him, he would probably want to sell his house
in Hembury. Mr. Bewdley's uncle, again ? H. Jones and Son
could not allow personal considerations to sway them in such
matters. Business was business, after all.

They reached Lingmarsh, and Tom drew up outside a shop
which bore the sign ' F. Grudge, Family Grocer.' " The key
of Cherry Trees is kept here," he said. " I'll just slip in and
fetch it." He entered the shop, to find Mr. Grudge serving a
customer with her weekly rations. " That's the lot, Mrs.
Chard," he was saying. " Sorry I can't let you have any more
marge, but that's all that's allowed." As the woman counted
out the money and put the various packages in her shopping
bag, Mr. Grudge turned to Tom. " Good morning, Mr. White.
What can I do for you ? "

" Good morning, Mr. Grudge. You might let me have the
key of Cherry Trees. I've got a client outside who wants to
inspect the property."

Mr. Grudge shook his head. " Sorry, Mr. White, but I

haven't got the keys. Mr. Jones has them. He came here one day last week, Wednesday I think it was, and asked me for the keys and never brought them back again."

This was a nuisance, but Tom had no doubt that it could be surmounted somehow. " Never mind, Mr. Grudge," he said. " I daresay I shall find a way of getting in." He left the shop and re-entered the car. " There's a minor hitch, Mr. Draycott," he said. " My cousin showed a client over Cherry Trees last week, and never returned the keys. He must have put them in his pocket and forgotten all about them. But I don't think that need worry us. We're sure to find some way of getting in."

" I sincerely hope we shall," Draycott replied, with a severity which indicated that he considered this gross carelessness on the part of Rufus. They drove away from Lingmarsh, along a narrow and winding lane which rose steadily out of the village. After a mile or so, Tom pointed to a house standing by itself, and just visible between the trees surrounding it. " That's Cherry Trees, Mr. Draycott."

" It certainly appears to have the virtue of seclusion," Draycott replied. " But that is all to the good. In the evening too close neighbours are apt to be disturbing. I must be allowed to pursue my studies in the intervals between taking my out-door exercise. The specialist raised no objection to that."

They drew up at the entrance, a rusty iron gate hanging crookedly on one hinge, and got out of the car. A path through the neglected front garden led them to the door. It was a grey, misty morning, and drops from the overhanging trees fell dismally on their heads. The front door was fitted with a Yale lock, and this was engaged. Lacking a key, there was obviously no means of getting in that way. " We'd better try the back," Tom suggested.

They walked round the house, picking their way through the clinging bindweed which had overgrown everything. The back door, though it badly needed a coat of paint, was stout, and resisted Tom's efforts. " It seems to be locked and bolted," he remarked. " Never mind, we're not beaten yet."

One by one he examined the sash windows on that side till he found one that seemed to suit his purpose. It was closed and fastened, but it fitted loosely in its frame, and the catch securing it seemed loose. He took a clasp knife from his pocket, opened it, and inserted the blade between the upper and lower sash, against the catch.

Draycott watched his efforts with an austere smile. " Have you ever been apprenticed to a house-breaker, White? " he asked.

" Not exactly," Tom replied. " But we house agents learn a trick or two." He worked away with his knife at the catch till he eased it quite back, and could raise the lower sash. He climbed in to find himself in the scullery. His first care was to shut the window and fasten it as securely as he could. Then he unbolted and unlocked the back door, to admit his client.

Draycott looked about him with interest. The house was sound enough structurally, and there were few signs of damp, though, like the garden, it had been terribly neglected. The atmosphere was heavy, with that peculiar lifelessness typical of houses that have not been lived in for some time. In places the paper was hanging from the walls, and flakes of whitewash from the ceilings littered the floor. " The owner says she can't afford to pay anyone to come in and clean up regularly," said Tom apologetically. " It's a pity, for an hour a week would have kept the place looking tidy. Shall we go along this back passage into the kitchen ? "

The kitchen was roomy and economically planned, with a comparatively modern cooker, and a large sink, with draining boards on either side. As he glanced at these, Tom uttered a sudden exclamation. " Why, bless my soul, there are the keys!"

He picked them up. There were two of them, a Yale key and another larger one of the ordinary household pattern. They were strung on a piece of wire, together with a label bearing the printed words, ' H. Jones and Son, Estate Agents, Hembury,' and beneath this in type, ' Cherry Trees, Ling-marsh.' " There are the keys, all right," Tom remarked. " My partner must have laid them down here when he was here the other day and forgotten them. I'll leave them with Mr. Grudge on the way back. Shall we look at the front rooms now, Mr. Draycott ?"

Draycott nodded his assent. At least he hadn't turned down the property at first sight, as Tom was half afraid he might. They inspected the two rooms described respectively as sitting-room and dining-room, then went upstairs. The view from one of the bedroom windows met with Draycott's approval. "A wonderful prospect across the valley," he said. "And the remoteness is not without its charm. The nearest house must be fully half a mile away. No danger of being disturbed by the activities of one's neighbours. A peaceful spot, most peaceful."

He stood at the window, looking out over the wide stretches of cultivated country. His estimate of the distance of the nearest house was probably correct. It was a beautiful old farm, surrounded by a cluster of barns and cottages. The only sound that came from it was the distant drone of a tractor, drawing a plough which turned up the earth in dark shining furrows. The mist was clearing slowly, giving a shadowy view of the top of the tower of Lingmarsh church standing out of the valley.

"This view must be entrancing in the sunshine," Draycott remarked, as though to himself. Then he turned from the window to Tom. "Cherry Trees certainly has possibilities, White. But you will understand that I can come to no immediate decision. I must discuss the matter with my wife, and bring her here to see for herself. May I take it that I can borrow the key from Mr. Grudge at any time?"

"Certainly, Mr. Draycott," Tom replied. "There will be no difficulty about that. And I have no doubt that I could arrange to drive you and Mrs. Draycott here at any time that suits your convenience."

Draycott shook his head. "We should not dream of putting you to that trouble. I know you are a busy man, White, and you must be doubly so just now, since you tell me that Jones is away. We can hire a car and driver. Alternatively, there is a bus service between Hembury and Lingmarsh. Now that we have seen the house, shall we explore the grounds? The particulars mention an orchard and a paddock."

They went out and made a tour of the estate, beginning with the paddock. This was not very exhilarating, for it had been allowed to run wild, and was sadly overgrown with weeds. Tom, in his professional capacity, tried to make the best of it. "I don't suppose you'll have much use for this, Mr. Draycott, unless you intend to keep poultry. I daresay one of the neighbouring farmers would be glad to rent it. The orchard,

I am glad to say, is in much better shape. It contains, I believe, some sixty trees in all. You will like to see them, no doubt."

They passed from the paddock into the orchard. A dozen rather aged cherry-trees were sufficient to justify the name of the house. The rest were apples, comparatively young and looking fairly promising. In the centre of this was a clearing, overgrown with rank grass, and in the clearing a small square building, built of brick, with a tiled roof from which protruded a single chimney. " That is the bungalow you saw mentioned in the particulars, Mr. Draycott," said Tom. " As I told you, it has latterly been used as an apple store."

" It appears suitable for that purpose," Draycott replied. " Can we look inside ? "

Tom approached the only door. It was locked, but the larger of the two keys opened it. They went in together, to find themselves in unexpected darkness. During the use of the bungalow, brown paper had been pasted over the window to exclude the light. There was moreover a queer unpleasant smell, which might be attributed to rotten apples.

Tom went up to the window and tore away a shred of paper, thus admitting sufficient light for them to see the interior of the room. It was empty and unfurnished, but for a small cooking-range at one side. Beside this was a door, closed, but evidently opening into the second room. Draycott looked about him for a minute or two. " The kitchen and living-room," he remarked. " The other must have been intended as a bedroom. I'll just peep into it."

The intercommunicating door was not locked, and opened as he turned the handle. The unpleasant smell immediately became more evident. Draycott stood in the doorway for a moment, peering into the almost complete darkness. " Come here, White, will you ? " he said quietly. " There's something in this room that isn't mentioned in the particulars. Does it come under the heading of landlord's fixtures, do you suppose ? "

Tom stepped up beside him. In the centre of the floor he could discern a dark and shapeless heap. Avoiding this, he entered the room, went to the window, and as before tore from it a shred of paper. The shaft of light fell on the heap, revealing it as the figure of a man, lying with his knees drawn up to his chin. Tom turned from the window and bent over the figure dressed in a dark overcoat, with a soft felt hat on the floor beside it. " Good heavens ! " he exclaimed, horror-stricken. " It's Rufus, and he's dead ! "

CHAPTER IV

DRAYCOTT ACCEPTED this statement with exemplary calm. " I thought it must be a dead body when I first perceived it," he replied. " I am afraid, White, that this settles the matter. My wife will never fancy the place, once she has learnt of the discovery we have made."

But Tom was too appalled to listen to him. " It's a matter for the police, Mr. Draycott," he said distractedly. " We must leave it exactly as we found it, and not touch anything. I say, it's pretty awful ! We shall have to go straight back to Hembury, and report the matter to the superintendent. You agree, of course ? "

" It would certainly seem the obvious course to take," Draycott replied. They left the bungalow, and Tom locked the door. He had already locked the doors of Cherry Trees itself. They went to the car, which Tom turned with some difficulty in the narrow lane, and set off towards Hembury.

Tom did not stop to leave the keys with Mr. Grudge, but drove on as fast as he could with safety. Neither of them spoke on the way. Tom was too occupied with his thoughts, which were grim enough, and Draycott respected what he supposed to be his concern at the loss of his cousin and partner. They reached Hembury, and Tom pulled up outside the police station. " You'll come in with me, won't you, Mr. Draycott ? " he begged.

The sergeant on duty received them with habitual police precision. " You wish to see the superintendent, gentlemen ? He is in his room. If you will wait here a moment, I will tell him you have called."

They waited uncomfortably for several minutes, until they were summoned to the superintendent's room. Superintendent Kingston had been stationed long enough in Hembury to have become acquainted with the more prominent citizens, and knew both Tom and Draycott well. " Sit down, gentlemen," he said. " You must excuse me for having been obliged to keep you waiting. Now I am at your service. What have you come to see me about ? "

Draycott glanced at Tom, as though to remind him that this was primarily his story. Tom must have rehearsed in advance what he would say, for his reply sounded strangely stiff and formal. " This morning I took Mr. Draycott to view a property which has been on our books for some time, Cherry Trees, Lingmarsh. We found there in a bungalow which stands in the orchard, the body of my partner, Mr. Rufus Jones. We left the body exactly as it was. I relocked the bungalow, and have brought the key here with me."

He laid the keys on the desk. Kingston made a note of the address. He had heard, in the way the police do hear such things, that Mr. Jones had not been seen in Hembury for the last few days, but had attached no importance to the report. " Have you anything to add to that report, Mr. Draycott ? " he asked.

" Nothing," Draycott replied. " Except to confirm what Mr. White has told you. It was I who saw the body first."

" You were together at the time ? " Kingston suggested.

Draycott nodded. " Yes, in the bungalow. I opened the door leading into the next room, and saw an object on the floor. I drew Mr. White's attention to this, and he identified it as the body of Mr. Jones."

" When did you last see your partner alive, Mr. White ? " Kingston asked.

" On Wednesday morning last," Tom replied. " He left the office about ten o'clock, intending to take a client to see Cherry Trees."

" Was the client a resident in this district ? " Kingston asked.

" No, he wrote to us from Manchester," Tom replied. " Podmore, the name was, to the best of my recollection. My partner was to——"

But Kingston held up his hand. " Thank you, Mr. White. I will ask you for a full statement later on. I need detain you gentlemen no longer just now. I will keep those keys for the present."

He put his finger on a bell-push on his desk, and the sergeant appeared. " You may show these gentlemen out, Sergeant," he said.

Finding themselves on the pavement, Tom and Draycott looked at one another blankly. Whatever they had expected, it had not been so summary a dismissal. " I will walk home to lunch," said Draycott. " My wife will be expecting me."

He went off, leaving his companion standing there. It would have been no use for Tom to go home, for Betty had warned him that she would not be in to lunch that day. She had to go to Baleminster on some Red Cross business or other. And Tom did not feel in the least inclined to face lunch in some public place. He went back to the office, which he found vacant but for the girl in the enquiry office. The rest of the staff, including Miss Chirton, had gone out for their mid-day meal. He went into his own room, and sat there miserably.

Kingston wasted no time. He was the type of man who liked to know the facts before he started asking questions about them. He first rang up Dr. Eleigh, asking him to meet him at the police station, within the next ten minutes. He then gave instructions that his car and driver were to stand by and that an ambulance was to be sent to Cherry Trees in an hour's time.

Dr. Eleigh turned up within the stipulated period. " What's this, Kingston ? " he demanded. " I was just sitting down to lunch when you rang up. You've arrested some poor driver for being drunk in charge of a car, and want me to give an opinion on his state of insobriety ? All right, I'll see him."

" It's worse than that, Doctor," Kingston replied. " I've just been told that Mr. Rufus Jones is lying dead in a house at Lingmarsh, and I'm going to take you out to see him."

" Rufus Jones ! " Eleigh exclaimed. " At Lingmarsh ? What did he die of ? "

" That's just what I want you to tell me," Kingston replied. " Come along, the car's waiting."

They got into the car and were driven off. " The address I am given is Cherry Trees, Lingmarsh," said Kingston. "Do you know it, Doctor ? "

" I do," Eleigh replied. " The owner was a patient of mine when she lived there. I used to go out and see her now and then. Who told you this amazing news, may I ask ? "

"Mr. Jones's partner, Mr. White," said Kingston. "He came to see me, He had with him Mr. Draycott, whom he had been showing over Cherry Trees."

Eleigh nodded. "That at least makes sense. I sent Draycott up to London last week to see a specialist, who told him he was to live an outdoor life in future. I told him he had better find himself a little place in the country, and mentioned Cherry Trees, saying that I knew it was for sale and was in the hands of H. Jones & Son."

They reached the village of Lingmarsh. The driver slowed up, about to ask his way to Cherry Trees, when Eleigh prompted him. "Straight on, past the church, then the first to the right. Drive on up the lane for about a mile. I'll tell you when you get there."

The driver followed these instructions, and the car pulled up at the gate of Cherry Trees. "I've never been here before," Kingston said as he got out. "Mr. White told me that he found the body in a bungalow in the orchard."

"Bungalow?" Eleigh replied. "Oh, the place that was used as an apple store, I suppose. I know where that is. Come along. What a state this place has got into, to be sure."

They reached the bungalow, and Kingston unlocked the door with the key Tom had left with him. He frowned as he saw the confused footprints on the floor of the kitchen. Those of the two latest visitors, no doubt, but they would make it impossible to trace any previous ones. Eleigh looked about him. "I don't see any body," he remarked. "It's the other side of that door, I suppose."

He opened the door and passed into the other room. Kingston remained in the kitchen for a few minutes, examining everything in it very carefully. Beyond some cigarette ash flicked off into the sink, he found nothing but a few shrivelled apples lying in odd corners. He went into the next room, to find Eleigh standing over the body. "He's Rufus Jones, all right," said the doctor. "And he's dead, very dead in fact. I can't tell you what he died of. For one thing it's too dark in here, and for another the body is in a state which is going to make determination of the cause of death far from easy. He'll have to be taken to the mortuary, where I can make a proper examination. And I'm not looking forward to that particular job, I can assure you."

"I've arranged for that," Kingston replied. "An ambulance will be along presently. He's been dead some time?"

Eleigh nodded. "Your nose can tell you that. Shut up in a small room with no ventilation and the door and windows closed. Some days, I should imagine. I'll do my best to make an estimate, later on, but you mustn't expect it to be very accurate. Now I think I'll take a turn in the open air till the ambulance comes."

Kingston examined the room minutely, but found nothing to enlighten him. It contained nothing whatever, except the body, not even a fireplace. Certainly nothing that could have retained finger-prints. There were no signs of any struggle having taken place. The dead man's clothes were not disarranged, and no trace of blood was visible anywhere. Kingston made careful notes and measurements of the position in which the body was lying, then went out to join Eleigh in the orchard.

Before very long the ambulance drove up. Under Kingston's direction the body was placed on a stretcher and carried to it. The driver looked about him in some dismay. "It's going to be a bit of a job to turn here," he said. "I noticed a gateway down the lane. If I was to back to that, I might be able to turn there."

"You needn't trouble to do that," Eleigh replied. "Keep on along the lane, the way you're heading now. After a while you'll come to a road. Turn right into that and you'll find it'll take you back to Hembury. It's some way further round, but that doesn't seem to matter much."

The driver accepted this advice, and drove off. Kingston locked up the bungalow and put the keys in his pocket. The police car, smaller than the ambulance, was with some backing and filling, turned outside the gate, and Kingston and Eleigh got into it.

"Can death have been due to natural causes?" the superintendent asked.

"My dear man, how do you expect me to tell you that?" Eleigh replied. "Jones may have had a heart attack, and fallen dead where he stood. I can't say till I've had a thorough look over him. I'll ring up the pathologist at Baleminster Hospital and ask him if he can come over and give me a hand

with the job. He's got more experience of these things than
I have. It depends on him when I can give you some sort of an
opinion. But it won't be till some time this evening, at the
earliest."

They reached Hembury, and there separated. Kingston
took as little time as possible for something to eat, then went
to the offices of H. Jones & Son. He was told that Mr. White
was in, and was shown to his room. Tom was sitting at his
desk, trying, without much success, to concentrate on the
work before him. He asked the superintendent to be seated,
and waited expectantly for what was to come.

"I have verified what you told me this morning, Mr.
White," said Kingston gravely. "You said that you had last
seen Mr. Jones alive at ten o'clock last Wednesday, when he
left here to meet a client. You were about to give me further
details when I interrupted you. May I have them now,
please?"

"Willingly," Tom replied. "I'll tell you all I can. On
Tuesday we received a letter from a client who had not been in
touch with us before. His name appeared to be Mr. Podmore,
but I can't be absolutely sure of that, for the signature was
scarcely legible. Anyhow, the letter was typed on the headed
notepaper of a firm, Podmores, Ltd., with an address in
Manchester. He said he was coming to Baleminster by the
11.10 a.m. train from London on Wednesday and asked to be
met at the station and driven to Cherry Trees. My partner
undertook to do this. I could not have done so, for I was
engaged all day at Wodely Manor, on a valuation."

"May I see Mr. Podmore's letter?" Kingston asked.

"I will ask our chief clerk, Miss Chirton, to find it," Tom
replied. He picked up his desk telephone. "Please ask Miss
Chirton if she will be good enough to come to my room." In
a few minutes she appeared. Tom had told her of his discovery
at Cherry Trees, but they had had no opportunity of discussing
the matter. "The superintendent wishes to see the letter we
had from Mr. Podmore on Tuesday morning, Miss Chirton,"
said Tom. "Will you find it for him?"

Miss Chirton shook her head. "I'm afraid I can't, Mr.
White. I have never seen that letter since I put it in Mr.
Jones's tray that morning. He never put it in his out tray. I
think he must have taken it with him when he went to meet

Mr. Podmore, thinking that it might be useful as an introduction to a client he had never met."

"I see," said Kingston. "Can either of you tell me the address from which the letter was sent?"

"Consort Square, Manchester," Miss Chirton replied. "If there was a number, I don't remember it. The name of the firm was Podmores, Ltd., Wholesale Grocers."

Kingston made a note of this. "Thank you, Miss Chirton. I needn't keep you now." When she had left the room he turned again to Tom. "Mr. Jones left here about ten o'clock. How did he propose to get to Baleminster?"

"In his car," Tom replied. "I saw him drive off in it."

"Baleminster's barely twelve miles from here by road," said Kingston. "It surely would not have taken Mr. Jones an hour and ten minutes to drive to the station there?"

"He said something about calling on one of our colleagues in Baleminster," Tom replied. "We people work together to some extent, you know. He didn't tell me which particular firm he meant to go and see."

"Is there any evidence that Mr. Jones did actually take his client to Cherry Trees?" Kingston asked.

Tom considered this for a moment. "Not I suppose what you would call definite evidence. The keys of Cherry Trees had been left with Mr. Grudge, the grocer in Lingmarsh. When I asked him for them this morning, he told me that Mr. Jones had called for them one day last week, he thought Wednesday, and had not brought them back. When Mr. Draycott and I got to Cherry Trees, we found the house locked. I managed to open a window and climbed in. I found the keys in the kitchen. They are the ones you have now."

"You've had no word from Mr. Jones, or from his client, since he left here on Wednesday morning?" Kingston asked.

"Yes, we have," Tom replied promptly. "We had a telegram from him. That at least I can show you." He opened a drawer of the desk, took out the telegram, and handed it to Kingston, who read it with interest. "Who is this Mr. Wilberton, to whom you were to apologise and pay special attention?"

"Another client," Tom replied. "The uncle of Mr. Bewdley of this town, whom no doubt you know very well. He had written to say he was calling here on Thursday, and wished to see Mr. Jones personally."

" Mr. Bewdley is away, somewhere abroad, I understand," Kingston remarked.

" He is," Tom agreed. " I fancy Mr. Wilberton took that opportunity of coming here. But that's beside the point. He did come, on Thursday afternoon. I didn't see him, but Miss Chirton gave him half a dozen orders to view, among them The Chestnuts. Mr. Haughley didn't take to him at all."

Kingston returned to the telegram. " This is very indefinite. ' Detained here' means, I suppose, detained in Baleminster. Have you any idea what could have detained him, Mr. White ? "

Tom exhibited signs of embarrassment. " Oh, I don't know, Superintendent. My partner was a man with wide business connections. As I told you, he talked about visiting some people in Baleminster. In the course of this visit, some business matter might have cropped up to detain him. At least, that's how I looked at it."

Tom's manner did not escape the superintendent. " Are you telling the exact truth, Mr. White ? "

" I'm only guessing," Tom replied hastily. " Of course, it may not have been business that detained him. He was a man with a very wide circle of friends and acquaintances. He might have met one of these, who persuaded him to stay in Baleminster."

Rumours of Mr. Jones's amorous tendencies had come to Kingston's ears. His partner must be assumed to be well aware of them, and that might be the cause of his embarrassment. " That sounds to me rather more likely, Mr. White. I must ask you to be perfectly frank with me. You think there was a lady in the case ? "

" Oh, no, I don't think that ! " Tom replied hastily. " What's the good of asking me ? It's no good guessing."

" Well, perhaps not," Kingston agreed, rather unexpectedly. " I'll keep this telegram for the present. You understand, of course, that this is a matter for the coroner, and that you will be called upon to give your evidence at the inquest. I have no further questions to ask you for the present."

He left the office and walked to the mortuary. The letter from Mr. Podmore, which had occasioned Mr. Jones's visit to

Cherry Trees, promised a valuable clue. It was not to be found in his room, and Miss Chirton had suggested that he had taken it with him when he set out to meet his client. If so, one might expect to find it in his pocket.

The body had been undressed, and lay covered with a sheet, ready for examination. The clothes had been folded up and placed on a bench nearby. Kingston went carefully through all the pockets, to find nothing in them whatever.

This seemed to him so extraordinary that he summoned the mortuary keeper. No, he hadn't taken anything from the pockets. Mr. Jones's clothes were just as they had been taken off him. The mystery remained unexplained. A man in Mr. Jones's position must always carry a certain amount of money with him, especially when he was going on an expedition. There were other things as well that occured to Kingston. Mr. Jones had left his office in his car. What about his driving licence? He was an habitual cigarette smoker. Kingston remembered the ash he had seen in the sink in the kitchen of the bungalow. Where were his cigarettes, to say nothing of a lighter or a box of matches? Above all, where was the letter, upon which so much seemed to depend?

Kingston returned to the police station, deep in thought. That someone had rifled Mr. Jones's pockets, before the body had been removed from the bungalow, seemed the only conclusion. And it dawned upon him that something else was missing too. Mr. Jones's spectacular car. What had become of that?

Later in the evening, Dr. Eleigh came in. " Well, Superintendent, we've just finished a most unpleasant job. I got the pathologist to come over from Baleminster, but he's had to hurry back, so I've come to tell you the result. To begin with, we found all the organs healthy enough. Nothing whatever to suggest that Jones succumbed to a sudden heart attack, or anything like that. In fact, we are of the opinion that death was not due to natural causes."

" What then? " Kingston asked. " Foul play? "

" It is very difficult to say," Eleigh replied cautiously. " You see, we have established without doubt that Jones has been dead for some days. That fact in itself makes it far from easy to determine the cause of death."

" Even to a layman, it's quite obvious that Mr. Jones had

been dead some days," Kingston remarked. " How many ? "

" We are not prepared to fix a time of death," Eleigh replied.
" You'll remember that I warned you we shouldn't be able
to. The most we can do is to give our opinion upon the limits
of the period. We believe the maximum to be six days, and
the minimum four. In other words, that death occurred on
Tuesday, Wednesday or Thursday of last week."

" Am I to understand that you can offer no opinion as to the
cause of death ? " Kingston asked.

" We can offer some negative evidence," Eleigh replied.
" We could find no wound or fracture. Jones was not shot,
stabbed or beaten to death. There are, however, certain marks
in the region of the neck. As the pathologist was careful to
point out, these may be no more than postmortem stains.
But there is another possibility. They may be the marks of
strangulation by the fingers of some person, standing behind
the victim."

CHAPTER V

AFTER THE doctor's departure, Kingston rang up the Chief
Constable of the County and reported the matter. After some
consultation, it was decided that the circumstances rendered
it advisable for the Criminal Investigation Department to be
informed. " You'd better run up to the Yard yourself,
Kingston," the chief said. " I'll let them know you'll be there
to-morrow morning. You'll see one of their people, and you'll
be able to tell them the story at first hand. Good luck to you."

On Tuesday morning Kingston took the early train from
Hembury, and arrived at Scotland Yard soon after ten o'clock.
The chief had carried out his undertaking, and he was ex-
pected. He was taken immediately to the room of Inspector
Arnold, who greeted him with the respect due to superior
rank. " Good morning, sir. Would you care to sit down ? "

" Don't call me sir, Mr. Arnold," Kingston replied, pro-
ferring his hand. " I feel a mere worm in this imposing building
of yours. As I daresay you've heard, we've had a spot of bother
in my home town, and I'd like to tell you all about it. I'll try
not to be too long-winded."

As he unfolded his story, Arnold made rapid notes. Kingston concluded with his conversation with Dr. Eleigh. " As usual, these medical men won't give themselves away," he went on. " However, they've gone so far as to admit that they don't believe that Mr. Jones died from natural causes. Suicide is impossible. If Mr. Jones had taken his own life, he couldn't then have locked up the bungalow and put the keys in the Cherry Trees kitchen. I don't see how he could have met with a fatal accident in such a place. So it seems to me that there's only one answer left."

" That the marks on the neck were in fact caused by strangulation by some unknown person," said Arnold. " Have you formed any suspicion as to who that person may have been ? "

Kingston smiled. " Well, Mr. Arnold, you have heard my story. We are told that on Wednesday morning Mr. Jones left his office intending to meet a client at Baleminster station and take him to Cherry Trees. I say, we are told, for the letter from the client making the appointment has apparently disappeared. We are also told that the client was unknown to Mr. Jones, or to anyone in his office.

" Now, if this is the truth, we are confronted by a most extraordinary theory. Mr. Jones met his client and took him to Cherry Trees. I say we are told. When they had entered the bungalow there, the client sprang upon Mr. Jones from behind and strangled him, then rifled his pockets. He left the bungalow, locking it behind him, and thoughtfully deposited the keys in the kitchen of the house. This done, he drove away in Mr. Jones's car for some unknown destination. Now, does all that sound very probable to you ? "

" Quite frankly, it doesn't," Arnold replied. " If this client, whose name is alleged to be Podmore, was indeed a total stranger to Mr. Jones, his motive can only have been the theft of his victim's personal belongings and his car."

Kingston nodded. " Exactly. Then there's that telegram I showed you a few minutes ago. According to the theory I've just outlined, it must have been Podmore, not Jones, who sent it. And that brings us up against two very awkward questions. ' Estates, Hembury ' is the correct registered telegraphic address of H. Jones & Son. Would a total stranger have known that ? Remember, Podmore had not seen the headed notepaper of H. Jones & Son, for no reply to his letter was sent.

" And this is the second question. The words in the telegram. ' Apologise Wilberton, pay him special attention.' Now, how in the world could Podmore have known that Wilberton was to call the next day, or that Jones regarded his visit as being of particular importance ? I refuse to believe that Jones chattered of his future appointments to a total stranger. He wasn't that kind of person."

" You're perfectly right," Arnold replied. " If the telegram was not sent by Jones himself, it must have been sent by someone who had a pretty intimate knowledge of his business affairs."

" That's nearer to the mark," said Kingston. " The people who have an intimate knowledge of his business affairs are to be found in Jones's office. I have an idea that his partner, young Tom White, knows, or at least suspects, more than he told me at our interview yesterday."

" You told me, I think, that Mr. White, besides being Mr. Jones's partner was also his cousin," Arnold remarked.

" That's right," Kingston replied. " I've always thought him a very decent young fellow. But his behaviour seems to have been a bit, well, apathetic, shall we say?. He received this rather curiously worded telegram, signed Jones, and apparently accepted it at its face value. ' Detained here over to-morrow.' But when to-morrow had passed, and still Jones did not turn up, White does not appear to have taken any steps to find out what had become of him. And he got distinctly flustered when I asked him if he could suggest what might have detained Jones. Still more so when I asked him whether he thought there was a woman in the case."

" What exactly made you ask him that last question, Mr. Kingston ? " Arnold asked.

" Well, I daresay you know how it is in a place like Hembury," Kingston replied. " It's only a small community, and we folk pick up a lot of tittle-tattle. Not all of it reliable, by any means, but winnowing away the chaff, a considerable grain of truth remains. Jones was a capable, successful, and so far as I know, straight man of business. A bachelor, and very well off, for apart from what he made himself, his father left him a lot of money. But he had one failing.

He was just a little too fond of running after women. And I have some reason to believe in some cases, married women at that."

" I see now what was in your mind," said Arnold. " The old familiar triangle. Jones, a married woman, and her jealous husband. Is Mr. White married, by the way ? "

" Yes, to a very charming and energetic girl," Kingston replied. " Mrs. White busies herself with Red Cross work. Devoted to one another, as far as one can tell."

Arnold nodded. " Well, Mr. Kingston, we'd better sum up the case. We don't know for a fact that Mr. Jones was murdered, though it seems pretty certain that he must have been. Nor do we know when, for the doctors won't say within three days. However, if he was seen alive on Wednesday, we can wipe out Tuesday. He may have been murdered on either Wednesday or Thursday.

" It seems to me the first thing to do is to interview Mr. Podmore. It's most unfortunate that his letter has not been found. But at least you have been told that the heading on it was Podmores, Ltd., Consort Square, Manchester, and that ought to be good enough. Not that it seems very likely that Podmore was the murderer, but we must hear what he has to tell us.

" Now, Mr. Kingston, the Assistant Commissioner has told me to hold myself entirely at your disposal. What I suggest is this. I'll go to Manchester straight away, and dig out what I can there. When I've done that, I'll report to you at Hembury, I hope to-morrow. And may I make another suggestion?"

" I wish you would," Kingston replied. " I came here for your advice."

" Then this is it," said Arnold. " How would it be if you tried to check up on Mr. Jones's movements after he left the office on Wednesday."

" I'll do that," Kingston replied. " And I shall hope to see you in Hembury some time to-morrow. I should like you to see Cherry Trees for yourself. Good-bye till then."

Arnold lost no time after Kingston's departure. He took a taxi to Euston, and found that a train left for Manchester in ten minutes' time. While he lunched in the restaurant car, he thought over what Kingston had told him. On the face of it, the evidence seemed to point to Mr. Jones having been lured to an empty house and there murdered. But why, and by whom? Not surely for the sake of the car and any valuables he might have, by a total stranger.

Feeling that speculation at this stage would be useless, Arnold spent the rest of the journey studying the notes he had made, so as to obtain a complete mastery of the facts. He reached Manchester at half past four and called a taxi, telling the driver he wanted to go to Podmores, Wholesale Grocers, in Consort Square, but that he didn't know their number. The driver replied that he knew the place, and deposited him at the doorway within a few minutes. He entered the premises, and, producing his official card, asked if he might see one of the directors.

He was immediately shown into a room, in which two comparatively young men were sitting. They both rose as he came in, and one of them spoke. " Well, Inspector, are we to consider this visit as an honour or a menace? But let me introduce the two heads of the firm. I am Robert Podmore, and this is my brother Ambrose. Won't you sit down and tell us why you have come to see us? "

Arnold sat down and, more for effect than anything else, produced his note-book. " Will you tell me which of you gentlemen wrote a letter early last week to H. Jones & Son, Estate Agents, Hembury? "

The two brothers exchanged puzzled glances. " I certainly didn't," Robert replied. " Did you, Ambrose? "

" Not I," said Ambrose. " I don't even know where Hembury is."

" The letter concerned a house known as Cherry Trees, Lingmarsh," Arnold persisted. " The writer asked if he could be met at Baleminster on Wednesday last, and taken to see the property."

Again the Podmores exchanged glances, more puzzled than before. " Honestly, Inspector, we neither of us have the foggiest ideas of what you are talking about."

" The letter was typed upon paper headed ' Podmores Ltd., Wholesale Grocers, Consort Square, Manchester '," said Arnold.

" That certainly sounds like ours," Robert replied. " May we see this letter? "

" I was unable to bring it with me," said Arnold.

" That seems unfortunate," Robert replied. " Had we been able to see it, we might have been more helpful. But I can assure you of this, Inspector, I was in Manchester all day last Wednesday."

" And you, Mr. Ambrose ? " Arnold asked.

" My answer is the same as my brother's," Ambrose replied. " And I can add this—Robert and I lunched with our respective wives at the Midland Hotel here last Wednesday. We're well known there, so if you're sufficiently interested you should be able to confirm that. The letter you speak of sounds to me suspiciously like a hoax."

" How do you account for it having been typed on your note-paper ? " Arnold asked. " One of your staff ? "

" It doesn't sound very likely to me," Robert replied. " All our staff are Lancashire folk, and so far as I know none of them have any interest in a property in the Hembury neighbourhood. I'm inclined to agree with Ambrose that the letter must have been a hoax, but I don't believe that any of our people perpetrated it. I can't quite see what they would have got out of it. In any case, all the staff were present here on Wednesday. That's so, isn't it, Ambrose ? "

His brother nodded. " It is so. There was no absentee during the whole of last week. You say the letter was typed on our note-paper, Inspector. That may be so, but it doesn't follow that it was typed here. Dozens of people, our customers mostly, come to these offices in the course of a week. Any one of them might pick up a sheet of our note-paper and put it in his pocket."

" May I have a sheet for comparison ? " Arnold asked.

" Certainly," Robert replied. He opened a drawer, took out a sheet, and gave it to him. " You have aroused our curiosity, Inspector. May I ask what is behind your enquiries ? "

Arnold hesitated, then he reflected that the news of Mr. Jones's death must very shortly become public property. " I will tell you, Mr. Podmore. There is reason to believe that Mr. Rufus Jones, the senior partner of H. Jones & Son, met the writer of the letter on Wednesday. He was not seen in Hembury until he was found dead in the premises of Cherry Trees yesterday."

Ambrose whistled softly. " Murder, eh ? Perhaps it's just as well for us that we've both got an alibi."

"It is," Arnold replied drily. "You are quite sure that neither of you knew this Mr. Rufus Jones?"

Both assured him that they had not. "We've neither of us ever been in that neighbourhood," said Robert. "We're Lancashire, born and bred. We both married Lancashire girls, and we both live in the suburbs of Manchester. Our business doesn't take us very far afield, for all our customers are within twenty miles of the city. And even when we're on holiday, we don't go further than Southport. Eh, Ambrose?"

"My wife and I, if you remember, ventured as far as Morecambe, a couple of years ago," Ambrose replied.

"I'd forgotten, for the moment," said Robert. "Very enterprising of you. But that's the extreme limit, Inspector."

Arnold took his leave, pretty well satisfied that the Podmores had told him the truth. However, he called at the headquarters of the City Police, where he sought the advice of a sympathetic inspector. "I dare-say you can tell me something about those two brothers?" he asked.

"Nothing that isn't to their credit," the inspector replied. "Podmores Ltd., is an old-established family business. Their father died three or four years ago, leaving it to them. And, from what I hear, they've gone ahead a lot since then. They're both hard-working, and they keep their noses right down to the grindstone. I believe they've neither of them been known to be away from the office for more than a week at a time."

"I'm bound to say they seemed all right to me," said Arnold. "They told me that on Wednesday last they lunched at the Midland Hotel with their wives. I'd be very much obliged if you'd check up on that for me."

The inspector promised to do this, and also to ascertain whether all the staff of Podmores Ltd. had been in Manchester that day. Arnold caught a train back to London, and divided the time of the journey between dinner and reflection. His time had not been entirely wasted, for he felt pretty well satisfied that the writer of the letter to H. Jones & Son had not been either of the Podmore brothers.

If indeed that elusive letter had ever been received. Kingston had repeated to him the statements he had heard. Both Mr. White and Miss Chirton declared that they had seen the letter. If it had never existed, there must be some measure of collusion between them. Since the letter was not to be found in the office, it had been suggested that Mr. Jones must have taken it with him. This could neither be proved nor disproved since Mr. Jones's pockets had apparently been rifled. On the other hand, the letter might have been wilfully destroyed after Mr. Jones's departure.

On the whole, Arnold thought it probable that the letter had existed. If so, who had sent it, and why? Kingston had outlined the obvious theory. That it had been sent by someone who wished to lure Mr. Jones to Cherry Trees, which, from Kingston's description, seemed to be an ideal site for murder. But this theory, followed to its logical conclusion, presented a number of difficulties.

Mr. Ambrose Podmore had remarked upon the ease with which anyone could secure a sheet of the firm's note-paper. Arnold was in agreement with that. He was quite prepared to believe that the letter had not originated from the offices of Podmores Ltd. It was difficult to imagine how anyone there could have known of the existence of Cherry Trees, or have had any motive for murdering Mr. Jones. And contact between a firm of wholesale grocers in Manchester and an estate agent in Hembury seemed difficult to establish. The two places were more than a couple of hundred miles apart, and there was no natural connection between them.

That the motive had been simple theft was unthinkable. Kingston's guess that a woman had been at the bottom of it was probably on the right lines. But any conjecture as to motive must wait until the facts were more fully established. All that was known with certainty at present was that Mr. Jones had been found dead at Cherry Trees. When he was killed was vague enough, for the possible period covered a couple of days. Even how he had been killed was no more than a possibility.

CHAPTER VI

KINGSTON LEFT Scotland Yard, intent upon following Arnold's advice, and took the next train to Baleminster. Arrived there, he went to the police station, where he procured a list of all the auctioneers and estate agents in the town. He proceeded to ring these up in turn. Had Mr. Jones of Hembury called on them in the course of the previous Wednesday morning? At the third or fourth attempt he received an answer in the affirmative. A clerk in the office of Messrs. Brockford and Kerry replied that Mr. Jones had called there that day.

Kingston walked to the office, a short distance away, and was shown into the presence of Mr. Brockford, to whom he explained his visit. " Yes, that's quite right," Mr. Brockford replied. " Mr. Jones did look in on Wednesday morning and I had some conversation with him. His firm and ours have often done business before. He told me that a client of his in Hembury had some furniture for sale, but that it wasn't enough to warrant the trouble and expense of holding an auction for that purpose alone. Mr. Jones suggested that the stuff might be sent here for inclusion in one of our periodical auction sales, if we could come to some agreement upon commission. That was easily arranged between us, and Mr. Jones said he would advise his client accordingly. I haven't heard anything from him since then."

" Can you tell me what time this interview between you and Mr. Jones took place? " Kingston asked.

" Between half past ten and eleven," Mr. Brockford replied. " I am sure of that, for Mr. Jones had to leave in a hurry. He looked at his watch and said he had only a few minutes to drive to the station, to meet a client who was to arrive on the 11.10 from London."

Kingston thanked Mr. Brockford and left the office. He went back to the police station, whence he rang up Hembury for his car to be driven to Baleminster to fetch him. Then he arranged for the number and description of Mr. Jones's car to be circulated to all police forces, with a request that if it were

seen he should be notified. This he regarded as a mere formality. Enough time had elapsed to enable the car to have
been disguised beyond the possibility of recognition. If
indeed it had not been disposed of entirely.

While he was waiting, he snatched a quick lunch, after
which he called at Baleminster Post Office. Then, when his
own car arrived, he told the driver the most direct route to
Lingmarsh. That was what Mr. Jones would have done after
picking up his client at the station. To make enquiries there
would be useless. Nobody there would be likely to remember
having seen a person answering to the description of Mr.
Jones. Or, if they did, to be able to say with any certainty
on what day and at what time. The most promising place
at which to pick up the trace was at Mr. Grudge's shop.

Kingston called there when he reached Lingmarsh. At the
mention of the keys of Cherry Trees Mr. Grudge became
slightly indignant. " I haven't got them, Superintendent ! "
he exclaimed. " I told Mr. White as much when he called for
them yesterday. You don't think I've stolen them, do you ?
Mr. Jones took them away last Wednesday, and I haven't
seen them since. He never brought them back here."

" That's not your fault, Mr. Grudge," said Kingston
soothingly. " You're quite sure it was on Wednesday that Mr.
Jones took them ? "

" Of course I'm sure," Mr. Grudge replied. " Wednesday's
early closing day. Mr. Jones came in here, between eleven
and twelve it must have been. He said he'd got a client
outside who wanted to see Cherry Trees, and could he have
the keys. I went and got them for him, and when I gave them
to him I told him that if he found the shop shut when he
brought them back, he'd have to knock on the side door."

" Did you see the client Mr. Jones was taking to Cherry
Trees ? " Kingston asked.

" Not very plain," Mr. Grudge replied. " I walked to the
door of the shop with Mr. Jones when he went out and I saw
that big car of his standing outside. And there was a gentleman sitting in the back."

" Do you remember what he looked like ? " Kingston asked.

Mr. Grudge shook his head slowly. " Not to know him
again, I don't. I didn't more than glance at him for a moment.
He struck me he must be feeling the cold, for he had a rug over

D

him and his coat collar was turned up to his ears. That's why I didn't properly see his face. He looked sort of thin and shivery like. Cherry Trees won't do for you, I thought. It can be bitter cold up the hill yonder in the winter time."

" The car didn't come back through Lingmarsh ? " Kingston suggested.

" Well, if it did, it didn't stop here," Mr. Grudge replied. " I've never seen the keys again from that day to this."

Kingston left the shop well satisfied with the results of his enquiries so far. There would have been no point in Mr. Jones telling Mr. Brockford that he was about to meet a client arriving on the 11.10 if he had not in fact been going to do so. The time of his arrival at Lingmarsh was in conformity with this. Mr. Grudge had only seen the client sitting in the car. In the back, not in the seat beside the driver. A very small point, but worth remembering.

He told his driver to take the lane leading past Cherry Trees. " You needn't stop there," he said. " I'm not going in. But I want to see the lane beyond the house. The way the ambulance went yesterday."

The lane, narrow and with none too good a surface, wound through undulating country. No houses actually abutted on it, though tracks led off to various farm buildings. The passage of the car attracted no attention. At one point, a tractor had to pull into a gateway to allow them to pass. With this exception, they had the lane to themselves until, two miles beyond Cherry Trees, it came into a road well known to Kingston.

This was far from being a main road. It wandered apparently at random across country, passing through various small villages as it did so. By turning to the right one could, if one followed the signposts carefully enough, reach Hembury ; in the other direction, one would eventually come upon the main road from London to Baleminster. It was not a road likely to carry any through traffic.

On his return to Hembury, Kingston learnt that the coroner had fixed the inquest for half past eleven next morning. This entailed a good deal of work on his part, which occupied him until the evening. He made no further enquiries that day, preferring to await Arnold's promised arrival.

He was inside the room at the police station when Arnold

was announced. " You couldn't have come at a better time, Mr. Arnold," he said. " The inquest is to be held in half an hour, and you'll be able to attend it. Only as an interested spectator, of course. We've just time for a quick exchange of news. How did you get on in Manchester ? "

Arnold gave a brief account of his enquiries there, to which Kingston listened with interest. " So the letter was a fake," he commented. " I think there must have been a letter of some kind, for my enquiries leave very little doubt that Jones did meet someone at Baleminster and drove him to Lingmarsh. I'll tell you all about it later on. We'd better be getting to the court now."

The jury of seven worthy citizens of Hembury chose their foreman, and the proceedings began. Tom White gave evidence of identification. He had seen the body, which he testified to be that of his cousin, Rufus Henry Jones, aged forty-five, single, whose address had been number twelve, King Street, Hembury. He had last seen his cousin alive about ten o'clock on the morning of Wednesday, 16th September, when he had set out in his car to meet a client by appointment at Baleminster station. This client had expressed a wish to view the property known as Cherry Trees, Lingmarsh.

" Was this client known to your cousin, Mr. White ? " the coroner asked.

" No, sir, he was not," Tom replied. " A letter, with the heading of a firm in Manchester, had been received in the office the previous morning. The signature of this letter appeared to be A. W. Podmore. Neither of us knew anyone of that name. We have failed to find the letter in the office. Probably my cousin took it with him."

The coroner looked slightly doubtful. " When your cousin failed to return, did you take any steps to discover what had become of him ? " he asked.

" Well, no, I didn't," Tom replied. " I was out all day, engaged upon a valuation. When I got back to the office, I found that a telegram had been received there, saying that my cousin had been detained."

Prompted by the coroner, Tom went on to describe how he and Mr. Draycott had found the body. He was followed first by Mr. Draycott, who told his story, and then by Pauline Chirton. She gave evidence of the receipt of the telegram, and confirmed Tom's statement that the letter was nowhere to be found. The coroner asked her whether she thought it likely that Mr. Jones had any considerable amount of money with him when he left the office. She replied that when he went out on business he always carried notes, to the extent of about twenty pounds, say, and his cheque book.

Dr. Eleigh was the next witness called, and he was followed by the pathologist. They had nothing to add to what Kingston had already been told. It seemed probable that strangulation had been the cause of death, which might have taken place any time within a period of twenty-four hours from deceased having last been seen alive. They were unable to give a more definite opinion.

The superintendent was the last to give evidence. He described his visit to Cherry Trees, and what he found there. He went on to stress the fact that nothing whatever had been found in the pockets of the deceased, and that so far his car had not been traced. From this he continued with his visit to Baleminster and Mr. Brockford's account of Mr. Jones's visit, which had ended with his departure at eleven o'clock. While in Baleminster the witness had visited the Post Office, where he had been given the original of a telegram handed in there at 1.25 p.m. on 16th September.

He handed the form to the coroner who, after examining it, passed it on to the jury. The message was pencilled in carelessly-formed but perfectly legible block letters. On the back was the address of the sender, in similar characters, ' R. Jones, Market Square, Hembury.'

As the members of the jury nodded their heads sagely over this, the coroner addressed the witness. " I presume that efforts have been made to trace the writer of the missing letter ? "

This gave Kingston his opportunity. He had no intention of saying more in a public court. There was no point in revealing the lines upon which the investigation was working. " The matter has been reported to the Criminal Investigation Department, sir," he replied. " I am assured they are instituting the necessary enquiries."

The coroner appeared satisfied. He had sufficient experience to be aware that to prolong the enquiry might serve only to defeat the ends of justice. He dismissed the witness and proceeded to address the jury. They would understand, from the remark of the last witness, that the police had the matter in hand. Meanwhile, they had heard sufficient evidence to enable them to arrive at a verdict, thus making an adjournment unnecessary. In considering how the deceased had met with his death, they should consider the medical evidence, and that relating to the circumstances in which the body was found. They would no doubt give due weight to the statements of two witnesses, to the effect that the bungalow was locked, and that the key was found elsewhere.

The jury was not slow to accept this pretty broad hint. A whispered conversation ensued between the members. It lasted only for a minute or two, and then the foreman stood up. " We are all agreed upon our verdict, sir. The deceased was murdered by some person or persons unknown."

As soon as the proceedings terminated, Kingston, followed by Arnold, left the court. " Well that's over, and we can get down to business," said the former, when they reached his room at the police station. " What do you make of it, Mr. Arnold ? "

Arnold filled and lighted his pipe before he replied. " That telegram you produced seems to me the crux of the matter. If it was written by Jones, he was alive as late as 1.25 p.m. May I have a look at it ? "

Kingston handed him the by now much fingered form, and he studied it carefully. " The fact that block letters were used doesn't necessarily imply a desire to escape from a natural handwriting," he remarked. " Every post office calls upon you to write your telegrams in block letters. These aren't very neat, I admit. But they may be due to natural slovenliness, rather than haste."

" It might be worthwhile to try to get hold of something written by Jones in block letters," Kingston suggested.

Arnold shook his head. " I doubt it. We should never get an opinion we could rely upon. You know how these graphologists contradict one another even in cases of ordinary handwriting. Block letters would give them far greater opportunity for differing. I think we shall have to decide for ourselves whether Jones wrote the telegram or whether he didn't."

" Very well, then," said Kingston. " Let's start with what we know. I think we may assume that the missing letter

existed, and for this reason. Jones told Mr. Brockford that he
had to meet a client at Baleminster station, who was to arrive
on the 11.10 from London. And again we can assume that he
did meet a client. When he called for the keys of Cherry
Trees, Mr. Grudge saw a passenger in his car, whom he described as a shrivelled up sort of person who seemed to feel
the cold. You're satisfied that this man couldn't have come
from Podmores of Manchester ? "

" I can't be absolutely satisfied till I've heard from the
police there," Arnold replied cautiously. " But from my
conversation with the two brothers, I think it very unlikely."

" Then we come up against some sort of hanky-panky right
away," said Kingston. " The enquiry can't have been genuine.
Why should anyone who merely wanted to look at Cherry
Trees with a view to possible purchase make an appointment
on paper which wasn't his and sign it in a presumably false
name ? But we're running ahead of ourselves. Let's get back
to this confounded telegram."

" Either Jones sent it, or someone else did in his name,"
Arnold replied. " Consider first the theory that he did send it.
That implies that he was back in Baleminster by half past one.
He must have shown his client over Cherry Trees, then driven
him back to the station to catch a train to London."

" How, in the light of that theory, can you explain how
Jones's body was found in the bungalow ? " Kingston asked.

" In this way," Arnold replied. " He returned there later,
possibly that afternoon. That's why he didn't give the keys
back to Mr. Grudge in the morning. He put them in his
pocket, knowing that he would want them again."

" And who murdered him when he got back to Cherry
Trees ? " Kingston asked a trifle scornfully.

" Someone who knew he was going back there, and was
waiting for him," Arnold replied. " I know this is only guess-
work, but, frankly, I'm not in love with the theory of murder
by a total stranger."

" I'll admit that I'm not, either," Kingston agreed. " Any
other point ? "

" Just this," said Arnold. " If Jones sent that telegram,
why did he ? Wouldn't it have been simpler for him to have
rung up his office ? "

Kingston's reaction to this question was very much what

Pauline Chirton's had been. " Perhaps he didn't want to give anyone at the office an opportunity of asking him what he was up to. Or there may have been another explanation. The telegram was sent in the middle of the lunch hour. Jones may have thought that if he rang up there would be nobody in the office to take the call."

" All right," said Arnold. " Now, let's consider the alternative theory, that it was not Jones who sent the telegram. That I suppose means that he was already dead, and that it was his murderer who sent it. But there again we come up against the puzzle of the total stranger. Two things. The telegram was sent to the firm's registered telegraphic address. And, more extraordinary still, it contains a reference to Wilberton. Now, I'll admit that a total stranger might easily have discovered the telegraphic address. But not that Wilberton was expected next day. Jones isn't likely to have mentioned that fact in the course of chatty conversation."

" Then you incline to the theory that the telegram was sent by Jones ? " Kingston asked.

" Not necessarily," Arnold replied. " This is what strikes me. Whoever sent it had a surprising knowledge of the affairs of H. Jones & Son. However, let's leave that for a moment, and try to reconstruct what actually happened. We needn't bother for the moment whether Jones was killed in the morning, or in the course of a second visit to Cherry Trees.

" Jones either took his murderer to Cherry Trees, or met him there. If he met him, it can only have been by appointment, one must suppose. Jones unlocked the door of the bungalow and they went in together. As Jones was leading the way into the inner room, the other sprang on him from behind, taking him off his guard, and strangled him. The murderer then proceeded to clear out his pockets, including his cash and his cheque book. He then left the bungalow, locking it behind him, and went into the house, where he most considerately left the keys in the kitchen. That done, he left the house by the front door, shutting it behind him, and drove off in Jones's car. Can you supply the motive ? "

Kingston smiled. " I'd rather leave you to supply it, Mr. Arnold."

" On the face of it, theft," Arnold replied. " We heard at the inquest that Jones usually had a good bit of cash about him.

Apart from that, there was the car. You tell me that it was big and new, and it must have been worth quite a bit. A professional car thief might have worked the dodge of making an appointment to view Cherry Trees. But, in my experience, that type of specialised crook never risks his neck by committing murder."

Kingston nodded. " Unless they're driven to it in self-defence. But there's no question of anything of the kind in this case. From all appearances the murder was treacherous and deliberate. You said, on the face of it. If the motive wasn't theft, what was it ? "

" You should be in a better position than I am to answer that question," Arnold replied. " You knew Jones and those he associated with, and I didn't. But this I will say. If the motive wasn't theft, it seems hardly possible that Jones's murderer can have been a total stranger to him."

CHAPTER VII

KINGSTON MADE no immediate reply. His thoughts were too chaotic to be readily put into words. Reports, each trifling in itself, from his subordinates. Chance words overheard, covert exchanges of glances when Rufus Jones's name had been mentioned. All these added together made up an impression, but hardly a clearly-drawn picture which he could lay before his colleague.

However, he made the attempt. " You want me to tell you about Jones ? All right. But, to begin with, you must understand that I never knew the fellow at all well. Nor did I ever have any dealings with him in my capacity as a policeman. We were acquainted with one another as ordinary fellow-citizens. And a purely negative acquaintance at that. There was no liking or disliking on either side. We spoke to one another, out of common politeness if we happened to meet. You follow me ? "

" Exactly," Arnold replied. " But you haven't told me your opinion of him."

Kingston smiled. " I doubt if I had one before this happened. And that may serve to illustrate what I've been trying to tell you. Or put it this way. A superintendent in charge of a place like this doesn't form any definite opinions about his fellow citizens unless they come within the range of the law. Jones never did. He was a successful business man, extremely capable in his own line, I believe. Men usually liked him on first acquaintance, but as they got to know him better, weren't inclined to trust him too far."

"A bit shady in his business transactions?" Arnold suggested.

"Oh, no, not that!" Kingston exclaimed. "I've never heard a hint of anything of that kind. I meant something quite different. Perhaps I should have said that it was younger married men who didn't trust him."

Arnold nodded comprehendingly. "Oh, I see. Any specific instances?"

"None," Kingston replied. "That's why I don't want to stress the point too heavily. But things do come to my ears, you know. I've heard of rows, with mysterious hints of women being the cause of them. Nothing definite, and certainly nothing upon which I was called to take action."

"I find this remarkably interesting," said Arnold. "Can one of these rows have culminated in murder?"

"I suppose that's not altogether impossible," Kingston replied quietly.

Arnold filled and lighted his pipe. "It's too early to jump to conclusions. But if jealousy had been the motive, where would you start looking for the murderer?"

"You saw young White just now," said Kingston. "What did you make of the way he gave his evidence?"

"He seemed straightforward enough," Arnold replied. "And what he said was confirmed in most essential points. But I did notice that he looked a bit uncomfortable when the coroner asked him what steps he had taken to find out what had become of his cousin. One would have expected him to have done something. This telegram says merely 'detained here over to-morrow.' It doesn't say anything about being away over the week-end."

"This is merely for your information, Mr. Arnold," said Kingston. "Tom White has a very charming young wife to whom he is apparently devoted. I have heard it whispered, no more, that Jones was in the habit of paying her attentions.

What truth there may have been in those whispers I cannot say."

Arnold smiled. "'You're being scrupulously fair. Tell me this. Who do you suppose, outside Jones's office, could have known of the impending visit of this fellow Wilberton?"

"That's not an easy question to answer," Kingston replied. "Mr. Wilberton was not a complete stranger, like the chap calling himself Podmore, who wrote the missing letter. You see he's the uncle of one of one of our more prominent citizens, Mr. Bewdley. Nobody here had seen him before last Thursday, though Mr. Bewdley was always talking about him. Mr. Bewdley had been trying to find his uncle a house in the town, so far without success. He's away just now, and isn't expected back for a while. Mr. Wilberton's connection with Mr. Bewdley would make it natural for Jones to tell his office to pay him special attention."

"I see," said Arnold. "His visit would have been in the nature of an occasion, as far as the people in the office were concerned, so much so that they may have spoken about it in advance to others. In fact, anyone in Hembury might have learnt that he was coming. But not, surely, a stranger like Podmore, coming from a distance."

"Mr. Wilberton did come here on Thursday," Kingston remarked. "And it seems he almost caused a riot. A Mr. Haughley, who lives in the town, was talking to me next morning, and he told me about him. The language he used about him was forcible. A great hulking gorilla of a man, and a coarse unmitigated bounder. He couldn't understand how a decent chap like Bewdley came to have such an uncle."

"A man can't be held responsible for his uncle, I suppose," Arnold remarked. "And this unpleasant person only comes into the picture because his name is mentioned in the telegram. You've answered my question. Almost anyone here might have got to know he was expected. In the course of his evidence, young White said that he was out all day on Wednesday making a valuation."

"He told me that when I talked to him," Kingston replied. "I had enquiries made, and as far as I can make out his statement was perfectly true. He was at a place called Wodely Manor, with a young clerk from the office, and didn't get back there till half past four, or thereabouts."

"The doctors say that Jones may have been alive after that," said Arnold grimly. "Have you any idea how young White spent the rest of the afternoon and evening?"

Kingston shook his head. "I've only got one trace of him. Jones lived in a house in King Street here, with a housekeeper, Mrs. Paston, to look after him. A very nice house it is, too. It was his father's before him. I went to see Mrs. Paston, but she's so deaf I found it very difficult to make her understand what I was talking about. However, she told me that she wasn't expecting Jones to come home on Wednesday night. Mr. White had come to the house to tell her that he had been detained at Baleminster. She thought that must have been between half past six and seven."

"White has a car?" Arnold asked sharply.

"Yes," Kingston replied. "The one he used to go to Wodely Manor. He keeps it in a garage behind the office. But look here. If Jones was still alive at half past four, what the dickens had he been doing with himself all the afternoon?"

Arnold puffed furiously at his pipe for a minute or two before he offered any suggestion. "Look here, Mr. Kingston!" he exclaimed suddenly. "What I am going to say to you will sound more unsubstantial than any fairy-tale. But we've got to consider the possibilities, however remote. The motive was jealousy, and Mrs. White was at the bottom of the affair. Any fundamental objection to that?"

Kingston shook his head. "None, that I know of."

"Then something like this may have happened. Jones receives a letter from a man who wants to look over Cherry Trees. It enters his head that Cherry Trees, isolated as it is, is the very place for a secret rendezvous. He knows that White will be occupied all day on Wednesday with the valuation at Wodely Manor. He asks Mrs. White to meet him that afternoon at Cherry Trees, and she consents."

Arnold paused, but as Kingston made no comment, he went on. "Jones meets his rather mysterious client, takes him to Cherry Trees, and brings him back to Baleminster. Having seen him off by train, Jones sends the telegram and has lunch. At the appointed time he drives to Cherry Trees again, where Mrs. White joins him. This is, say, between three and four o'clock.

"Later, White, having looked in at his office, goes home and finds that his wife isn't there. Something, you can't expect me to guess what, gives him an inkling as to where she may be. He, in his turn, drives to Cherry Trees, and finds the pair of them in the bungalow. In a fit of fury he strangles his cousin. That's only a rough outline. I leave it to you to fill in the details."

"What about the disappearance of the car, and the rifling of Jones's pockets?" Kingston asked.

"That's easy," Arnold replied. "When White came to his senses, he realised that he would have to cover his tracks, for his wife's sake as well as his own. Part of his method would be to make theft appear his motive for the murder. Any normally intelligent chap would think of a thing like that."

Kingston laughed. "You've got it all pat, Mr. Arnold. I won't damp your ardour by pointing out one or two minor difficulties involved in your theory. Seriously, though, you may not be so very far wide of the mark. But I can't imagine Betty White behaving as you suggest. It seems to me more likely that if she was involved in any way, it was by acting as a decoy."

"It's your turn, Mr. Kingston," said Arnold politely. "May I hear your theory?"

"I can't claim it as my theory," Kingston replied. "It's no more than an amendment of yours. Betty White and her husband had resolved to do Jones in at the first convenient opportunity. It may be that since the opportunity didn't come, they contrived it. I mean that the so-called Podmore was no more than a stooge, put up to the game by White. A perfectly harmless practical joke, of course, merely to lead Jones up the garden path."

"It's a pity that letter can't be found," Arnold remarked. "We might have traced its origin by the typing."

"Finding the machine in the offices of H. Jones & Son?" Kingston replied. "Well, perhaps. But you may be sure the letter has been destroyed long ago, and I don't suppose that whoever typed it kept a carbon copy. The next step was taken by Betty White. She saw Jones, and told him that she had heard from Tom that he was going to Cherry Trees. If he happened to be there in the afternoon, she might run out and meet him. That gets over the snag of how White found out where she was. The sequel fell out as you've outlined it."

" That's all very well," said Arnold. " But why should this young couple have wanted to make away with Jones ? "

" Perhaps Betty White resented his attentions," Kingston replied slowly. " But there may have been more in it than that. Now that you've brought White into the foreground, there's something I'd better explain to you. It concerns the late lamented Jones.

" Henry Jones, his father and the founder of the firm, was one of those lucky chaps. Or perhaps it wasn't luck, but an unfailingly sound sense of business. I don't know, for I never met him. Anyhow, everything he touched turned into gold by magic. He'd buy a derelict farm for a song, and sell it in a few minutes' time for ten times what he gave for it. Anyhow, that's the legend locally.

" However it may have been, he died worth a lot of money. He was a widower, and his only child, Rufus, inherited the lot. And Rufus, whatever his faults may have been, inherited not only the money, but his father's business ability. I have of course no personal knowledge of his financial affairs, but I have never heard of him throwing money about. I daresay that his only extravagance was the pursuit of his amorous adventures. It seems to me very likely that we shall find that he died at least as rich as his father.

" And that brings us to the point. Jones may have made a will, leaving his money to some person or persons of whom we have no knowledge. If he didn't, young White is, to the best of my belief, his only surviving near relative."

Arnold chuckled. " So we come down to earth. We descend from the high regions of romantic jealousy to mere sordid gain. Well, I'm bound to say I prefer a financial motive for murder, if only because it's the commonest. I shouldn't be a bit surprised if you'd hit the nail on the head, Mr. Kingston."

" I'm only guessing," Kingston replied modestly. " There's just this about it. The Whites must be pretty hard up. I've heard, from a reliable source, that Tom had to realise every penny of his assets to buy the partnership with his cousin. I don't know what share the junior partner gets of the profits of the firm, but, judging from the way the Whites live, it can't be very spectacular. And I don't suppose he had much prospect of improvement while the senior partner lived.

Whether or not they murdered Jones between them, the Whites can hardly be expected to regret his death."

Arnold nodded. " The motive's there all right. And the opportunity, too, it seems to me. As for probability, your theory sounds far more likely than murder by the man who signed himself Podmore, with a motive of theft. Of course, this man must have played a part in the affair, though possibly an unconscious one. His use of a presumably false name and a sheet of stolen note-paper shows that. I'm very much inclined to your idea that he was a stooge. But surely, when he hears of Jones's murder, he'll come forward ? "

Kingston shook his head. " Would you, in his place ? Would you come forward and admit that you had been alone with Jones in the place where his dead body was found, in the face of the evidence given at the inquest, that Jones had not been seen alive since ? You'd run a considerable risk of putting your head in the noose if you did. Besides, this stooge may not be a highly respectable member of society. He may have his own personal reasons for avoiding an appearance in the limelight."

" Yes, that's true enough," Arnold agreed. " At least we know he exists, for Mr. Grudge saw him. Not that his description of him helps us much. It doesn't seem likely that anyone but White, and possibly Mrs. White, can have put him up to the game. And where did they dig him out from ? Can he be one of your local worthies ? "

" I doubt it," Kingston replied. " A local would run too much risk of being recognised, by Jones or someone else, who would know that his name wasn't Podmore, and that he wasn't interested in buying Cherry Trees. He's more likely to be someone the Whites knew before they came here."

" In that case, it's not going to be easy to trace him," said Arnold. " We're bound to suppose that Jones drove him back to Baleminster station, whence he took train back to wherever he came from. If he chooses to lie doggo, I don't quite see how we're going to unearth him."

" We shall have to do without him," Kingston replied. " It seems to me that the first thing we ought to do is to find out where Betty White spent that afternoon. How about calling on her, you and I ? "

" Might that not be a bit too hasty ? " Arnold objected. " I make a rule never to question a suspect until I've got something definite to go upon. Apart from the obligation of cautioning them, which obviously puts them on their guard, it discloses the lines the police are working on. Can't we begin by tackling someone who knows both Whites fairly intimately? "

Kingston considered this for a few moments. " Miss Chirton, who works in the office. You saw her at the inquest. She's a highly intelligent woman, and of course knows all about Tom White. I happen to know that she and Betty White go about together quite a bit."

" She seems the very person," said Arnold. " We might have a chat with her. But not, I think, in the office."

" We'll ring her up and ask her to come here," Kingston replied. " But look at the time, Mr. Arnold ! It's nearly two o'clock, and we haven't had lunch yet. Let's go out and have a snack, and we'll get down to business afterwards."

Arnold thought that an excellent idea, and they went out together. After a quick lunch, they came back to the police station. As they entered, the sergeant on duty spoke to Kingston. " Excuse me, sir. Mr. Scrimp of Potash Farm rang up a few minutes ago. He wanted to speak to you, but when I told him you were out he gave me a message. He said that a car had been abandoned on his land, and he told me the number. It was the number of Mr. Jones's car, sir."

" Thank you, Sergeant," Kingston replied. Then he turned to Arnold. " Potash Farm is not more than two or three miles from Cherry Trees. I think we'd better go and see Mr. Scrimp right away."

CHAPTER VIII

THEY SET OFF at once in the superintendent's car. " Scrimp is a decent chap," said Kingston, as they drove towards Lingmarsh. " Apt to get a bit merry when he's had a drink or two, but a thorough good farmer who knows his job. I was able to do him a good turn a little while back, and since then I'm included in his list of friends. He often looks in to see me when he comes into Hembury."

" Do you suppose he knew Jones ? " Arnold asked.

" Bound to have," Kingston replied. " All the farmers round about knew Jones. Farmers and auctioneers keep in pretty close touch, as a rule. But I don't suppose that Scrimp knows anything about what happened last Wednesday. This is Lingmarsh, and there's Mr. Grudge's shop. We turn to the right up this lane, and you'll see Cherry Trees for yourself."

Kingston stopped the car outside the gate. " There you are, this is the place. You can just see the bungalow through the trees yonder. Like to get out and have a look at it ? "

" Hardly worth wasting time just now," Arnold replied. " We'd better see that car first."

Kingston drove on along the lane, which was as usual deserted. He drove on for a couple of miles, or rather more, till he came to a gate, on which was painted the name, ' Potash Farm.' Arnold got out and opened this, being careful to shut it again when the car had passed through. They went on for nearly half a mile up a rough farm road, till they came to a farm-yard. " Ah, there's Scrimp himself," said Kingston.

A burly, red-faced man, dressed in a tweed coat, breeches and gaiters, was giving instructions to the driver of a wagon and a pair of horses. " Hallo, Super ! " he exclaimed heartily as Kingston and Arnold got out of the car. " You've come about that car, I daresay. I'll take you along and show it to you myself. But you and your friend will come in and have a drink first ? I've got some parsnip wine, as good as you've ever tasted."

Kingston answered for both of them. " Not just now, if

you'll forgive us, Mr. Scrimp. We haven't any too much time to spare. Let me introduce you to Mr. Arnold, from Scotland Yard."

Scrimp shook Arnold's hand vigorously. " Pleased to meet you, I'm sure, Mr. Arnold. We country folk seem a bit strange to you, I daresay. Well, if you gentlemen won't come in, we'll be getting along. No good taking your car, it's only a hundred yards or so, and the way's a bit rough. I'll have to get it made up before we start carrying the beet, next month."

Under Scrimp's guidance they set off. He led them across the yard, and along a track which seemed to run more or less parallel to the farm road by which they had approached Potash Farm. It certainly deserved the epithet rough, for it was liberally pitted with deep pot-holes, which they had difficulty in avoiding. " It's in a terrible state," said Scrimp apologetically. " I'll have to have it made up again before beet-lifting comes along. You see, we don't use it much unless we're carrying something off the farm. Then it's handy as another way out on to the lane."

" It's not a Class A road," Kingston replied. " How did you come to find this abandoned car ? "

Scrimp jerked his thumb over his shoulder. " Mark, him you saw me speaking to when you drove up, he found it. I sent him along to the old pit this morning to fetch a load of gravel. And when he came back with it, he told me there was a car standing in the pit. I thought that a bit queer, so I went along myself to have a look. And when I'd seen it, I thought you'd best be told, Super. I fancied to myself that I'd seen that same car before."

The estimate of a hundred yards or so turned out to be rather optimistic. It was fully a quarter of a mile before the track entered a small spinney, in which it gradually became a ravine between sloping banks on either side. " It's not very far now," said Scrimp encouragingly. " The pit's only just round the bend. It used to be used for getting road-metal in the old days, but that's over and done with now. I only take a load from it now and again, when I want to make my ways up."

They reached the pit at last. It had been dug, long ago, out of the bank on the right hand side of the track. The floor was about the size of a tennis lawn, and here and there fair-sized trees were growing on it. The greater part of the sides was overgrown with weeds and brushwood, and at one point a bare face of flinty gravel was exposed. Tracks of wagon wheels led to and from this.

But the car was the centre of interest. It had been driven into the pit, and then obliquely across the floor of it. Apparently blindly, for the front bumper was hard up against one of the young trees, which it had bent over. Kingston looked at the number, then turned to Scrimp. " You said that you had an idea you'd seen this car before ? "

Scrimp nodded sagely. " That's right, Super. There's only one about these parts that had so posh a car as that. If it isn't the one I've seen Rufus Jones about in, it's the very spit of it, that's all I can say."

" You can't tell how long it's been here ? " Kingston asked.

" There's no telling that, Super," Scrimp replied. " I doubt whether anyone's been along this way since harvest was over. There's nothing to bring them, you see. And if I hadn't sent Mark for that load of gravel this morning, it might not have been found till we start sugar-beeting next month. Now I'll be getting along back. You gentlemen will do as you think best, and if when you've finished you like to drop in at the farm and have something, you'll be welcome."

" Your friend is hospitable," said Arnold, as Scrimp disappeared up the track. " And it was tactful of him to leave us to it. We'd better look over the car, I suppose."

Hitherto they had been standing in the entrance to the gravel-pit, facing the back of the car. From that aspect it appeared undamaged. But as they approached it, and came level with the front doors, a very different state of affairs revealed itself. The exterior of the car was unscratched, even the bumper which rested against the tree was not buckled. But the windscreen was starred in three or four places, and, looking inside, Arnold could see that the leather upholstery of the front seats was covered with scratches, and in one place actually torn.

He tried the door on the driver's side, and, finding it unlocked, opened it. " Just look here ! " he exclaimed. " I suppose one of Mr. Scrimp's bulls can't have got in ? The inside of the car is a complete wreck."

And so it was. Everything breakable seemed to have been

broken. The floor-mat had been torn from its fastenings, and lay in an untidy heap. The wooden instrument board was scarred and splintered, and nearly all of the glasses covering the dials of the instruments were shattered. Even one of the cranks controlling the windows had been wrenched off.

" Can you beat it ! " Kingston exclaimed. " How the dickens can this have happened ? It wasn't the shock of hitting the tree that did it. If it had been violent enough for that the bumper would have been bent. It looks to me as if there'd been some sort of a scrap on the car. What do you think ? "

" It looks to me precious like it," Arnold agreed. " But who were the scrappers ? and was the car driven in here before or after they'd had their set-to ? It's only the front that's been wrecked. I can't see any signs of damage in the rear. Or outside either, for that matter."

The two of them stood silently appraising the damage. Until suddenly Arnold exclaimed, " Look at that clock ! It's one of those electric gadgets, driven off the battery. The glass over the face of it is shattered and splinters have got wedged behind the hands, stopping it, naturally. And you see the time it's stopped at ? Ten minutes to six."

Kingston saw the trend of Arnold's mind. " Last Wednesday afternoon. We can bank on that. Whoever took the car from Cherry Trees wouldn't have driven it round England before depositing it here. He, or she, brought it here straight away. The time corresponds exactly with what we've been thinking about, and the motive for murdering Jones obviously wasn't to steal his car. What beats me is how all this damage came to be done. But we'll talk about that later. Let's see where this track comes out."

They had not far to walk along it. Barely a hundred yards from the gravel-pit the track emerged from the spinney, and ran level with the surrounding ground. It topped a slight rise, from the summit of which the lane was visible, quite a short distance away. Where the track came out into the lane were a couple of gate posts, but no gate. The place of this was taken by an old and rusty chain, one end fixed with a staple, the other hooked over a bent nail.

" Isn't that just like a farmer ! " Kingston exclaimed. " Make do with any old thing rather than buy a new gate.

Handy for whoever was driving the car, though. We'll get it out by the way it went in. That is, if it'll go."

They returned to the abandoned car and he opened the bonnet. "Doesn't seem anything amiss here. I wonder if she'll start. " he remarked as he climbed into the driving seat. The ignition key was in the switch. He turned this and pressed the starter button. The battery had run down very low, and the engine turned slowly and reluctantly. But after two or three attempts it fired, and, after a cough or two, ran sweetly enough.

"That's good!" said Kingston. "Jump in, and we'll drive back to Hembury. Never mind about my car. I'll send a couple of my chaps out to fetch it."

Kingston drove the big car to Hembury without incident and parked it in the yard of the police station. He and Arnold searched it thoroughly, without finding anything of interest. No clue whatever as to who had driven it to the gravel-pit. "What do you make of it all, Mr. Arnold?" Kingston asked when they were back in his room.

"There's plenty of scope for guessing," Arnold replied. " But, before you do that, let's get the facts as straight as we can. We've no actual proof that the car was driven to the pit on Wednesday evening. But the time at which the clock stopped is highly significant. It didn't stop till the glass was broken and jammed the hands. We can assume pretty safely that the glass wasn't broken when Jones set out on Wednesday morning. So the damage can't have been done before ten to six that afternoon. Which seems definitely to put the morning client out of the picture."

"It does," Kingston agreed drily. "He's not our man. Go on."

"The gravel-pit next," Arnold replied. " Mr. Scrimp tells us that none of his people have been near it for weeks, it's completely hidden from anyone going along the lane. No stranger would drive through the chained gateway on the odd chance of finding beyond it the ideal place in which to deposit a car he had no further use for.

"Next, the damage to the car. How are we to account for that? I said just now that the clock didn't stop before Wednesday afternoon. But it may have stopped at ten to six on some morning or afternoon of a subsequent day. I think we must assume that the car was abandoned on Wednesday afternoon. Then here's a possibility for you. When abandoned the car was undamaged, and unlocked. Subsequently a pair of trespassing children found it and amused themselves by wrecking it. Children are destructive little brutes by nature, but I can't imagine them doing all that damage. And why did they confine their efforts to the front of the car?"

Kingston laughed. "I'm not much taken by that possibility, Mr. Arnold. You'll have to try again. As soon as I looked inside that car I said there had been a scrap in it, and I'm still pretty sure I was right."

"Very well, then," Arnold replied. "Here's a suggestion for you. We've already discussed the probability of Jones having returned to Cherry Trees on Wednesday afternoon, having made an appointment to meet someone there. The murderer reached the spot some time before six. He found Jones not in the house or the bungalow, but in his car, outside the gate. Perhaps Jones was tired of waiting for someone who hadn't turned up, and was on the point of giving it up and driving home."

Kingston nodded. "That's beginning to sound more like it. I'll finish the story for you. The murderer got in beside Jones and tried to strangle him. Jones not unnaturally reacted to this, and there was a violent struggle, kicking and striking out in that confined space. Perhaps the murderer had brought a weapon of some kind with him, a cosh, if you like. That would have accounted for the damage. In the end he got the better of Jones and strangled him.

"He then had two problems to solve. To get rid of the body, and of the car. He realised well enough that the longer he could delay the finding of either, the better for his get-away. He daren't leave things just as they were, for someone might come along that way at any time. The car was the least important of the two things he had to get rid of. The gravel-pit would do well enough for that. It wouldn't really matter if one of Scrimp's men happened on it next day.

"But the body was an entirely different proposition. That must not be found until it had reached a state at which any opinion as to cause of death, or even perhaps identity, would be difficult to form. I might put in a word there. One of the reasons for the pockets being emptied may have been to hinder identification.

" What then was to be done with the body ? Why, dump it in the bungalow. It doesn't seem very likely that the murderer could have done that single-handed. And, having got it there, to lock the bungalow door, leave the key, together with that of the house, in the kitchen, leave the house by the front door, taking care that the automatic lock worked, and clear out ! "

" That last is a very neat point," said Arnold approvingly. " The keys not being available, no one could enter either house or bungalow, short of breaking in. No unauthorised person was likely to do that."

" And the surviving partner of H. Jones and Son would take jolly good care that no client was taken to view Cherry Trees until a sufficient time had elapsed," Kingston replied darkly. " And then he contrived that the client, not himself, should make the discovery. It comes to this, as you must see as well as I do. Everything points to young White, probably with the assistance of his wife."

Arnold nodded. " I'm inclined to agree with you, Mr. Kingston. But we're a very long way yet from having built up a case against them. I think our next step should be to have a chat with Miss Chirton."

Kingston glanced at the clock. " She ought to be leaving the office pretty soon. I'll ring her up and ask her if she'll be so good as to step in here when she does."

They were still discussing the case when Pauline Chirton was announced. She was quite unruffled, and smiled modestly at Arnold when Kingston introduced him. " I'm sorry to put you to this trouble, Miss Chirton," said the superintendent. " It's about something you said at the inquest this morning. When you were asked if Mr. Jones usually carried much money on him. Can you tell us any more about that ? "

" Well, as it happens I can," she replied. " After I got back from the inquest, I asked the people in the office if any of them knew when Mr. Jones had last drawn some money. One of the clerks told me that Mr. Jones had sent him to the bank just before it closed on Tuesday with a cheque for twenty-five pounds. The clerk drew the money in pound notes and gave them to Mr. Jones. He was the clerk whom Mr. White took to Wodeley Manor next day."

Kingston found the introduction of White's name most

opportune. " Oh, yes, of course. Mr. White was out all day on Wednesday. Who actually took in that telegram ? "

" I did," Pauline replied. " As I was coming back to the office after lunch. The telegraph boy and I reached the door together, and I took the telegram from him."

" Mr. White didn't even run home for lunch ? " Kingston suggested.

Pauline shook her head. " He told me before he started that he was taking some sandwiches with him. He said it would take up too much time to come home for lunch. Besides, Mrs. White was out."

Kingston and Arnold exchanged a quick glance. " Mrs. White does a lot for the Red Cross, I believe," said the former. " I expect she was out on some business connected with that, wasn't she ? "

" I couldn't say," Pauline replied. " I was with her a day or two before, Monday evening, I think it was, and she told me she would not be at home on Wednesday. She said she had to go to Baleminster, and might be there all day. But she didn't tell me what she was going for."

" Shopping, perhaps," Kingston remarked. " You ladies like to take your time over that. And Baleminster is an easy journey from here by car. Mrs. White drives a car, I suppose ? "

" Oh, yes," Pauline replied. " She's a very good driver. But she can't have driven into Baleminster that day, for Mr. White's car was out at Wodeley Manor. She must have gone by bus or train."

" Yes, of course," said Kingston. " Oh, by the way, Miss Chirton, that letter from Manchester hasn't been found yet ? "

Pauline shook her head. " I'm pretty certain it's not in the office, for I've hunted for it everywhere. I'm quite sure that Mr. Jones must have put it in his pocket when he'd read it."

" A very natural thing for him to have done," Kingston replied. " Did Mr. Jones open the letter himself ? "

" Oh, no," Pauline replied. " I open all the letters myself, unless they are marked ' Personal,' as soon as I get to the office in the morning. I opened that one among the rest on Tuesday, and put it in Mr. Jones's tray."

" What did you do with the envelope ? " Kingston asked.

Pauline smiled. " We don't keep the envelopes, Mr. Kingston. They go into the waste paper baskets. The office boy empties them into a sack of the waste paper collection."

" And what becomes of the sack, Miss Chirton ? " Kingston asked.

" The dustmen take it away on Friday mornings and leave another in its place," she replied.

" I see," said Kingston. " Now, about that telegram, once more. You had it when you got back from lunch on Wednesday, and of course read it. Did you ring up Mr. White at Wodeley Manor, and tell him about it ? "

" I didn't think that necessary," Pauline replied. " I showed it to Mr. White as soon as he arrived back. That was about half past four. Mr. White was just as surprised as I had been."

" Surprised that Mr. Jones had been detained ? " Kingston suggested.

" Well, not exactly that," she replied, a trifle uneasily. " We supposed that Mr. Jones had been detained on business. What really surprised us was that he wasn't back on Thursday to meet Mr. Wilberton."

" It must have seemed rather odd," said Kingston. " Do you know what time Mr. White left the office that evening ? "

" No, I don't," Pauline replied. " I didn't see him go. But he wasn't there when I left between half past five and six."

" Thank you, Miss Chirton," said Kingston. " I'm sorry we've kept you so long talking. What we really wanted to know was about the money Mr. Jones might have had on him. What you've told us is most valuable. If he drew a cheque for twenty-five pounds on Tuesday afternoon, he probably had most of it on Wednesday. Now, if you'll come with me, I'll show you safely off the premises."

CHAPTER IX

KINGSTON RETURNED, smiling contentedly. " Not too bad, eh, Mr. Arnold ? "

" I congratulate you, Mr. Kingston. Your method filled me with admiration. You put it to her in such a way that she can't have had the slightest idea what you were really after. And without knowing it, she gave us quite a lot of extremely useful information."

" Just a minute before we discuss that," said Kingston. " We can't leave that car standing about in the yard here indefinitely. I know that Hembury Motors Ltd. have one or two lock-ups at their place. I'll ring their manager and ask him if he can house the car in safety for a while."

He made the call, and after a short conversation reported to Arnold. " That'll be all right. I spoke to Thornham himself. He's the manager. He's got a spare lock-up, of which we can keep the key. And he'll send round at once and fetch the car. Now, what have you got to say about Miss Chirton ? "

" A most capable young woman, with all her wits about her," Arnold replied. " And I don't believe she knows any more about the affair than she's prepared to tell us. And that was quite a bit, when you come to think it over. Several very important points.

" Take them in the order in which they came out. White did not come home to lunch on Wednesday. That is at least an indication that he knew his wife wouldn't be there. She wasn't absent from Hembury without his knowledge. No question of her taking advantage of his being out all day to go away herself.

" Mrs. White told Miss Chirton on Monday, on Monday, mark you, that she wouldn't be at home on Wednesday. The letter from the so-called Podmore hadn't been received at the office then. But it must have been composed. Had Mrs. White any knowledge of the contents of that letter ? Or was it just coincidence that she had arranged to be away from home on Wednesday ?

" Mrs. White told Miss Chirton that she had to go to Baleminster. Whether she had to or not, I think it's probable she did go there. On the same day Jones went to Baleminster, thence to Cherry Trees, and back to Baleminster. Did he and Mrs. White meet there that afternoon ?

" Miss Chirton tells us that Mrs. White is a very good driver. Capable perhaps of driving Jones's car at a pinch. She may have driven it to the gravel-pit, while her husband tidied things up at the bungalow.

" White got back to the office about half past four. He and Miss Chirton had some conversation about the telegram, which surprised them. She looked a bit bothered when you asked her why they were surprised. Perhaps she thinks now that White oughtn't to have been surprised. After that, apparently, she didn't see him. The time he left the office isn't established. Perhaps in time to drive to Cherry Trees and get there before six."

" Very well put, Mr. Arnold," said Kingston. The slightly strained politeness between the local superintendent and the officer from the C.I.D. was still apt to show itself. " But young White is a pretty cool customer. Jones was to have held a farm sale next day, and he held it for him. They tell me that when the sale started he apologised for the unavoidable absence of his partner, which nobody could regret more deeply than he did himself. He's not the sort of chap to confess to the crime, however hard we were to drive him."

" Mrs. White might turn out to be the weaker vessel," Arnold replied. " But it's hardly come to that yet. As I believe I remarked before, it's no use tackling suspects until one is sure of one's ground. By which I mean at least some evidence which would stand up to cross examination in the court."

" I quite agree," said Kingston. " I'm not suggesting that we rush things. But already our evidence, circumstantial though it is, is pretty strong. We have both motive and opportunity. And I'll go further, and ask you who but Mrs. White would have lured Jones to Cherry Trees that afternoon. Any attractive woman, you might reply if you were sufficiently cynical. Miss Chirton answers to that description, but I think we are agreed that we can leave her out. What other woman could have known that Jones was going to Cherry Trees that day?"

"There's this possibility," Arnold replied. "Jones picked up some woman in Baleminster and drove her to Cherry Trees in his car."

Kingston shook his head. "That won't do. Jones wasn't murdered by any woman single-handed. Why, man, look at the state of the car! Only two men, struggling desperately together, could have wrecked it to that extent. And, again, if a woman had succeeded in strangling Jones in his car, she couldn't possibly have dragged his body to the bungalow by herself. No, it's a sure thing that the woman had a man to help her."

He paused, digging holes in his blotting-paper with the point of a pencil. "The very fact that the letter has vanished is evidence in itself!" he exclaimed abruptly. "Miss Chirton is convinced that Jones took it with him. He may have done so, in which case it was removed from his pocket with the rest of the stuff. It's just as likely he left it in the office, and that White picked it up and destroyed it. As you pointed out yourself, Mrs. White seems to have known what was in it before it was delivered. I'll bet it was posted a lot nearer home than Manchester. That's why I asked Miss Chirton about the envelope."

"Her reply was natural enough," Arnold remarked. "Business firms file the letters they receive, but not the envelopes with them."

"They didn't file this one," Kingston replied viciously. "But you're quite right, Mr. Arnold. It's not the slightest use our asking the Council to let us go through the waste paper their people collected last Friday. How should we recognise that particular envelope if we found it? I'll bet whoever sent it wasn't obliging enough to use an envelope with the name of Podmores Ltd. printed on it. And if, as I suspect, it was posted anywhere but in Manchester it would be more hopeless still. I believe——"

He was interrupted by the buzz of his telephone. He answered the call with a curt, "Show him in." A minute later a youngish man appeared, and laid a key on the superin-tendent's desk. "I thought I'd better bring you the key myself, Mr. Kingston. The car is safely in one of our lock-ups.

I'm bound to say it looks a good deal worse for wear, than when I last saw it. Do you want us to do anything about that ? "

" Not just yet, Mr. Thornham, thank you," Kingston replied. " When did you last see the car ? "

" On Monday of last week," Thornham replied. " We sold Mr. Jones the car, and we've always serviced it for him since. He drove it into our place to have that done on Monday the 14th. And I don't know whether this will interest you, Mr. Kingston. We keep a register of all the cars we service regularly. The date of each servicing, the work done and so forth, and the mileage shown at each date."

He took a note-book from his pocket. " I jotted down the figures in case you might want them. Our record shows the mileage of Mr. Jones's car on the 14th as 7,517. The mileage now shown is 7,569. The car has run only fifty-two miles since Mr. Jones took it out from our place on the afternoon of the 14th."

Kingston made a rapid note of these figures. " Thank you, Mr. Thornham. I'm very much obliged to you. I'll keep the key for the present, and let you know later on what I want done with the car."

" That was highly intelligent of him," he went on, when Thornham had gone out. " Take a paper and pencil and work it out for yourself. Jones drove from here to Baleminster, about thirteen miles. From Baleminster to Cherry Trees. It's ten miles from Baleminster to Lingmarsh, and at least a mile to Cherry Trees. Call it eleven miles, and a bit over. Back to Baleminster, another eleven miles. Again in the afternoon to Cherry Trees, eleven miles. Finally, someone drove the car from Cherry Trees to the gravel-pit, say three miles. Now just add that lot up, and see what it comes to."

" Forty-nine miles," Arnold replied, with commendable promptness.

" Near enough," said Kingston. " The distances I gave you were only approximate, and Jones may have made a detour round Baleminster while he was there. It fits in so exactly with what we've been talking about that it's almost proof by itself. When we were interrupted just now, I was going to say that I believed it was quite likely that the letter was posted in this very town."

Arnold smiled. " We can't prove that, anyhow. But I agree with you that it's probably a local crime, so to speak. That being so, I can't see that I can do much good by staying here. It all depends upon whether we can ferret out anyone who saw the Whites, or either of them, between half past four and half past six. And you, with your local contacts, are far more capable of doing that than I am."

Kingston agreed to this, and promised to let Arnold know at once if any fresh information was forthcoming. He took him to the station, and saw him off on his way back to London.

Arnold was not sorry to get away from Hembury. It seemed to him that the superintendent had got the bit between his teeth, and that there was a risk of his being too precipitate. He might even twist the facts to fit in with his theory, a mistake which Arnold knew from experience to lead to failure. Not that Arnold had any doubts of the guilt of the Whites. But that was a very different matter from being able to prove a case against them. After all, that case, as it stood at present, was based largely on conjecture. The best plan, he felt sure, was to adopt a waiting policy. If the superintendent chose to take a false step, Arnold, absent from the scene, could hardly be blamed for the consequences.

He was in his room at Scotland Yard on Thursday morning when his telephone rang. Superintendent Kingston wished to speak to him from Hembury. In a few moments he heard Kingston's voice. " That you, Mr. Arnold? Good morning. I thought I might as well ring you up. Rather a queer thing."

" A fresh development?" Arnold asked. " Anything sensational?"

" Oh, no," Kingston replied. " A bit odd, that's all. A chap has just been in to see me. An elderly man who's got a farm near Lintford, about two miles from here. He told me that as he had to come in on business, he thought he'd better drop in and tell me that he'd seen Jones on Tuesday evening, the 15th."

Arnold did not at once see the significance of this. " Very thoughtful of him, but he might have saved himself the trouble. We know from many sources that Jones was alive and well next morning."

" Wait a minute," Kingston replied. " This chap told me that he had made up his mind to sell his farm and retire. He wrote to Jones at his home address, one day the week before last, asking him to come and see him one evening without mentioning the matter to anyone, as he did not want his intentions to leak out yet. Jones turned up in his fine big car about seven on the evening of the 15th, and the chap took him round the farm. Now just you put that in your foul pipe and smoke it."

Kingston rang off, leaving Arnold in a state of considerable amusement. One of the Superintendent's beautifully constructed pieces of evidence had fallen like a pack of cards. Jones had driven to the farm near Lintford and back, a total distance of at least twenty miles on Tuedsay evening. The mileage recorded since Monday should then have been nearer seventy-two than fifty-two. No wonder the superintendent's voice had sounded bitter.

Seriously though, how was this discrepancy to be accounted for? As Arnold asked himself this question, one way of accounting for it occurred to him. The about ten miles from Hembury to Lintford, with possibly a further short distance to the farm, corresponded, as near as made no matter, with the eleven miles from Baleminster to Cherry Trees. If then, after his journey to Cherry Trees on Wednesday morning, Jones had not returned to Baleminster, the recorded mileage would be correct.

But Arnold thought that wouldn't do. It raised too many problems. The old question, if Jones hadn't sent the telegram, who had? Where had the car been from its arrival at Cherry Trees, at a time which could be fixed by Mr. Grudge's statement, until shortly before the clock stopped at ten to six? It must have been motionless for some six hours. If outside Cherry Trees, someone must surely have passed along the lane and noticed it.

That was up to Kingston. He might make use of his local contacts, as Arnold had suggested. Again, where had Jones been all this time, to say nothing of his mysterious and elusive client? Arguing together in an empty house, until in desperation, the client murdered Jones? Ridiculous, of course. The client's motive for murder could have been theft, and he obviously hadn't stolen the most valuable thing, the car.

There must of course be some perfectly simple solution. The mileage recorder had stopped working. They did, sometimes.

The cable either broke or came loose. Anyhow, it was to be hoped that the incident would teach Kingston a lesson. He had displayed far too great an aptitude to accept as convincing evidence events capable of a totally different interpretation. The evidence of the mileage recorder had completely broken down. But that merely meant that it must be discarded as unreliable. It did not mean that it could be used as an argument in support of the innocence of the Whites.

For of their guilt Arnold was pretty well satisfied. If they hadn't conspired to kill Jones, who had? But he was very well aware that this question would cut no ice with a judge, who would demand what definite evidence there was against the accused. And for the present Arnold could only reply that there was none.

As Arnold reflected upon this, it struck him that it was just the sort of problem that would appeal to a friend of his. Desmond Merrion, at present a man of means and leisure who had, during two wars, served with distinction in the Intelligence branch of the Admiralty. He had almost an uncanny gift of ferreting out the truth, in Arnold's opinion, by unorthodox methods and the use of a particularly vivid imagination. Nevertheless Arnold had no scruples in seeking Merrion's aid in the solution of his most difficult cases. The problem confronting them now was not to detect the culprits, but to unearth the necessary evidence against them. And Arnold felt pretty certain that Merrion, if his interest could be aroused, would revel in the job.

Merrion, with his wife Mavis, lived at High Eldersham Hall, in East Anglia. They had also a small pied-a-terre in London, a set of rooms in St. James's. Merrion, who had various rather vague and not particularly onerous business connections, frequently spent a few days in London. Arnold had a call put through to the rooms. After a decent interval, he was informed there was no reply.

The inference was that Merrion was at home in the country. When he came up to London he always brought his confidential man-servant, Newport, with him. They would not both be out in the morning. So Arnold had a call put through to High Eldersham Hall. There would be somebody there, anyhow.

There was. As soon as Arnold was connected, he recognised a familiar voice. " How are you, Newport ? " he asked

cordially, for he and Newport were old acquaintances. " Can
I speak to Mr. Merrion ? "

" I'm afraid you can't, Mr. Arnold," Newport replied with
polite regret. " Mr. and Mrs. Merrion are away."

" That's unfortunate," said Arnold. " Can you give me Mr.
Merrion's address ? "

" I'm afraid I can't even do that, sir," Newport replied.
" Mr. Merrion told me before he left that it was no good
writing to him, for neither he nor anyone else knew what port
the ship might call at, or when."

" The ship ! " Arnold exclaimed. " What ship ? I thought
Mr. Merrion's nautical cases were over long ago."

" Oh, it's not that, sir," Newport assured him. " Mr.
Merrion has gone as a passenger this time. You see, Mr. Arnold,
he's gone for a cruise in the Eastern Mediterranean, and I
don't expect him back for a month at least."

CHAPTER X

FOR A LONG time it had been evident that the roof of the main
block of High Eldersham Hall would have to be taken down
and rebuilt. The old timbers supporting the lead were honey-
combed with worm, and the lead itself was cracked with age.
The architect whom the Merrions consulted took a breezy
view of the situation. " No good trying to patch things up,"
he said, after a day spent crawling about above the ceilings of
the attics. " It's too far gone for that. The best thing, and
the cheapest in the long run, would be to take the whole thing
down, and put up light steel supports instead of wood, and
copper instead of lead. And I'd recommend you to have the
work done as soon as possible, Mr. Merrion. I wouldn't answer
for what might happen if we had a heavy fall of snow next
winter."

Merrion sighed. " Steel and copper ? It sounds more like
re-roofing a factory than one of the stately homes of England.
However, I suppose you know best. I daresay we can find the
money somehow. Eh, Mavis ? "

This had been in June. Tenders were put out, and one of
them accepted. It was finally arranged with the successful

contractor that the work should be put in hand early in September. " Well, that's that," said Mavis resignedly. " It's got to be, I suppose. But don't imagine that we're going to stay here while all the fuss is going on. It means some dreadful resort, I suppose, where you'll be bored stiff within a week."

" I've got another idea about that," her husband replied. " What about going to sea ? "

" What ? " Mavis exclaimed. " In a liner ? You'll have to think again, Desmond. Neither you nor I is the sort to be herded together like a flock of sheep, with some raucous-voiced entertainment organiser as shepherd. You might as well ask me to spend a few matey weeks in a holiday camp."

" Calm yourself, my dear," Merrion replied. " I wasn't thinking of a liner. No Luxury Cruises to the land of Sunshine for us. But there are freighters, carrying not more than twelve passengers, which potter about from port to port. No dressing-up, no regimentation, do just as you like. How does that appeal to you ? "

" It sounds more like it," said Mavis doubtfully. " One doesn't sleep in a hammock in the forecastle, I take it ? "

Merrion laughed. " Even the crew don't do that now-a-days. Very often every man has a room to himself, and the passenger cabins are usually larger, if not so ostentatious, as those on a liner. Incidentally, there's no rationing at sea, and drinks are a lot cheaper. What about it ? "

" If your picture isn't overdrawn, I'm game," Mavis replied. " All right then. You set to work to find this dream ship of yours, and I'll promise to come with you."

Merrion got into touch with various travel-agents. His conditions were first that the voyage must begin early in September, and, since the contractors had estimated that the work at High Eldersham Hall would take about six weeks, that the round trip must take about that time, Second, as Mavis stipulated, that the ship's destinations should lie in a warm climate.

It took him some time to find what he wanted. He received a letter informing him that the Norwegian freighter *Ballerina*, approximately three thousand tons, was scheduled to start from London on or about 2nd September, returning to a North European port. The ports of call were Piraeus, Istambul and or Ismit, Cyprus, Beirut, and or Tripoli, Lebanon. The

F

round trip was expected to take from six to nine weeks. A double cabin was available, and would be reserved for Mr. and Mrs. Merrion upon receipt of fare.

" It all sounds delightfully vague," said Mavis, when she had read the letter. " What exactly does it mean ? "

" Put the word 'exactly' out of your head for good and all," her husband replied. " It means that you and I shall spend a few weeks drifting about the Eastern Mediterranean. Nobody, not even the owners themselves, know where the good ship *Ballerina* will call. The ports mentioned are those for which she has, or expects to have, cargo. By the time she sails, she may have cargo for other ports as well. When she has discharged her outward cargo, she will poke about from port to port until her holds are full, picking up homeward cargo wherever it may offer. And that cargo may not be consigned to London. We may be pushed off the ship at Le Havre, Dunkerque, Antwerp, Hamburg, almost anywhere, in fact. And get it firmly fixed in your mind that the business of a freighter is to carry cargo. Passengers are only a side-line, and must be prepared to take the rough with the smooth. Does all that appal you ? "

Mavis shook her head. " Not in the least. It sounds enormous fun. Send them the money for the fares. It seems ridiculously cheap. I only hope it won't be nasty."

Rather exceptionally, the sailing date was not unduly delayed. On the morning of Thursday, 3rd September, Merrion received a telegram, informing him that he and Mrs. Merrion should be on board the *Ballerina*, lying at Jarl Wharf, West India Dock, by six o'clock that afternoon.

Since they had been waiting, with their belongings packed, for the last two days, this was easy. He loaded up their car with the luggage and, taking Newport with them, set out for London. To drive down the West India Dock road was simple enough, but to find the correct entrance to Jarl Wharf was another matter. However, after enquiries, Merrion drove through a gateway on to a space cumbered with lorries, vast packing cases, sacks, steel drums and what not. And against the quay, beyond all these, lay the *Ballerina*.

Merrion's heart warmed to her at first sight. She was a squat, sturdy motor-ship, with sampson-ports, two stumpy masts, and a short false funnel. Curiously enough, in these

materialistic days, she had a figure-head, the head and bust of
a woman, holding what appeared to be a palm-branch, or was
it an ostrich feather, across her breast? Merrion supposed
that she represented a ballerina. He was delighted to notice
that the ship was fitted with electric winches, which worked
in almost uncanny silence. There would be no deafening
clatter when the ship was in port, loading or unloading cargo.

All this at a glance. The next problem was to get on board.
The *Ballerina* was loading at four of her five holds, and the
narrow quay seemed almost unapproachable. However,
between them they carried the luggage from the car to the
gangway, dodging electric trucks and enormous loads swinging
overhead. There was no smartly-uniformed steward to greet
them. But for the stevedores in and around the holds, and the
men at the winches, there was nobody to be seen. As usual,
with a freighter in port, the officers and crew seemed to have
disappeared. They dumped the luggage in the alleyway, and
bade farewell to Newport, who was to drive the car back to
High Eldersham Hall, of which he was to be in charge during
his employers' absence.

They had allowed themselves plenty of time, and it was
barely four o'clock. To all appearances they were the first
passengers to embark. Merrion, following his nautical instinct,
soon discovered a small smoking-room, in which was a bell-
push. He pressed this, and after an interval, a fair-haired
statuesque girl appeared. Before long they learnt that her
name was Cinevra, which became corrupted by English tongues
to Cinema, or even Cineraria.

She looked at the Merrions speculatively. It was her first
voyage as a stewardess, her first time at sea, in fact. No one
had initiated her into the procedure. Besides, her English,
which all Norwegians learn at school, was already more than
half forgotten. " You, passengers? " she asked painfully,
delving in her memory for the words. " What names, please? "
Merrion told her, and she repeated the name. " Ah, yes. Tree
an' fo'. Will you come, please? "

" What's that? " Merrion asked. " Three and four? We
booked a double cabin, not two single ones."

This was beyond Cinevra's comprehension, and she shook
her head dolefully. Then she brightened up and smiled. " I
fetch steward. You like—what you say—some tea."

"We should like nothing better," Mavis replied. As Cinevra vanished, she turned to her husband. "I didn't expect to find a stewardess on a freighter. At least that's what I suppose the girl is. But it looks to me as if we should have to learn Norwegian, Desmond."

Merrion laughed. "I ought to have warned you. Scandinavian ships always carry stewardesses. Perhaps only because they're cheaper than men, I expect. As for learning Norwegian you'll find it a lot easier to brush up that girl's English. She already knows our English weakness for tea."

A few minutes later an individual in his shirt-sleeves appeared, tall and broad-shouldered, bringing with him a faint but unmistakable aroma of alcohol. Merrion discovered later that his English was really only fluent when he had had a drink or two. "Mr. and Mrs. Merrion? Glad to see you. I show you your cabin. Where you put your baggage?"

"We left it in the alleyway," Merrion replied. "Seven pieces."

"I send boy to fetch it," said the steward. "You come with me. I show you cabin." He led them down to the deck below, upon which the saloon and cabins were situated. He produced a couple of keys, and unlocked doors numbered three and four. "Best cabins in ship," he went on. "Bathroom just here and toilet opposite."

Merrion was about to expostulate, when he produced yet another key, with which he unlocked a sliding door between the two cabins.

"See!" he said, as he slid the door back.

"Two cabins. Make them into one for married couples. You let me know of anything you want. I go to find boy."

The cabins were relatively spacious, each with a wide settle facing forward and overlooking number two hold, at present a yawning gulf into which strangely shaped bundles were being lowered. Merrion felt the beds. "No hammocks here, or even bunks. And beds, with spring mattresses too. Think you'll be comfortable!"

"I'm sure I shall," Mavis replied. "I really didn't expect anything quite like this. You can get up first in the morning, and leave me the whole space to dress in."

The boy appeared with the first batch of luggage, a blue-eyed, fair-haired young Viking. He was rather shy or had no

word of English, but he grinned ecstatically when Mavis pressed
half a crown into his hand. " More than his day's pay, I
daresay," Merrion remarked. " The Norwegians sign them on
young and cheap. Even chaps who mean to become officers
have to start on the bottom rung of the ladder and work
themselves up. Here he comes with the rest of the stuff. I
wish I knew how to say thank you in Norwegian. We needn't
start unpacking now. Let's go and see if we can find the tea
that girl promised us."

They reached the smoking-room as Cinevra was setting a
tray on one of the tables. She smiled at them encouragingly.
" Good tea. I just make it. You pour ? "

Upon being told that they would, she disappeared. Mavis
poured out a cup of tea and tasted it. " Hardly what we're
accustomed to at home, but not too bad. I daresay we shall
get used to it." Later in the voyage she discovered that it
was the topsy-turvy habit on board the *Ballerina* to boil the
water for making tea in a saucepan, and to make the coffee in
a kettle. They were sipping their tea and nibbling the biscuits
which accompanied it, when a man strolled into the smoking-
room with an unconscious air of possession.

He was short and stocky, with a round weather-beaten face,
deep-sunk brown eyes and a mass of black hair. He was wearing a rough tweed jacket, a pull-over, and a pair of flannel
trousers. " You passengers ? " he asked, while they were still
wondering who he might be. " I kaptan, name Larsen, Hans
Larsen."

They stood up and introduced themselves. Captain Larsen
chuckled engagingly as they shook hands. " You expected
kaptan in gold lace and brass buttons and fine cap with
badge ? Not till we get to sea. And that will not be till to-
morrow's tide, about eleven. We wait for fifty ton sugar,
coming first thing in morning."

" Time's nothing to us, Captain," Merrion replied. " This
is a nice ship you've got."

Larsen shrugged his shoulders in an unsuccessful attempt
to conceal his pride in the *Ballerina*. " Good ship. Getting
old though. Built in Oslo fifteen years ago. I kaptan since
the war ended. All the passengers English this trip. Usually
we bring some Norwegians from Oslo. You must all try to
teach me English."

Mavis smiled at him. " No need for that, Captain. Your English is perfect already."

Larsen shook his head. " Oh, no, not that. I serve in tanker under English flag in war. But my English it get rusty, like the tanker. Now, I tell you this. On Norwegian ship you do what you like. Go where you like, up on bridge, down on main deck. And you see bell there ? If you want anything, ring it."

He went out, leaving them to finish their tea. " Decent chap," Merrion remarked. " And a good seaman, like all Norwegians, I don't doubt. He meant what he said when he told us on Norwegian ships you do what you like. A smack at our posh liners, I daresay. You won't find much spit and polish on this ship."

They went down to their cabin and started unpacking. Mavis was bound to admit, but with some encroachment upon her husband's half, she found plenty of room for her clothes. By the time they returned to the smoking-room it was full of people. Merrion did not attempt to sort them out. He knew from experience that it was impossible to differentiate those who were to become his fellow-passengers from their friends who had come to see them off and the shipping agents and their families, who infest a ship on sailing day. He strolled out on to the boat deck, exceptionally spacious for so small a ship, found a wooden chest marked ' Lifebelt,' sat on it, and lighted a cigarette.

After a while Mavis joined him. " I thought I should find you out here," she said. " I ran into that steward just now. He seemed slightly drunk, but he told me that supper would be served at seven o'clock."

" Drunk, is he ? " Merrion replied. " He's lucky. Got a private stock of his own, I suppose. We shan't get drunk this evening, not on board, at all events. All the drink is under the seal of Her Majesty's Customs, and that isn't supposed to be broken until we're outside the three mile limit. I don't some-how fancy supper washed down by good plain water. What about going ashore and having dinner and something to drink ? "

Mavis agreed, and they set out. The policeman at the dock gates warned them that on their return they would be asked to produce their steamer ticket before they would be allowed to re-enter. There was no difficulty about that, for Merrion had them in his note-case. They took a bus into the heart of London, had their meal, and were back soon after ten. There was no difficulty about picking out the *Ballerina*, for she was brilliantly illuminated, in contrast to her sisters, the English freighters lying in the dock. Parsimony forbade their wasting fuel on running dynamos when in port. By the time they boarded her, the smoking-room was deserted. They went below and turned in.

Merrion was the first up in the morning. All the holds were working merrily, and he knew he would only be in the way if he went on deck. He strolled into the saloon, where he found Cinevra and another girl laying the tables. This other girl, addressed as Nina, was younger, with a soft voice and mischievous eyes. They smiled good morning at him, and went on with their duties.

The saloon was airy, and by no means cramped. In the centre was a large round table, laid for eight. Besides this, at opposite sides of the room, were two small tables. One of these was laid for three, the other was evidently not to be laid, for it was covered with cups and plates. A roomy sideboard and the necessary chairs completed the furniture.

Merrion noticed that Cinevra was laying a wide paper envelope, with a name written on each at each plate. Trying not to look inquisitive, he made the circuit of the round table. In the place facing the door of the saloon was an envelope on which ' Kaptan Larsen ' had been written in indelible pencil. Continuing in a clock-wise direction, he read the name on the rest. Mrs. Stewart-Patterson, on the captain's left. Mr. Pulham, Mrs. Lavenham, Mr. Merrion, Mrs. Merrion, Clarice Mallory. Finally, on the captain's right, Mrs. Mallory. Cinevra had not yet laid the envelopes on the smaller table, so he could not learn the names of those who were to occupy it.

He went back to the lounge, to watch through the scuttles there the loading of the ship. The sound of a gong, banged by an apparently furious hand, awakened him from his reverie. Breakfast, no doubt. Not wishing to be the first arrival in the saloon, he went down to the cabin. Mavis had not yet finished dressing. When she had, they went into breakfast together.

They were not the last to appear. The captain had taken

his seat but the chairs on either side of him were vacant. In fact, at the round table only two other seats were occup'ed, those of Mrs. Lavenham and Mr. Pulham, who were politely handing one another the toast and butter. She was a handsome woman, approaching middle age, and displayed some reserve towards the conversational advances of her neighbour. He was a fussy little man in the late sixties, garrulous, and in table manners, not over refined.

At the side table sat three men. By his uniform, and the gold stripes set on purple on his sleeve, Merrion knew the one in the centre to be the chief engineer. He was talking to his two companions in picturesque and not very intelligible English. One of these was a man about sixty, big, burly, and jovial, with rather coarse features and a loud voice. The other looked slightly younger, quiet, slim, with a slight stoop and the face of a student.

As the Merrions, after bidding the captain good morning, took their seats, another passenger came in. She was a slightly wizened elderly woman, with a determined, though not an unfriendly expression. Anyone could tell at first glance that she was Scottish, but, as though to eliminate all possible doubt, she wore a tartan skirt. Limping slightly, she supported her steps to the table with the aid of a shooting stick. An unusual implement to bring on board ship, Merrion thought. This was Mrs. Stewart-Patterson.

Scarcely had she taken her seat when an excited voice became audible and a flurry at the saloon door. Merrion was to learn that Mrs. Mallory was one of those women who created an air of commotion wherever they go. She appeared, a youngish woman with an ingenuous expression, leading by the hand a large and stolid female child of about ten. " Come along, darling. There are only two seats left, so they must be ours. Oh, we're sitting next to the captain ! How nice ! Good morning, Captain. I'm sorry we're late, but it took such a long time to get Clarice dressed. Good morning, everybody. Sit down there, darling, that's right. Look, your name's on the envelope."

Having thus concentrated all eyes upon herself, Mrs. Mallory sat down. Before long she was chattering to the captain in a highly-pitched voice. " I'm travelling to join my husband in Athens, you know, Captain. He's got a very

as odd. Across her legs was a large sketching-block, supported with one hand, while in the other she held a pencil. This was no pose, for she was sketching away assiduously, paying little attention to Mr. Pulham, who was standing by her admiringly. Merrion wondered whence her inspiration came. Situated as she was, the only object within her view was an unfinished power-station.

A group of three was leaning over the rail, watching the loading of bags of sugar from a lighter which had come alongside. Mrs. Mallory in the centre, with Mr. Wilberton and Mr. Bewdley, one on each side of her. Mr. Wilberton was telling a story, at which Mrs. Mallory smiled at appropriate intervals. Every now and then her narrator appealed to Mr. Bewdley. " That's right, isn't it, Horace, my boy ? " Sometimes Mr. Bewdley replied, " perfectly right, Uncle Jasper." More often he contented himself with merely nodding. No doubt he had heard the story many times before. He seemed more interested in the sugar, or perhaps his own thoughts.

Clarice was sitting in a chair by herself, intent upon a copiously illustrated book. Merrion was inclined to be sorry for her loneliness, but he soon discovered that she was like that. Not exactly shy, but reserved and rather unapproachable. She could not be described as an attractive child, for she was lumpish and her movements gauche. Besides, she was slightly cross-eyed, but her expression was not devoid of a certain sly intelligence.

Mavis and Mrs. Lavenham were sitting together, chatting away as if they had known one another all their lives. Mrs. Lavenham was knitting with amazing speed and dexterity, hardly ever bestowing a glance at her work. Merrion was glad that Mavis had chummed up with her, for she seemed the most congenial passenger on the ship. She was certainly vivacious, suitably dressed, and extremely good-looking, especially when she smiled. Merrion went up to them, and Mavis introduced them. " Have you met my husband, Mrs. Lavenham ? "

Mrs. Lavenham was patently genuine. " I sat next to Mr. Merrion at breakfast, but we didn't speak. I've been married long enough to know that men should never be spoken to at breakfast. Do tell us, Mr. Merrion. Your wife and I have both been wondering. Where is the place the captain said we were to call at first ? "

Merrion's naval experience had given him some knowledge of the Mediterranean. " Kalimata," he replied. " It's a small port in southern Greece. I've never been there, but I've been told it exports currants."

" It seems most romantic ! " Mrs. Lavenham exclaimed. " I don't mean the currants, of course. Just think of it, Mrs. Merrion. Men like Adonis and women like Aphrodite, though with rather more clothes on, I hope. What are we going there for, Mr. Merrion ? "

" Not to admire the inhabitants, I imagine. I shouldn't pin my hopes too high, Mrs. Lavenham. From what I've seen of modern Greece, they're not likely to look as you seem to expect. I've been talking to the carpenter. He told me that he had sailed on United States ships, and he speaks a wonderful brand of American. The fore deck is littered with steel drums. I asked him what was in them, and he told me they were empty, and that we were to discharge them at Kalimata. It seems that the natives fill them with grape juice, and send it back to England to be made into British wines."

" Even less romantic than the currants," Mrs. Lavenham remarked. " Oh, whatever's that ? "

The compressed air whistle with which the *Ballerina* was fitted had a curiously heart-gripping note. It was a blast from this that had caused Mrs. Lavenham's exclamation. " A signal that we're just about to push off, I expect," Merrion replied. He strolled to the rail, and the two women rose and followed him. On the quay-side men were standing by the warps, and a raucous voice from the bridge was yelling orders.

One by one the warps were cast off. There was a tremor and muffled rumbling as the engine turned dead slow astern. The *Ballerina* began to move almost imperceptibly towards the lock gates. " How lovely ! " Mrs. Lavenham exclaimed. " We're off ! "

But to Mrs. Stewart-Patterson, still perched upon the hatch cover, the departure seemed less alluring. " Oh, we're moving ! " she exclaimed. " How provoking ! My sketch isn't half finished, and I shall never be able to finish it now." She laid aside her sketch-block and pencil, and groped for her shooting-stick, but failed to find it. " Oh, wherever has my stick gone ? I can't get out of my chair without it."

Mr. Pulham, to whom the appeal was addressed, looked

vaguely about him. Merrion had turned at the sound of Mrs. Stewart-Patterson's voice, and saw the shooting-stick. It had slipped off the hatch and was lying on the deck beside it. He returned it to her, and she seemed duly grateful. " Thank you so much. I can hardly move a step without my stick, yet I always seem to be losing it. I lost it once on the *Acropolis*, and it took me ever so long to find it. Do tell me your name. I'm so terribly deaf that I can never catch names unless they are shouted at me."

Merrion told her and introduced Mavis. Mrs. Stewart-Patterson rose majestically from her chair with the aid of her stick. " I must take these things down to my cabin somehow," she remarked expectantly.

Mr. Pulham hastened to pick up her sketching-block, stool and rugs. Merrion offered her his arm to help her down from the hatch. She set off, followed by Mr. Pulham with her impedimenta. A procession that was to become familiar on the *Ballerina*. Mrs. Stewart-Patterson, stumping along on her stick, in her train one, or sometimes two, of the other passengers, bearing their tribute.

Meanwhile the *Ballerina* was backing her way into the lock. Beyond it, a tug was waiting to get her into position in the river. The lock gates opened, and the tug slung her slowly round until her head was pointing down the stream. The tug cast off, and with a swish of compressed air, the *Ballerina's* main engine went ahead. The voyage had fairly begun.

By the time that lunch was over, Gravesend was reached. Merrion, leaning on the rail, watched the change of pilots. He had seen it before, times innumerable, but the deftness with which the operation was carried out still interested him. As the pilot-boat sheered off, he took a chair to the end of the boat deck and set it up in a position from which he could see on either side. The marvel of London River always fascinated him. The endless procession of vessels of every type, from tall, smartly-painted liners, through every variety of trading craft, down to tawdry mud-hoppers. With, here and there, in lovely contrast, one of the few surviving brown-sailed barges, tacking across the fairway.

One by one the familiar landmarks came in sight. The clustered oiltanks of Thames Haven, Canvey Beacon, Sheerness faintly under a pall of smoke, the long pointing finger of

Southend pier, the undulating skyline of the Isle of Sheppey.
Finally, the first of those strange monstrosities, the anti-
aircraft defences built upon the sands.

The afternoon brought to light those roughnesses inevitable
on the first day out, before passengers and ship's routine have
adjusted themselves to one another. A hand on Merrion's
arm told him that Mavis had come to his side. " Look over
there," he said, pointing over the starboard bow. " See those
things, perched up on stilts in the water ? Like so many
herons. No, not herons, something much uglier. Pterodactyls,
perhaps. Just imagine what life must be like in one of them."

" Life is becoming pretty hectic on board," Mavis replied.
" Mrs. Mallory is raising Cain because it's getting on for
half past four, and she can't see any signs of tea being got
ready."

" Afternoon tea is an insular vice," said Merrion. " I don't
suppose it comes into the catering scheme of a Norwegian
freighter. That we were given a cup yesterday was, no doubt,
an act of grace."

" That may be," Mavis replied. " But Mrs. Mallory says
she's going to have her tea or know the reason why. And I'm
bound to say Mrs. Lavenham and I are on her side. Do come
and see if you can't do something about it, Desmond."

Merrion allowed her to lead him to the smoking-room. " Oh,
Mr. Merrion ! " Mrs. Mallory exclaimed as he appeared.
" We're all dying for our tea, and there's no sign of it. Do you
think you can speak to the captain ? "

Merrion smiled. " I don't think we need appeal to the
highest level, at all events in the first instance. Let's try
ringing the bell, and we'll see what happens."

He rang the bell, well and firmly. They could hear the faint
tinkle of it somewhere below. After a long interval, the
steward, in shirt-sleeves, appeared, his bleary eyes showing
that he had been indulging in a siesta. " You want something ? " he asked, in a none too gracious tone.

" We want our tea ! " Mrs. Mallory replied. " Surely it's
time it was served ? "

The steward's answer implied rebuke. " We not give tea
on this ship. Besides, there isn't anyone to get it. Stewardesses
and cooks, they not on duty in afternoon."

" That's nonsense ! " Mrs. Mallory exclaimed. " I'll get it

myself if you'll show me where to get the things. And I'll
pay for it too, if that's the difficulty."

The steward shook his head. For a few minutes he seemed to
find the problem insoluble. Then he assumed the air of a
Nordic Solomon. " You have coffee after lunch, yes? Very
well. You not have coffee after lunch, you have tea in afternoon. How you say to that?"

There was a chorus of approval. "Wait a minute," said Mrs.
Mallory. " I'll go and find the others and ask them."

She went out, to return in a couple of minutes. " They're
on deck, and I've spoken to them. They all say they would
rather give up coffee after lunch for tea in the afternoon."

The steward inclined his head. " Very well, I will arrange.
One of the girls will get tea now."

A second occurrence of friction was lubricated by Merrion
himself. Some little time after tea Merrion entered the
smoking-room to find the men of the party assembled there.
Mr. Wilberton was complaining to his nephew. " It's not
good enough, Horace. I'm always accustomed to having a
whisky at this time of day. When I booked the passages I
was told there would be plenty of drink on board. But I'm
damned if I can get hold of any."

Mr. Pulham piped up at this. " It's most annoying. I've
just been down to the steward, to ask him to let me have
some cigarettes. I understood from what he said that everything is under seal, and that he isn't allowed to break it
until we're three miles from land, and that won't be till
we've dropped the pilot off Dungeness. We shall have hours
to go yet."

An idea occurred to Merrion. It might work, or it might
not. There was quite a good chance, for the mentality of the
steward seemed hardly above average. Merrion strolled out
on deck and looked about him. The *Ballerina* was now in the
middle of the estuary, not very far from the Tongue lightship.
On the starboard beam the Kentish coast was a good four
miles away, and, in a slight haze rising from the water, looked
further still.

He went below, and along the alleyway to its after end,
where the steward's cabin was placed. The steward, in his
shirt-sleeves as usual, was making entries on a series of papers
laid out on his desk. " Sorry to disturb you, steward," said

Merrion ingratiatingly. " Will you oblige me by coming on deck for a moment ? "

The steward followed him out of the end of the alleyway. " You see that land over there ? " said Merrion, pointing. " How far off do you think it is ? "

" It is long way," the steward replied. " About five mile, I should t'ink."

" All that," Merrion agreed. " And there's no land any nearer, as you can see for yourself. Now, what about letting us have a drink ? "

The steward's mind worked logically. He had been told not to break the seals till the ship was three miles from land. That limit had apparently been passed. " Certainly, Mr. Merrion," he replied. " I go to open up now. You ring bell and tell the girl what you like."

Merrion returned to the smoking-room. " I've worked the oracle," he announced. " I have convinced the steward, by the evidence of his own eyes, that we are at this moment more than three miles from land, and he has gone to break the seals. What he'll say or do when we've turned the corner and he sees the North Foreland barely a mile away, I don't know. But that's his funeral, not ours."

Mr. Wilberton was so delighted that he insisted upon standing Merrion a drink, and rang the bell, at which Cinevra appeared. " Now, what are you going to have ? " Mr. Wiilberton asked. " Mine's a double whisky."

Merrion, with some knowledge of Norwegian habits, ordered an aquavit. This intrigued Mr. Bewdley, who had never heard of that particular beverage and said he would have one too. Mr. Pulham was content with a bottle of beer, explaining that he never drank anything stronger than that. Mr. Wilberton, as always, had a story about that. Something to the effect that when he had been ill a year before his doctor had told him he oughtn't to drink spirits. He had replied that spirits would do him less harm than any of the doctor's filthy medicines. " Pretty good, that ? No, ha, ha ! "

The meal that followed at half past six was described as supper. It consisted of mutton chops, followed by the delightful Scandinavian practice of smorgesbrud, which, literally interpreted, means butter and bread. These were certainly included, but a host of other dishes accompanied them. The sideboard was covered with cold food of every kind, meat, fish, salads of every description. One took a plate and helped oneself, choosing this and that as one's fancy directed. " Well, I'm bound to say they don't do one so badly on this ship," Mr. Wilberton remarked, as he visited the sideboard for the second time.

When he had finished his meal, Merrion went up on deck. The *Ballerina* was running southward through the Downs, and the coast looked alarmingly near. Alarming, that was, for the steward's peace of mind. But that phlegmatic individual did not show up. Not until next morning when they were safely in mid-channel, with no land in sight, did he, happening to meet Merrion, shake his head at him reproachfully.

Later, in the smoking-room, Merrion found himself talking to Mr. Bewdley over a glass of beer. By way of conversation, Merrion had said that he and his wife had had to leave home while repairs were carried out, and had thought that a sea-voyage was as good a way of spending the time as any.

Mr. Bewdley glanced across the room, to where Mrs. Mallory was talking vivaciously to Mr. Pulham and Mr. Wilberton. " It was my uncle, or rather my aunt, who persuaded me to come. I can't say I was particularly anxious to be away so long. I'm one of the directors of a firm in a place called Hembury."

" I don't know anyone living there," Merrion replied. " But I've driven through Hembury often enough."

" Then you must have seen our mill," Mr. Bewdley replied. " You can't have missed it, for it's the ugliest thing in the town. An eyesore, my friend Mr. Houghley calls it. All the same it plays its part in the nation's food supply, and does pretty well, I'm glad to say. Radlett and Son is the name of the firm."

" I know them by repute," said Merrion. " And I've seen the mill. I should describe it as a landmark rather than as an eyesore. Your uncle is another of the directors ? "

" Oh, no," Mr. Bewdley replied. " It's rather ridiculous that he should be my uncle, for there's barely ten years between us. However, he likes to emphasise the relationship. His idea may be that by treating me as his nephew he keeps me in my proper place. No, he and his sister, my aunt, live in Birmingham. He had an extremely flourishing business

G

there, which he sold for a considerable figure quite recently, and now he's at a bit of a loose end."

He had lowered his voice, and now glanced in his uncle's direction. But he need have had no apprehensions that what he was saying might be overheard. At a near-by table Mavis and Mrs. Lavenham were talking to Mrs. Stewart-Patterson. Their raised voices, as they strove to make her hear what they were saying, drowned all other conversation.

Mr. Bewdley went on : " At a loose end. And it doesn't seem to agree with him. Have you ever noticed that when men who have worked hard all their lives retire, something in their make-up seems to slip a cog ? I don't mean that Uncle Jasper is going off his head. Far from it, he's still the same shrewd old sinner that he always has been. But at times he seems to lose control of himself. Drinks too much, flies into ungovernable rages, and says and does the most unexpected things. My aunt is getting very worried about him."

" I daresay he'd be better if he had something to occupy his mind," Merrion remarked.

" That's just it," Mr. Bewdley replied. " That's what we all think. As a matter of fact, for some time past, I've been trying to find him a house in Hembury. With a bit of garden you know, where he could occupy himself, if only in bullying the gardener. But he's very difficult to please. What put it into his head to come on this voyage, I don't know. But, since he had made up his mind to it, we all thought it might be a good thing. However, my aunt had her fears how he might behave among strangers. She was afraid he might get himself into some sort of trouble. So she begged me to go with him, and in the end I agreed."

Cinevra made her appearance, bearing a tray with a bowl of fruit, plates and knives. She put this on a vacant table, and the various groups into which the party had split coalesced.

CHAPTER XII

" It's GETTING quite a family party," Mavis remarked to her husband in the privacy of their cabin, on the second day out. " And I mean that literally. The members of most families I know don't by any means always manage to hit it off. But they are at least bound by a common interest, as we are."

" We're getting to know one another, certainly," Merrion replied. " And we exercise forbearance, probably because we have never met before. It would be fatal to undertake a voyage with people one knew really well. Everybody would be acutely conscious of everybody else's irritating habits. As it is, there is only limited opportunity of observing those habits. You get on all right with these people ? "

" Quite as well as could be expected," said Mavis. " It's the women you mean, I take it. Mrs. Lavenham I like very much. She's straightforward, honest to goodness, and talks sense. Mrs. Stewart-Patterson is a bit difficult, but one must make allowances for her, she's so terribly deaf. From what she says she must be a formidable old woman at home in Scotland. She seems accustomed to being obeyed, if you know what I mean."

Merrion nodded. " I do. She's already taken to ordering Mr. Pulham about like a page-boy. However, he doesn't seem to mind. Rather flattered, in fact. And Mrs. Mallory and that amazingly stolid child of hers ? "

" They're a queer contrast," Mavis replied. " Clarice is certainly stolid. It's the most difficult thing in the world to get a smile out of her. Her mother isn't. At the slightest provocation, she'll talk upon any conceivable subject, whether she knows anything about it or not. Preferably with the men of the party. You see, with the exception of her daughter, she's the youngest female passenger, and she likes to exploit the fact. I don't mean that unkindly in the least. Anyway, she's leaving us at the Piraeus."

" I'll tell you something in confidence," said Merrion. " Keep it to yourself, for the captain doesn't like passengers to get hold of things until he's certain of them himself. He says they only badger him with questions, which is perfectly true. He's a simple soul in his human relations. Not in the least interested in passengers, whom he regards as so many items of living cargo, but wrapped up in his wife and small grandchildren. I was yarning with him this afternoon, and he took me into his cabin and showed me their photographs."

" Is that what you were going to tell me in confidence ? " Mavis asked.

" Sorry," her husband replied. " I was running a bit off my course. No, it was this. He said we may expect two more passengers, picking up one at Cyprus, and another at Beirut."

" Male or female ? " Mavis asked.

Merrion imitated the captain's gesture. " He could not sigh. I gather that all he was told was that he should have the cabins available. They aren't likely to make much difference to us, either way."

" I don't suppose they will," Mavis agreed. " I'll ask you the question you asked me. How do you get on with these people ? "

" Meaning the men ? " Merrion replied. " Oh, well enough. Bewdley tops the list. He's a quiet sort of chap, and never puts himself forward. But get him to himself, and he's very good company, in his own quiet way."

" I'm not particularly taken by his uncle," Mavis remarked.

" Neither am I," Merrion agreed. " I keep out of his way as far as possible. That's not difficult, for he seems to prefer Mrs. Mallory's company to that of anyone else on board. And she doesn't seem to resent his heavy-handed pleasantries. Wilberton is a blusterer by nature, and when he isn't blustering he's telling stories of such inordinate length that the point, if any, is swamped in a mass of verbiage."

" And the fussy little Pulham ? " Mavis asked.

" He amuses me," Merrion replied. " He's here, there and everywhere buzzing round like a blue-bottle. Fussing round Mrs. Stewart-Patterson, if she's about. On the bridge, talking to the officer on watch. Telling him how the ship should be navigated, I daresay. Cornering the captain, and bombarding him with silly questions. He told me himself that he had spent half an hour in the pantry, teaching Cinevra and Nina how tea should be made. Somebody will turn and rend him before long, I don't doubt."

"Mrs. Lavenham, perhaps," said Mavis. "He had the impertinence to address her as Mrs. Lavvy, and it's more than she can bear. Oh, well, we shall all get on each other's nerves now and then, I suppose. Perhaps we shouldn't be altogether flattered if we knew what our fellow-passengers thought of us."

The *Ballerina* rounded Ushant, and as she ploughed her way southward the weather grew gradually warmer. The sea remained almost unnaturally calm, even the dreaded Bay was asleep, breathing regularly in a long slow swell. Mr. Pulham, whose remarks were always banal, kept repeating the out-worn phrase, 'as smooth as a mill-pond.'

So the *Ballerina* thumped her way along at a steady thirteen knots. Thumped was the word, for there was no escaping from the sound of her Diesel engine. Fortunately, one very soon got used to it. But, on one occasion, the chief invited Merrion into the engine-room. To his ear, accustomed to the more harmonious song of the steam turbine, the discord down there was appalling. So deafening was the clamour that only by dint of shouting within an inch of one another's ears could the men make themselves heard. It seemed marvellous that metal, let alone flesh and blood, could stand it. At Merrion's remark, when they had left this inferno behind them, the chief only smiled. "Noisy? They all do. But they cheap."

Across the bay of Cap Ortegal. Finisterre rounded, a course nearly due south. The wicked-looking Berlingas, the Lisbon pilot-boat cruising off the mouth of the Tagus. Cape Vincent, and into the strange milky atmosphere of the Levanter, so common at the mouth of the Straits.

Then, one glorious evening, the unforgettable silhouette of Gibraltar, crowned with a misty cloud. To give his passengers the best possible view, the captain steered into the bay, before rounding the point. Mrs. Stewart-Patterson shook her head sadly. The captain wouldn't stop while she made a sketch. Even Mr. Wilberton was reduced to silence. Mrs. Mallory remarked that she felt like writing poetry. Cinevra asked Merrion if anybody lived on the Rock, to which he replied that they could not only live on it, but in it as well. Mr. Pulham, presumably with some dim memory of having heard of apes and scorpions, assured everybody within hearing that the caves were full of chimpanzees and serpents.

By next morning the *Ballerina* was well into the Mediterranean, a disappointment to some of those who had never
sailed that sea. The Levanter still blew lightly, with a chilly
touch that raised grey waves, just tall enough to make the
ship pitch slightly. Clarice announced at breakfast unexpectedly, for she rarely spoke at meals, that she had seen the
sea more blue at Brighton. Mrs. Lavenham, who most
unfortunately was a bad sailor, bravely appeared. But her
usually expressive eyes were glassy, and she confined herself
to a single cup of coffee, the eggs and bacon which Cinevra
set before her remaining untasted.

However, by noon they had run out of the Levanter, into
brilliant sunshine and a sparkling calm. Everybody's spirits
rose, each affected in a different way. After lunch, Mrs.
Stewart-Patterson cornered Mavis. " The light is really
wonderful, my dear. I want to make sketches of all the
passengers, so that I shall have something to remember them
by when the voyage is over. And I should like to begin with
your husband, for he has such an interesting face. Do you
think you could ask him if he would sit for me ? "

Merrion raised no objection. After all, what he wanted to
do was to sit and watch the sea and the passing shipping.
Mrs. Stewart-Patterson stumped about the boat-deck with
her stick until she had found the exact spot to suit her.
Merrion was made to drag a chair there, and to shift about in
it until the right position was found. Then Mrs. Stewart-
Patterson arranged herself, with the assistance of Mr. Pulham.
One chair to sit on, another upon which to rest her feet. Two
rugs, to protect her from any possible draught. Her stool,
which was fitted with an extension to support the sketching-
block, at her side. The shooting-stick, where she could reach
it at any time. At last, gazing intently at her sitter, she took
her pencil in hand.

Everyone found something to do. Even Mrs. Mallory,
hitherto restless, produced a garment of some kind, at which
she sewed spasmodically. Clarice, whose appetite was insatiable, munched chocolates while she peered at her illustrated book. Mrs. Lavenham knitted with her amazing
dexterity, read a book and chatted to Mavis, all at the same
time. Mavis was crocheting a pullover, destined for her
husband. If it wasn't large enough, it would do for Newport,

more slightly built. Mr. Bewdley, whose mind was never very far from his business, sat thinking, making occasional notes of matters to discuss with his fellow-directors on his return. Mr. Pulham spent much of his time in the smoking-room, writing interminable letters to everyone he knew at home. What he found to write about so voluminously, nobody could guess. His fellow-passengers, perhaps.

Only Mr. Wilberton was frankly bored. He had confessed as much to Merrion that morning. " If I'd known we should be at sea so long, I wouldn't have come. Those damned agents told me we should always be putting into some port or other. I didn't come to hang around like this doing nothing. I want to see the sights in these foreign places we're supposed to be going to. Night-clubs, and that sort of thing, you know. I tell you what. If this ship is going to take so long getting home as it's taking getting out, I shall leave it and fly home."

Merrion wondered what he expected to find in these foreign places. His imagination had pictured something remarkably gay and exotic, no doubt. Meanwhile, Mr. Wilberton consoled himself with frequent glasses of whisky. Drinking these, with intervals of vulgar pleasantries to Mrs. Mallory, seemed his only occupation. It was not to be expected that reading appealed to him much. As for looking at the sea ! To Mr. Wilberton's eyes, the sea appeared no more than a lot of water. And water was a liquid in which he could feel no interest whatever.

Unfortunately, too, he threatened to become a focus of discord. One morning he was sitting on deck, with a glass of whisky balanced on the arm of his chair. Mr. Pulham, bustling about on some fussy errand of his, was unlucky enough to brush off the glass with a cushion he was carrying, and it fell with a crash on the deck. He was full of apologies, and said that of course he would buy Mr. Wilberton another drink. But Mr. Wilberton, infuriated, turned upon him, calling him a meddlesome busybody. He'd knocked over the glass on purpose, because he was a snivelling beer-drinker, and couldn't bear to see another drinking whisky like a man.

Then again, in a particularly convivial moment, he made the mistake of attempting to treat Mrs. Lavenham with the same sort of familiarity with which he treated Mrs. Mallory. Mrs. Lavenham, after her first gasp of outraged surprise, told him in no measured terms to go away and stay away for good. Her expression of scorn and contempt would have shrivelled up anyone less thick-skinned.

This sort of thing was bound to create friction. It even threatened to split the passengers into two opposing camps. There were some who seemed disposed to excuse Mr. Wilberton's behaviour. It was due only to his natural hastiness. Beneath his somewhat crude exterior, there throbbed a heart of gold. Why, he would spend hours amusing his hearers with his never-failing anecdotes. You couldn't expect a man of his age and experience to sit down and do nothing but twiddle his thumbs, could you?

It was to be expected, of course, that in public at least, Mr. Bewdley should do his best to excuse his uncle. Mr. Wilberton was apt to be hot-tempered, and to act on the impulse of the moment. But these outbursts were only sparks struck from a generous and exuberant nature. He meant no harm, forgot what he had said or done within a few moments. Mrs. Stewart-Patterson couldn't understand what it was all about. Deaf as she was, she had gained only a confused idea of what had happened. She had somehow got it into her head that Mr. Pulham had deliberately thrown Mr. Wilberton's drink overboard. As for Mrs. Lavenham, well, men aren't as a rule impertinent to women unless they have received some encouragement. In Mrs. Stewart-Patterson's opinion, people had no right to speak so hastily of Mr. Wilberton.

But the principal advocate for the defence was Mrs. Mallory. Who could restrain themselves from being rude to Mr. Pulham? A fussy, ridiculous little man, always poking his nose in where he wasn't wanted. And what right had Mrs. Lavenham to put on airs? She mustn't expect to be treated as a cut above everyone else. For her own part, she, Mrs. Mallory found Mr. Wilberton a very cheerful travelling companion.

Partly as a result of this, Mr. Pulham began to find himself rather at a loose end. He would not speak to Mr. Wilberton, and kinship made it natural to extend the same treatment to his nephew. Mrs. Stewart-Patterson ceased to encourage him to act as her page-boy, and even those who sympathised with him in his quarrel, had very little time for his fussy attentions. In one of his frequent confidences, he imparted to Merrion that in his opinion, present company excepted, of course, the rest of the company were a pack of snobs. As for that fellow Wilberton and his supercilious nephew, he hated the sight of them.

So it came about that his fellow-passengers rarely saw Mr. Pulham except at meals. By way of expressing his disapproval, he took to frequenting the pantry and the crew's quarters. He could be seen helping Cinevra and Nina in their duties, even participating in the washing-up. The crew were accommodated aft, and number four hold was where they mainly fore-gathered. Mr. Pulham, a comic picture in a nightshirt tucked into a pair of white shorts, and heelless slippers on his feet, was frequently seen there. The more ambitious and younger members of the crew pounced on him. Not because of any honour they felt at a passenger seeking their company. Norwegians are not like that. But because it was a heaven-sent opportunity of getting lessons in English for nothing.

Captain Larsen was one of those people who seem oblivious of what is going on around him, yet by some mysterious intuition are aware of every detail. He wisely left the naviga-tion of his ship to his officers, rarely appearing on the bridge except when entering or leaving port. He seemed to spend most of his time in a chair on the boat-deck with his eyes closed. Merrion shrewdly suspected that this appearance of slumber was no more than a protective device. Not even the most inquisitive passenger would molest a man trying to snatch half an hour's sleep as a respite from his arduous labours.

But the captain's idle hours aroused the curiosity of some, perhaps even shocked them. Mrs. Mallory in particular, whose ideas of the duties of a master mariner were hazy in the extreme. " Don't you ever steer the ship, Captain ? " she asked him one day at lunch.

Captain Larsen chuckled happily at the suggestion. " No, I not steer, Mrs. Mallor'. You see, if took wheel, I might fall asleep, and then where you find yourself ? But you need not have fears. If I run ship into danger, Mr. Wilberton save you, no ? "

Captain Larsen was well aware of Mr. Pulham's habits, of which he disapproved. True, he had said himself that on a Norwegian ship one was free to do as one liked. What he had meant was that passengers were not subjected to any regimentation. But certain reasonable limits were implied. The passengers had plenty of room in which to disport themselves. The crew, when off duty, had similar facilities. But undue fraternisation between passengers and crew was not to be encouraged. It led to misunderstandings and jealousies.

In his quiet way, Captain Larsen tried to drop Mr. Pulham a hint. " I scarcely seen you all day, Mr. Pulham," he said to him one day at supper. " You not like sittin' on boat-deck ? "

" No, I don't, Captain," Mr. Pulham replied firmly, his mouth full of smoked salmon. " I prefer talking to friends of mine who are always pleased to see me."

This was in the Sicilian Narrows. Pantellaria had been sighted that afternoon, a tall outline seen indistinctly through the veil of Mediterranean haze. " We don't seem to be getting on together as well as we did," Mavis remarked to her husband in the cabin as they prepared for bed.

" What can you expect ? " Merrion replied philosophically. " Nine people, of varying character and interest have been cooped up together for a week. At sea, too, with very little avenue of escape from one another's company short of jumping overboard. It's only natural that some of us should rub the others up the wrong way. Don't you worry about it. These people will get a chance of stretching their legs on shore before long. And they'll be so glad to get back to the ship that they'll swallow their mutual dislikes. You see if they don't."

Mavis looked doubtful. " I don't see what going on shore has got to do with it."

" Just this," her husband replied. " The antagonistic won't tramp the unfamiliar streets together. They'll get away from one another for a bit, and so relieve the tension. Mr. Wilberton will seek out his night-clubs, possibly in the company of Mrs. Mallory. Mr. Pulham will comb the Levantine ports for a lively milk-bar. We, I imagine, shall not trouble our heads much about any of them."

" I'm not troubling now," said Mavis. " I find it all most amusing. We might have found ourselves among a much worse crowd. And I'm very glad indeed that I've met Mrs. Lavenham."

At supper on Saturday, 12th September, eight days from the departure of the *Ballerina* from London, Captain Larsen made a remark. " All you get up early to-morrow morning ? "

"Why should we get up early?" Mrs. Mallory asked. "To-morrow's Sunday. In England we usually stay in bed a little later on Sunday mornings. Is it a habit in Norway to get up earlier?"

Captain Larsen shook his head. "You get up early for first sight of Greece. We reach Kalamata soon after breakfast time."

CHAPTER XIII

MERRION DID get up early. He put on his dressing-gown and went on deck, to see land on either side. The *Ballerina* had entered the Gulf of Messenia, and was now heading north towards the port of Kalamata. In the dawn the view was entrancing. The sea, a deep blue for once, and on the distant shores mountains rising chain after chain towards the cloudless sky.

He returned to the cabin, to report to Mavis, still in bed. "Gulf of what did you say?" she asked sleepily. "It sounded like Messina, which I thought was in Sicily."

"So it is," Merrion replied. "This is the Gulf of Messenia, a very different matter. And magnificent it is. I'd hop out and have a look, if I were you."

By the time the breakfast gong was sounded, Kalamata was visible in the distance ahead as a vague cluster of buildings. A new air of excitement pervaded the saloon. As soon as Captain Larsen came in, he was bombarded with questions. What sort of a place was Kalamata? What did one do there? How long would they stop?

But Captain Larsen refused to be drawn. "I cannot sigh. Only once before have I been here, and then I did not go ashore. To me, a sailor, all ports very much alike. You go ashore, spend money, and what you have for it? Nothing. But you not spend much money. Sunday, all shops shut."

"But we shall stay here longer than to-day, surely, Captain?" Mr. Pulham asked.

Captain Larsen shrugged his shoulders. "That depends. If agent has got a gang to work Sunday, we leave this afternoon. If not, to-morrow. You ask me after we tie up alongside."

The Merrions watched the entry into port. Outside the breakwater the *Ballerina* hove to, to allow the pilot to come aboard from his extremely noisy motor-boat. From where they stood, leaning on the rail just abaft the bridge, they could hear him giving his orders. " Why, the man's speaking English ! " Mavis exclaimed.

" It's the language of the sea," her husband replied. " And what else could he speak ? The officers wouldn't understand Greek, and a Greek pilot could hardly be expected to be a fluent Norwegian scholar. You'll find all these chaps speak English. Nautical English, that is."

The *Ballerina* went slowly ahead again, and as she rounded the breakwater the town became visible, drenched in the sunshine of an already blazing hot day. The Merrions could make out a straggling water-front of undistinguished houses, with here and there a stunted tree. Piles of rubble were gaps of desolation. The Merrions were told that Kalamata had been bombed by Germans, Italians, British and Americans. To say nothing of having been machine-gunned intermittently by one or other of the contending Greek factions. At intervals a swirl of dust would rise and sweep across the sun-baked buildings.

Mavis surveyed the scene. " So this is Greece," she said without much enthusiasm. " Are we going ashore, Desmond? "

" I don't know," her husband replied doubtfully. " The place looks to me exactly like what the British seaman calls a dump. Let's not decide till we hear what the orders are."

The ship drew slowly alongside the quay, where a languid group awaited her arrival. Customs officers, police, two or three important-looking officials. They were joined, at a run, by a perspiring little man, carrying an enormous satchel. He danced about the quay until the ship's side was within reach. Then, without waiting for the gangway to be lowered, he leapt aboard. " Kaptan ! Kaptan ! " he shouted excitedly.

Someone directed him to the bridge, and a moment later he appeared on the boat-deck. Seeing the passengers assembled there he took off his hat and bowed profoundly. " I the Company's agent," he declared proudly. " What you want, you ask me." Then he tapped his breast impressively. " And I Norwegian Consul."

The captain, who had seen his arrival, came down from the bridge and took him into his cabin. " He seems to have a

pretty soft job," Merrion remarked. " I don't suppose the
Company's ships call here very regularly. And as for being
Norwegian Consul, that can't take up much of his time."

The excitable little man was followed more decorously by
the rest of the shore party. The usual examination and stamp-
ing of passports followed. The Merrions returned to the rail
and leaned over it. Beneath them the dusty quay-side baked
in the overpowering sun. The only relief was a dusky and
cavernous cafe, outside which the branches of an almost
leafless tree gave an illusion of shade. In this a few scattered
men, in various stages of undress sat imbibing coffee.

As the Merrions watched, other men arrived, in twos and
threes, on brightly painted bicycles. They coalesced into a
swarm, until they were joined by a big man in a small ram-
shackle car. They swarmed round him as he got out and
addressed them. His audience punctuated his speech with
shouts and waving arms.

" Do we witness the birth of a rebellion ? " Mavis asked.

" Very likely," Merrion replied. " Subversive politics are
the curse of this country. But I'm more inclined to think that
he's merely telling them what to do. Yes, I thought so."

The speech ended, and the man clambered on board the
ship. At the same moment the captain appeared from his
cabin, and the passengers surrounded him, clamouring their
questions. He held up his hand in an appeal for silence. " We
sail at half-past two," he announced. " You can go ashore
now, if you please. But you must be on board again before
sailing time. The ship wait for nobody."

The passengers dispersed, all but the Merrions. Captain
Larsen turned to them. " We got a gang to work till all the
drums are discharged. Three hours, the foreman he says."

" Your agent did a good job of work, then," Merrion replied.
" I thought he seemed a bit excited about something."

" Excited ? " Captain Larsen said scornfully. " I expect he
always like that. He come aboard to beg cigarettes. But he
brought me a message from the owners. We sail straight from
here to the Piraeus. I tell Mrs. Mallor' that. She be glad to
know. You go ashore ? "

Merrion turned to Mavis. " What do you think ? "

" I'm not very keen," she replied. " It seems terribly hot
and dusty, and there doesn't seem much to be seen."

Captain Larsen nodded approvingly. " I think you right. You take your chairs up on bridge. Cooler there, under awning. I go to see Mrs. Mallor'."

The Merrions followed the captain's advice. From the bridge they had an excellent view of the quay and the town beyond it. They watched the remaining passengers streaming down the gangway. " Like so many children released from school," Mavis remarked. The work of unloading had already begun, and the empty drums were being dropped on the quay with resulting clangs of metal. " These chaps aren't wasting much time," Merrion observed. " They're on piece-work, I expect. My word, it's hot, even up here ! I shan't be sorry to get to sea again."

Before very long Captain Larsen ascended the bridge ladder carrying a chair and followed by Cinevra bearing a tray with glasses and three bottles straight from the refrigerator. " I sit with you here," he said. " You like our Norwegian beer on a hot day, yes, Mrs. Merrion ? "

" I think it's the best I ever tasted," Mavis replied, truthfully enough. " It was nice of you to think of it. It was the very thing I wanted."

They raised their glasses, uttering the magic word ' Skol ! ' Captain Larsen gestured towards the quay. " This place no good. What you say, one horse, dust and dirt everywhere. You quite right not go ashore. Wait till Piraeus. Then Athens, perhaps."

" I hate asking questions, Captain," said Merrion diffidently. " I feel quite ashamed of us English when we bombard you with them. But I'll venture on this one. Are we likely to be at the Piraeus long enough for my wife and me to have a run round Athens ? "

For once the captain could say. " Plenty time. We have cases of machinery and some general cargo to discharge. We get there early in morning, but it will take us all day. You take Mrs. Merrion see Athens. Not half hour by taxi from Piraeus customs house to Acropolis. That what you want to see ? "

" I'd love to see it ! " Mavis exclaimed. " I've never been there before."

Captain Larsen chuckled. " You find it hot. Hotter than here perhaps. And it's climb, climb, all the time, and no cool

beer when you get there. Ah, that little man! He want to
see me again, I expect."

The agent, still clasping his enormous satchel, was hurrying
along the quay to the gangway. The captain finished his beer,
then descended the ladder. "He's a very decent chap,"
Merrion remarked. "Well, it's the Acropolis for you to-
morrow, my dear. Think you can manage it in this weather?"

"Of course I can," Mavis replied. "What about asking Mrs.
Stewart-Patterson to come with us and show us round? She
told me the other day that she lived in Athens at one time."

"Mrs. Stewart-Patterson!" Merrion exclaimed. "My dear
girl! What about the captain's climb, climb all the time?
Why, she'd never do it, even with that shooting-stick of hers."

"You don't know that old woman as well as I do," Mavis
replied. "If she makes up her mind to do a thing, she'll do it,
climb or no climb. I know she's longing for the chance of
seeing the Acropolis again, for she told me so herself. And she
told me her legs are a lot better since she's been on board."

Merrion shrugged his shoulders. "Very well. Ask her, by
all means. But don't expect me to carry her. I shall have
enough to do to carry myself, if it's as hot as this."

As they sat there, the first of the passengers who had gone
on shore appeared, walking down the quay. These were Mrs.
Stewart-Patterson and Mrs. Lavenham. It seemed that Mavis
had been quite right about the former, for she was stumping
along quite rapidly with the aid of her stick. In spite of
its being Sunday, Mrs. Lavenham had somehow acquired a
huge bunch of flowers, of which she was passionately fond.

The next to appear, surprisingly enough, were the three men
of the party, together. "There, what did I tell you?"
Merrion exclaimed. "They've obviously patched up their
quarrels, for they look as merry as sandboys."

One of them certainly was, for his loud laughter reached
them through the hot air. This was Mr. Wilberton, in the
centre of the line abreast, with the other two one on either
side of him. As now and then he took an uncertain step, Mr.
Bewdley laid a hand on his arm to steady him. When they
reached the gangway, Mr. Wilberton lurched forward and
began to ascend it. It swung under his heavy tread, threaten-
ing to overbalance him. However, he reached the head safely,
and a few minutes later appeared on the boat-deck. Looking

up, he caught sight of Merrion. " Hallo, my boy ! " he roared.
" You ought to have come ashore with us. They've got no
whisky, but they gave me some stuff with a name which
sounded like oozoo. Not bad, when you get used to it."

" So that's what the matter is with him," Merrion remarked
to Mavis. " It's terrible stuff. He'll have a hang-over which
won't improve his temper, I'll be bound. We'd better be going
down, it's almost lunch time."

Not until lunch was half way through did Mrs. Mallory enter
the saloon, in a great state of fluster and dragging Clarice
behind her. " Oh, Captain, I'm so sorry we're late ! " she
exclaimed. " We've been all round the town looking for the
Post Office, and when at last we found it, it was closed. I
wanted to send a telegram to my husband, telling him to meet
us at the Piraeus. I can't possibly manage by myself, with all
the luggage we've got. I don't know——"

Captain Larsen interrupted her. " You not worry, Mrs.
Mallor'," he said soothingly. " Your husband, he in touch
with the company's agent in Athens, I expect. He know now
that we shall be at the Piraeus in the morning."

The last of the drums were swung ashore as Merrion regained
the deck. The agent, with his satchel looking bulkier and
heavier was on board, and insisted on shaking hands with such
of the passengers he came across. Just before the gangway
was raised, he scuttled ashore, and stood on the quay, waving
his hat. The *Ballerina* sailed punctually on time.

That afternoon was spent coasting along the eastern shore
of the Gulf, a marvellous panorama of steep hillside, dotted
with villages. Beyond them, the mountains towered, stark
and rugged in the powerful sunlight. By nightfall the ship had
sighted Cape Malca, and entered the channel between it and
Kythera. Mrs. Lavenham, standing on the rail between
Merrion and Mavis, pointed to the twinkling lights on the
mainland. " Isn't it queer ? "

" What do you find queer, Mrs. Lavenham," Merrion asked.
" That an isolated village on the extreme southern tip of
Greece should apparently enjoy the blessings of electric
light ? "

Mrs. Lavenham laughed. " No, it wasn't that. I was thinking of the difference between those people over there and us.
We're just a handful of strangers, thrown together by chance

for a few weeks, probably never to meet again. Whereas those people have lived together all their lives, working, if they do work, eating, sleeping, intriguing, making love and inter-marrying. There can't be anything each one of them doesn't know about the others."

" I don't suppose there is," Merrion replied. He kept the rest of his thought to himself. That, by the end of the voyage, there wouldn't be much that the passengers on the *Ballerina* didn't know or invent, about one another.

By dawn, the ship had reached the entrance to the Piraeus. Merrion had again got up early, but the morning haze hid from him the hills of Athens in the distance. After a delay of a couple of hours they came alongside, and the usual formalities were gone through. The *Ballerina* had tied up on the side of the harbour furthest from the town and custom house. When the captain came in to breakfast, he anticipated any interroga-tion. " If you go ashore, you have to land at custom house. A launch come by-and-by and take you across harbour. I cannot say when we sail, but you must be here aboard by half-past four."

The launch duly came, bringing with it Mr. Mallory, into whose arms his wife fell dramatically. A long delay ensued, caused apparently by Mrs. Mallory's last minute packing. At last her baggage, tons of it, it seemed, was lowered into the launch, and all the passengers followed. Mrs. Stewart-Patterson descended the iron ladder with the utmost agility. But Mr. Pulham was not so fortunate. He missed the side of the launch and continued down the ladder until his feet were in the water. However, amid the unrestrained laughter of his fellow-passengers, he was hauled aboard, and with an agonised shriek, the launch set out across the harbour.

There was an affecting scene at the custom house, Mrs. Mallory bidding farewell to everybody, with the exception, Merrion noticed, of Mr. Wilberton. The Merrions broke away in company with Mrs. Stewart-Patterson. That indomitable old lady had taken the management into her own hands. She had got someone to telephone to a friend of hers who lived in Athens, and that somebody had brought a message that the friend would meet her at the foot of the Acropolis at half-past twelve, and take her to lunch. " So we have plenty of time," Mrs. Stewart-Patterson said triumphantly. " It's only half-

H

past ten now. We'll take a taxi, and I'll show you everything."

She was as good as her word. They drove to the Acropolis and, in the full glare of the sun, climbed the steep and ascending steps, Mrs. Stewart-Patterson in the van. The ring of her stick on the stones led the way, the Merrions, streaming with perspiration, following in her wake. She was insistent that they must miss nothing. The Parthenon, the Temple of Victory, everything on that scorching hill-top must be explored. At last, on the stroke of half-past twelve, dauntless and unwearied, she led them down again.

Her friend, a younger woman, was waiting for her. The Merrions did not wait for an invitation to lunch. Mavis explained mendaciously that they wanted to look round the city before returning to the ship. The friend told them to jump into the car. They did so, and she dropped them at the Hotel Britannique. " Well, what would you like to do next ? " Merrion asked, when they had thanked her and she had driven off.

" I'm not going a step further," Mavis replied. " I'm utterly worn out, and if I'm not revived quickly I shall collapse on the pavement. Look ! There are people in that cafe over there drinking what looks very like beer. I think I might just be able to stagger as far as that."

The cafe turned out to be a very pleasant place. They had quite a lot of iced beer, light but thirst quenching, and then an excellent lunch. " I'm feeling a little stonger now," Mavis remarked as she sipped her coffee at the end of the meal. " What do you suggest now ? "

" Sightseeing without exercise," her husband replied. " We'll take a taxi, and tell the man to drive us round a bit, then back to the ship. There must be a road round to the other side of the harbour."

This programme was carried out. The driver of the taxi they hired spoke a little broken French, a language with which they were both familiar. Merrion made him understand what they wanted, and after an hour or so round Athens and its suburbs, he brought them on to the quay, within fifty yards of the *Ballerina's* gangway. The fare he asked was quite reasonable, and upon Merrion giving him a tip in addition equivalent to five shillings, he nearly fell out of his seat with gratitude.

They found they were the first passengers to return. Captain Larsen, his cap drawn over his eyes, was reclining in a chair in a shady corner of the boat-deck. But he was not so fast asleep as he appeared, for he was instantly aware of them. " You back, then ? Have a good time, yes ? "

" Marvellous ! " Mavis replied. " I feel I could write a guide-book on the Acropolis. But you were right about the heat, Captain. My clothes were sticking to me all over."

Captain Larsen chuckled. " I told you. Why you go and look at lot of old ruins ? Plenty of them in England, I think. Never mind, cooler when we get to sea. We sail at six for Alexandria."

The remaining passengers arrived together. They had assembled at the custom house, whence a launch had brought them across the harbour. The Merrions gathered something of their adventures. Mrs. Lavenham's had not apparently been very exhilarating. " I got landed with Mr. Pulham," she confided to Mavis. " I never had such an awful day in my life ! To begin with, he wouldn't have a taxi to Athens, though I offered to pay for it. He insisted on taking a tram, which shook me to pieces. Then he would dawdle about the town, stopping people and asking them where we could get a cheap lunch. Fortunately, most of them didn't understand him. However, we did get a lunch of a sort, in a queer little place that reeked of garlic. Then a tram back again, and half an hour's waiting for the launch in that beastly custom house. I'm worn out."

Mrs. Stewart-Patterson, on the other hand, was as lively as a cricket. She came on board carrying two large parcels in addition to her stick. " I wish I could have stayed with you and your wife, Mr. Merrion," she said. " We could have done a lot more sight-seeing together. As it was, my friend and I did a lot of shopping. All my friends expect me to bring them something back when I go abroad."

Mr. Bewdley had spent an instructive day. " I wanted some information about the olive oil trade, in connection with my business," he told Merrion. " I went to the Consulate, and they gave me the addresses of two or three of the leading men in the town. Charming fellows they turned out to be, and they told me all I wanted to know. One of them insisted upon driving me back to the custom house in his car."

This left Merrion wondering how Mr. Wilberton had amused himself. It was not till after supper that he learnt. He was alone on deck, watching the light dying over the receding coast, when Mr. Wilberton came up to him. " Sorry to be leaving, old boy ? " he asked. " I am. Had a jolly good time. Mrs. Mallory asked me to meet her husband and lunch with them. We shall miss that woman, she was the only one on the ship with any go in her."

CHAPTER XIV

THE NEXT DAY, Tuesday the 15th, was passed at sea, with a distant view of the eastern tip of Crete in the morning. The bay of Alexandria was reached on Wednesday morning, and the *Ballerina* was berthed by ten o'clock. At once, vendors of merchandise and touts of every description swarmed aboard. Some of these the stalwart Egyptian police ejected with violence. But others remained. Captain Larsen announced that the *Ballerina* would be in port all day, and the passengers need not be on board till supper-time.

Mr. Pulham burst into the smoking-room where they had all assembled, with the exception of Mrs. Lavenham. There had been a slight swell during the night from which she had suffered. She had told Mavis that she would spend the day lying down and getting over it. " I say ! " Mr. Pulham exclaimed. " I've been talking to one of the chaps who came on board. He's all right and he talks quite decent English. He's got a big car which will take six besides himself, and he says he'll drive us round for two or three hours, and show us the sights. It'll only cost one pound Egyptian per head, which is pretty reasonable. There are seven of us now, but I daresay he could squeeze one more in."

" You needn't worry about that, Pulham," said Mr. Wilberton. " I'm not going. I don't want to see the sights. I'm going to scout round by myself, and see if there's any fun in the place."

" Mrs. Lavenham doesn't want to go, either," Mavis remarked. " She isn't feeling very well."

"And you can count me out, too," said Merrion. "I've been here before, and I'm not particularly anxious to see it again. I shall stay on board and look after Mrs. Lavenham."

Mrs. Stewart-Patterson could not understand what was being talked about, but when the proposition was explained to her, she became immediately enthusiastic. "Oh, yes, I'd like to go. I'll take my sketching-block with me. I daresay I shall have time to put in a few outlines, which I can fill in afterwards."

They started off after lunch, Mavis, Mrs. Stewart-Patterson, Mr. Pulham, and Mr. Bewdley. This last, apprehensive of what his uncle might get up to by himself, had offered to accompany him, but had been rebuffed. "You mind your own business, Horace, my boy, and I'll mind mine. You always look down your nose if there's any chance of a lark. You'll enjoy yourself, rubber-necking with the rest of the flock of sheep."

Mrs. Lavenham had emerged from her cabin looking distinctly wan. She couldn't stay there any longer, for she felt suffocated, and must have some fresh air. Merrion carried a chair on to the bridge, and helped her up to it. When he had made her comfortable she promptly fell asleep.

Merrion, finding himself alone, was by no means bored. Alone, for the captain had gone ashore with the agent, and Mrs. Lavenham, in her present somnolent condition, could hardly be described as a companion. He remained on the bridge, interested in the activities about him. Cargo was being discharged methodically. More steel drums, this time full, and from the wording on them apparently containing the raw materials of coca-cola.

On the wharf where the *Ballerina* lay, a regular market had been set up. Half a dozen stalls, each with its voluble proprietor, on which everything, from sticky sweet-stuffs, to elaborate and gaudy hand-bags, was displayed. Round these the crew and the four stewardesses of the *Ballerina* circled, longing though mistrustful purchasers. Four stewardesses, for, in addition to Cinevra and Nina, the ship carried two others, who waited on the officers. The only means of communication between buyer and seller were a few words of halting English. Merrion watched with amusement one of the ordinary seamen, a fair-haired giant, haggling for a pair of ladies' slippers. A present for his girl in Norway no doubt.

As he watched, there came an unexpected diversion. A car drew up, deposited one of its inmates on the quay, and departed. Merrion recognised the passenger so summarily dumped as Mr. Wilberton. He staggered a few steps, turning his head from side to side unseeingly, then collapsed upon a heap of rugs beside one of the stalls.

Nobody paid any particular attention to him. It was no business of the stall-holders, and the crew had so often been in a similar state from a spree on shore that it was no novelty to them. But Merrion felt he had better do something about it. He went down the gangway and laid his hand on the other's shoulder. " You'd better come on board with me, Mr. Wilberton," he said persuasively.

" Thanks, old boy," Mr. Wilberton said thickly. " Don't know what's come over me. Must be the sun. Or something I've eaten disagreed with me. Feel deadly sick. I don't know——''

His speech became inarticulate. Merrion dragged him to his feet, supported him up the gangway, and deposited him on the bed of his cabin. Mr. Wilberton grunted, and collapsed into unconsciousness.

Merrion felt pretty certain that the sun could not be held responsible for his condition. He had probably been given some concoction to drink, wood alcohol most likely. The way the car had driven off after dumping him on the quay was in itself suspicious.

In due course the shore party came on board, having, by their own accounts, seen everything there was to see. Merrion drew Mr. Bewdley aside, and told him of his uncle's condition. " The best thing is for him to sleep it off," he said. " He probably won't feel any too good for the next day or two, but there's not much to be done about that."

Mr. Wilberton's adventure remained something of a mystery. It did not become a matter for smoke-room gossip, for Merrion told nobody but Mavis, and Mrs. Lavenham had been fast asleep at the time. It was not until next morning that Mr. Bewdley confided in Merrion. " Uncle Jasper has only just woken up, and says he feels awful. He's going to stay where he is for the present. I asked him what had happened to him, and he told me he'd met a couple of very nice chaps, who took him out to lunch. He says he doesn't remember anything after that."

Merrion smiled. " I daresay he doesn't. And I'm afraid he'll get a bit of a shock when he feels well enough to go through his pockets. One has to be careful about very nice chaps in a port like Alexandria."

Discharging took rather longer than had been expected, and the *Ballerina* did not sail until nearly midnight. Next day, Thursday the 17th, was spent at sea. It was quite calm, and Mrs. Lavenham had completely recovered. Mr. Wilberton appeared at lunch, unduly silent and woe-begone. The chief, who must have heard something from one of the crew, was a man of experience in such matters. " You not look very well, Mr. Wilberton," he said. " You come with me to my cabin. I give you something buck you up, eh ? "

The chief's prescription must have done Mr. Wilberton good, for by supper he had almost regained his usual poise. While it was still light, the central massif of Cyprus became visible in the far distance. But it was not until next morning that the *Ballerina* entered the harbour of Famagusta. Asked how long she might be expected to remain there, Captain Larsen could not say. They had a lot of cement to unload. It might take two days, perhaps three. He'd be able to tell them more that evening.

Mrs. Lavenham left the breakfast table rather hastily. Mavis, fearing that she might be feeling ill again, after an interval went to her cabin. " Oh, do come in, Mrs. Merrion ! " she exclaimed. " And please shut the door. I'm in hiding."

Mavis laughed. " In hiding ? And who or what on earth from ? "

" Mr. Pulham," Mrs. Lavenham replied. " I know he's going to ask me to go ashore with him, and after my experience in Athens I simply couldn't bear it. I asked Mrs. Stewart-Patterson just now if I might go with her. She said I should be welcome, but that she was going to spend all day sketching among the ruins we passed as we came in. And I was looking forward to seeing something gayer than ruins."

" That's easily arranged," said Mavis. " You tell Mr. Pulham that you'd already arranged to go with us. My husband and I mean to get a taxi, find a bank, cash a fat cheque there, since Cyprus is in the sterling area, and then we can enjoy ourselves. We'd simply love you to come with us."

" Oh, that is good of you ! " Mrs. Lavenham exclaimed. " May I ? You're sure your husband won't mind ? "

" He'll enjoy it as much as I shall," Mavis replied. " That's settled. We'll start as soon as you're ready."

Merrion, who thoroughly enjoyed Mrs. Lavenham's company, was delighted. A taxi proprietor was standing at the foot of the gangway, and led them to the dock gate, outside which a car was waiting. They drove to the bank, where both Merrion and Mrs. Lavenham cashed travellers' cheques, receiving Cyprus currency in exchange. Thus furnished, they spent an hour or so shopping. It was very hot, and by the time they had finished, they all felt in urgent need of refreshment. The owner of a shop, whose advice Merrion sought, recommended the King George Hotel.

They summoned a taxi again and drove there, by a circuitous route, so that they might see something of the town of Famagusta. The King George Hotel, when they reached it, came fully up to expectations. A wide terrace, shaded with awnings, looked out over the bathing beach, and an almost cool breeze blew in from the sea. They sat there, drinking iced beer, after which they had lunch.

" Well, what next ? " Merrion asked, when they were ending their meal with coffee and Cyprus brandy. " I don't feel inclined to go back to the ship. If she's unloading cement, it'll be more than a trifle dusty. I've an idea. They tell me that one of the things we ought to see on the island is Kantara Castle. About an hour's drive, and there's a hotel near by where one can get a cup of tea. What about it ? Taxis seem to be remarkably cheap here."

Both Mavis and Mrs. Lavenham agreed enthusiastically. A taxi was found, and they set out. The road ran at first across the flat plain, fertile, but now parched at the end of the dry season. Then, after winding perilously through a couple of villages, their narrow streets thronged with laden donkeys, it began to climb into the hills. Tortuously, but magnificently engineered, the gradients never excessive. Until at last the driver stopped and pointed to a ruin hardly distinguishable from the living rock on which it was founded. " Kentara," he said, with his strange Cypriote intonation. " You climb up ? "

Since the only way to the castle was by a steep, narrow and shadeless track, the three decided to remain content with the view from the road, thereby missing the chance of a glimpse of the Taurus mountains in Anatolia, far away to the north-west. But the view towards them from the eastward was magnificent. A vast semi-circle of untroubled sea spread from Famagusta, a speck on the coast line to the south, to Cape Andreas, the north-eastern part of the island.

They feasted their eyes on this until Mavis clamoured for her tea. The driver took them back a short distance by the way they had come, and pulled up outside a small hotel, standing by itself among the hills. As they were getting out another car passed, going in the direction of Kantara. As it went by a head popped out of the window and shouted a greeting. It was Mr. Pulham, and with him in the car were the second officer and the two officers' stewardesses.

" I can't help feeling sorry for Mr. Pulham," Mrs. Lavenham remarked. " He's so very much the odd man out. None of us have any time for him, so he has to fall back on foreigners, who probably don't understand a quarter of what he says to them."

" I don't think you need be sorry for him," Merrion replied. " He probably enjoys posing as the generous passenger who doesn't mind standing a trip into the country. And, after all, he very rarely says anything worth understanding. And there's this about it. If they don't know what he's talking about, there's very little risk of their interrupting him."

They lingered over tea, then drove back to the ship. By the time they arrived, discharging was just finished for the day, and the crew were washing a thick layer of cement from the decks. To avoid this, they retired to the smoking-room, where a few minutes later Captain Larsen joined them. " You enjoy yourselves ? " he asked, in the tone of a parent welcoming his children back from a party.

They assured him that they had enjoyed themselves immensely. " That good," he said. " You have two day more here, perhaps three. Not finish unloading to-morrow. Next day Sunday, no work. Perhaps finish Monday morning. I cannot say. Then we go Limassol, a few hours along coast."

It could only have been the captain's disgust at the prospect of an idle day in port that made him so unusually communicative. The ladies went to change for supper. Merrion, feeling in urgent need of a drink, asked the captain to join him. Two bottles of beer were brought, and seeing that the captain was enjoying his, Merrion ventured on a further question. "What about that passenger you were expecting to join us here, Captain?"

"He join us at Limassol, so the agent tell me," Captain Larsen replied. "Funny name, sound like Grampus. The agent not know him. He say he Englishman, come here on business, Government, maybe. Nobody here know him. Perhaps he—what you say?—hush-hush man. Better say nothing to others."

Mrs. Stewart-Patterson came in, complete with stool, sketching-block and stick. She had had a most enjoyable day, and everyone had been so good to her. She had even been allowed to sketch the interior of a mosque. She hadn't finished. Did the captain think she would have time to go ashore again for an hour or two to-morrow?

Captain Larsen assured her that she would, then, probably to avoid further questioning, left the smoking-room. Mrs. Stewart-Patterson assembled her gear, and Merrion helped her to carry it down to her cabin. As he came up again, he met Mr. Bewdley and his uncle. Mr. Bewdley drew him aside. "I think that adventure in Alexandria has taught my uncle a lesson," he whispered. "He's been as good as gold all the time we've been ashore. It's true we spent most of the day going from one cafe to another, but he didn't drink anything stronger than beer. I only hope the reformation will last for the rest of the voyage."

The only absentee at supper was Mr. Pulham. After that meal it was the chief's invariable habit to fiddle with the wireless in the smoking-room. Wherever the *Ballerina* might be, at sea or in port, he always seemed able to coax a budget of news from some station or other. But this evening he went off to his own quarters. A few minutes later, the first officer put his head in at the smoking-room door and beckoned to the captain. It was easy enough for Merrion to sense that something was amiss.

After an interval he strolled out on deck, to see Captain

Larsen leaning over the rail, watching the gangway. He turned swiftly at the sound of approaching footsteps. " Ah you, Mr. Merrion ! " he exclaimed. " Always trouble in port. No rest for me until we get to sea again. What you think now ? Two girls from officers' saloon gone ashore and not back yet. Pantry-boy, he serve their supper, and they not like it. That what first officer wanted to see me for. Want me to log them. What good that do ? "

" Very little, I imagine," Merrion replied. Knowing that the truth must out, he thought the captain might as well hear it at once. " We saw them in a car this afternoon with Mr. Pulham and the second officer."

" Mr. Pulham ? " Captain Larsen exclaimed. " That man a nuisance. Never had passenger like him, always upsetting the ship. I not mind his taking girls ashore, but he had no business keep them when they should be on duty. What I say to him ? "

" You dropped him a hint once, Captain," Merrion replied. " He didn't seem inclined to take it, you remember."

" I wish he fell overboard," Captain Larsen exclaimed viciously. " I give him one more chance, then I tell him. He can do what he likes himself, but he not make others break rules."

Merrion fully appreciated the captain's mood of annoyance. This minor worry, following the prospect of a wasted day in port, had ruffled his usually sunny temperament. " Look here, Captain," he said. " It wouldn't do you any harm to have a day ashore. Mrs. Lavenham, my wife and I are going to drive to Nikosia to-morrow and have lunch there. Why don't you come with us ? "

Captain Larsen shook his head. " You very kind, Mr. Merrion. I like to come with you there, not with any others. But if I go, ship fall to pieces. All right at sea, officers know what to do. But in port, no. Agent, he come aboard with orders. They say, you see captain. Captain gone ashore. What ? "

Before Merrion could reply, Captain Larsen pointed to a car driving along the quay towards the ship. It stopped and out of it bundled the two truant stewardesses, who made a dash for the gangway. They were followed by the second officer and, more leisurely, by Mr. Pulham. There was something about him, as he paid the driver, rather fumblingly, that suggested his determination not be be hurried by any-body.

Captain Larsen disappeared into his cabin. Merrion guessed that he could not trust himself to speak to Mr. Pulham just then. Mr. Pulham made his way on deck and, seeing Merrion alone there, lurched up to him. "Hallo, old fellow!" he exclaimed boisterously. "I say, I've had a rattling good day, with three of the very nicest people I've ever met. And I say, old chap. They make topping brandy here, and it's cheap too. As a rule I never drink anything but beer. But they persuaded me to try some brandy, and I'm bound to say I enjoyed it." He yawned widely. "I say, I'm feeling rather tired. I'll go and sit down, if you'll excuse me."

Merrion smiled to himself at the unexpected effect strange places had on people. That, for example, the normally abstemious Mr. Pulham should have become happily tight on Cyprus brandy, a state he would have regarded with horror in the conventional setting of his suburban home. That he himself, again, should be positively looking forward to a long drive in excessive heat, for the double purpose of seeing a town in which he had no particular interest, and of buying a meal which would certainly be no better than he could have had on board for nothing. Come to think of it, why go voyaging at all?

But these philosophic reflections did not spoil next day's enjoyment. They reached Nicosia about eleven, where Mavis and Mrs. Lavenham discovered to their horror that the shops closed early on Saturdays. They must do some shopping, now they had come all this way. The pretext being that in Cyprus one could buy English goods manufactured for export only.

Merrion deposited himself in a convenient bar and waited for them. He was as content there as anywhere else. More so than he would have been on board the *Ballerina*, where cement dust would have penetrated every sweating pore. All the same, he fully shared Captain Larsen's desire to be at sea once more. Too long a stay in port made him feel fidgety.

The party of three lunched, drove round the town, and returned to the ship. However restive Merrion might feel, the rest were thoroughly enjoying their stay in Cyprus. Mr. Wilberton had discovered some kind of cabaret, to which he hastened after supper. Mrs. Stewart-Patterson, indefatigable

as ever, had filled up her original sketch-block and bought
another. She had mislaid her shooting-stick in the old town of
Famagusta, but a small boy had retrieved it for her, receiving
as reward a pat on the head and a shilling. Mr. Pulham was on
shore with, of all people in the world, the phlegmatic steward.

Sunday dawned sultry, with a threat of thunder. Merrion
and Mavis did not feel inclined to go on shore again, and Mrs.
Lavenham agreed with them. For one thing, the shops would
not be open, and even to walk as far as the dock gate in such
weather would be a considerable effort. Even Mrs. Stewart-
Patterson was content to employ her new sketching-block on
deck, drawing the caiques lying in the harbour.

The day passed uneventfully, and Monday came. At
breakfast Captain Larsen announced that they would probably
sail for Limassol soon after midday. Immediately nearly
everyone remembered something that he or she must get
before they left Famagusta. Such a general exodus ensued
that the Merrions were very soon the only passengers left on
board.

Captain Larsen came up to them. "What they all go
ashore for ? Shopping ? Why they not wait till they get
back to London ? I go home, my wife say to me, ' You brought
anything for me ? ', and I say ' Nothing. If anything you
want, I buy it for you in Oslo ! ' "

By lunch time, the shoppers had all returned, laden with
parcels, and very soon afterwards the *Ballerina* cast off. The
afternoon was spent coasting along the southern shore of
Cyprus, until the anchor was dropped off the port of Limassol,
shortly before supper. "When can we go ashore, Captain ? "
Mr. Wilberton asked, when that meal began.

Captain Larsen shrugged his shoulders. "Agent's boat
alongside, you go off with him, if you like. But you not get
back to-night. We stay out here. Perhaps boat to-morrow,
I cannot say."

It certainly was rather tantalising, lying less than a mile
off-shore, with the lights of the town beckoning invitingly.
But the passengers had to make the best of it. Captain Larsen
explained to Merrion that the depth of water at the quay was
only sufficient for lighters and other small craft.

Tuesday morning came, and Mrs. Stewart-Patterson
appeared on deck before breakfast, clad in a voluminous robe,

and announcing her intention of bathing from the gangway. The sea looked so tempting that she couldn't resist it. Someone suggested the possibility of sharks, but she scouted the idea. No shark was going to deter Mrs. Stewart-Patterson from doing what she wanted. She flung aside her robe, revealing a smart bathing-dress, and dived in, to display her abilities as a remarkably good swimmer. Merrion, leaning over the rail, watched her emerge. Not quite as a second Aphrodite rising from the same Cyprus seas, he thought.

Soon after breakfast a motor-boat came off, the man in charge of it announcing that he would take passengers ashore for two shillings a head. They all crowded into it, the Merrions included, Captain Larsen adjuring them that they must be back by lunch time. Arrived at the quay, the party split up. The Merrions, with Mrs. Lavenham, strolled about, looking at the shops, then, taking a taxi, drove out to a cafe on the shore a little distance from the town. Merrion had beer, and the ladies ices.

They were back on board by the appointed time, to find the *Ballerina* surrounded by lighters, into which cargo was being discharged. There was no means of going ashore again after lunch, even had they wanted to. The Merrions and Mrs. Lavenham leaned idly on the rail, watching the process of unloading. After a while they saw a motor-boat approaching from the shore, and soon they were able to see a man sitting in it, a suit-case on either side of him. " That must be our new passenger ! " Mrs. Lavenham exclaimed. " How exciting ! I wonder who he is."

CHAPTER XV

MERRION LAUGHED. " We shall very soon know. I've come to the conclusion that there are three stages of acquaintance on board a ship like this. In the first stage, one becomes aware of one's fellow-passengers as human beings. In the second, one decides whether or not one likes each particular individual. In the third, one learns their version of their life-histories. The captain told me that this man's name was Grampus."

" Nonsense ! " Mavis exclaimed. " It can't be. A grampus is a creature that puffs, isn't it ? "

" Well, this fellow may puff, for all you know," Merrion replied. " Here he comes."

The boat reached the gangway, and the man stepped on to it, followed by the boatman, carrying his suit-cases. He was on the tall side, ungainly in build, and skinny. His face was clean-shaved, and rather expressionless, and he wore tinted glasses, with heavy tortoise-shell rims. So much they could see from above, before Cinevra appeared to conduct him to his cabin, the one vacated by Mrs. Mallory.

Later on, when the discharging was nearly finished, the agent came off, and after completing his business with the captain, got into conversation with Merrion. He was one of those people who seemed to have an insatiable curiosity regarding his fellow-beings, and asked a lot of questions about the passengers on board, who they were and all about them. Merrion parried these as best he could.

But the agent was most intrigued by the new arrival. " His name is Grampound," he said in a hushed voice. " Mr. Stephen Grampound. I can't make out who he is or what his business can be. All I know is that he booked his passage in London weeks ago. I've found out that he flew to Cyprus last week, and that since then he's been staying in Nicosia. That's the seat of the island Government, as no doubt you know."

The agent lowered his voice still further. " It's my belief he was sent here on some secret diplomatic mission. Something to do with the fuss that's being kicked up in some quarters here for the handing over of the island to Greece. Or it might even be concerned with the building of a naval base here. Whatever it is, the man's as close as an oyster. He came into my office this morning to ask what time the ship sailed, but I couldn't get anything out of him. That shows that he's on some secret business or other."

Merrion found the agent's logic diverting. It had apparently not occurred to him that nobody would care to reveal his business, however straightforward it might be, to one so patently inquisitive. And it seemed unlikely that Mr. Grampound, having terminated some secret and mysterious mission, should have chosen to return by the slowest of all available routes.

The *Ballerina* weighed anchor just before supper. Mr. Grampound appeared at that meal, having been allotted the seat on the captain's right, formerly occupied by Mrs. Mallory. He was quiet and reserved, almost shy, saying as few words as possible. Captain Larsen, his curiosity probably aroused by the agent's rather awkward guesses, tried to draw him out, but failed.

The following morning found the ship at Beirut, astonishing in its wealth of new buildings and luxurious high-powered cars. Mrs. Stewart-Patterson had a friend, or the friend of a friend, at the Legation, and set off there as soon as the landing formalities were over. Mr. Pulham went on shore by himself. He had confided in Merrion that he had spent nearly all his money in Cyprus, which may have accounted for the solitariness of his expedition. He was followed by Mr. Bewdley and his uncle. The Merrions and Mrs. Lavenham were the last to leave the ship. Nobody gave a thought to the self-effacing Mr. Grampound.

The Merrion party had decided to see something of the town and to lunch there. This they did, most adequately, returning to the ship in time for tea. In the smoking-room they found a woman they had not seen before, with vivacious expression and bright eyes. "My name is Cassidy," she announced in rich Irish brogue. "And I am the new passenger."

Miss Cassidy proved an acquisition. Not only had she an inexhaustible fund of amusing Irish stories, but she was a most interesting woman. She was in the diplomatic service, transferred to Beirut from Cairo some months earlier. Now she was going home to Ireland on three months' leave, and didn't seem to care how long it was going to take her to get there.

By the end of the evening Miss Cassidy had passed the stage of being a new arrival, and had become one of the curiously assorted group of passengers. As contrast to Mr. Grampound, who seemed deliberately, though quite courteously, to keep himself apart.

It was not until the *Ballerina* had left Beirut at noon on Thursday that Captain Larsen announced the next port of call, Istambul. Miss Cassidy was thrilled. She had heard so much of Istambul, and had always wanted to go there. It had to be explained to Mr. Wilberton that Istambul was the name by which Constantinople was now known. Even that did not improve the sulky temper into which he had lapsed. He had heard from Mr. Pulham, who had been talking to the officers that it would take two days and more to get there. At lunch Merrion overheard him regretting loudly that he hadn't left the ship at Famagusta, spent a few days in Cyprus, and gone home by air.

If Mr. Wilberton was becoming so obviously bored, the rest of the passengers were thoroughly enjoying themselves. The next couple of days passed agreeably. On Friday evening, after supper, Merrion was alone on deck, leaning on the rail and looking at the lights of Rhodes, twinkling in the distance. It was dark, and until he spoke Merrion did not realise that the shadow which had taken its place beside him was Mr. Bewdley. He asked what lights they were over there, and Merrion told him. " Have you talked to Mr. Grampound, Mr. Merrion ? " he asked abruptly.

" The best answer to that question is that he hasn't talked to me," Merrion replied. " He seems rather lost on board here, and I've done my best to be friendly. But I haven't found him very forthcoming."

" The same with me," said Mr. Bewdley. " I've done my best to make him talk about himself, for that, in my experience is the subject most people prefer. But all that I got out of him was that he was recovering from a nervous breakdown. He had to go to Cyprus on a matter of important business. His doctor had told him that it would do him a lot of good, when

I

that was finished, to take as much time as he could coming
slowly home by sea."

" A prescription the doctors are very fond of," Merrion
replied. " They don't always seem to realise that though a
sea voyage may be an excellent tonic physically, the psycho-
logical results are often disastrous."

Merrion could hear Mr. Bewdley chuckle. " My uncle, you
mean ? Oh, yes, he's thoroughly down in the dumps. Being at
sea depresses him. He'll cheer up again when we get to
Istambul. Are you ever haunted by a resemblance, Mr.
Merrion ? "

" Frequently," Merrion replied. " One racks one's brains
for the origin of the resemblance."

" It's not quite that in my case," said Bewdley. " The
original is a boy whom I have not seen for very many years.
I have not even heard of him since I last saw him in most
unfortunate circumstances. If he is still alive, he will now be
in his forties. And there is something about Mr. Grampound
that reminds me of that boy. The likeness is far too vague to
explain. Nothing more than the shape of his head, perhaps."

" You imagine he might be the man into whom the boy has
grown ? " Merrion asked.

" I wouldn't put it as strongly as that," Mr. Bewdley replied. " It is merely that I am haunted by a resemblance
which may be no more than a figment of my own imagination.
I have, I assure you, said nothing of this to Mr. Grampound
himself. There is a skeleton in our family cupboard, Mr.
Merrion."

He spoke so seriously that Merrion tried to laugh him out of
his haunting. " Mr. Grampound is certainly not of the fleshy
type. But all the same, I should hesitate to describe him as a
skeleton."

But Mr. Bewdley was not to be diverted. " You know very
well what I mean, Mr. Merrion. There is, or was, a member of
the family whom for years we have done our best to forget."

" Have you spoken of this to your uncle ? " Merrion asked.

" Most certainly I have not ! " Mr. Bewdley exclaimed
emphatically. " My uncle's discretion in such a matter could
hardly be relied upon. To mention it to him might cause
considerable unpleasantness, and that I am anxious to avoid.
You won't say anything about this, Mr. Merrion ? "

" Of course I shan't," said Merrion. " And if I were you, Mr. Bewdley, I shouldn't think any more about it."

Mr. Bewdley laughed mirthlessly. " Didn't I tell you I was haunted ? That's why I felt I must talk about it to somebody, and you seemed the most suitable person. I hoped that unburdening my mind might help to lay the ghost. Perhaps it has already."

He left the rail abruptly, and wandered off into the darkness, leaving Merrion marvelling afresh at the curious effects of a sea-voyage upon individuals. Here was Mr. Bewdley, a by no means imaginative man of business, talking about ghosts and haunted by resemblance. We should see his uncle simpering over a volume of sentimental verse next.

Rather less than twenty-four hours later the *Ballerina* entered the Dardanelles. The prospect of being in port again the next day roused Mr. Wilberton from his sulkiness. He even tried his heavy-handed witticisms on Miss Cassidy, to be countered by a flow of Irish irony which effectively silenced him.

Merrion looked out of his cabin scuttle early on Sunday morning. The pink dawn revealed on the port bow the minarets of Istambul in all their oriental loveliness. He dressed and went on deck. The *Ballerina* was moving towards the entrance of the Bosphorus, and the whole panorama of Istambul was clearly visible. The ship lost way as the pilot-boat appeared. The pilot came aboard, and the engine turned again. Merrion supposed that they would now head into the Golden Horn. Instead of which the ship's head turned to starboard before she dropped anchor about a mile from the Asiatic shore, and the pilot left her.

Merrion had no objection, for from where they lay the view of Istambul was fascinating. But some of the other passengers exhibited impatience. " How long are we going to stay here, Captain ? " Mr. Pulham asked at breakfast.

" I cannot say," Captain Larsen replied. " We wait for berth, all day perhaps."

Mr. Wilberton swung round in his chair. " What's that ? We're to be stuck out here all day ? You can lower one of those boats of yours and put us ashore, can't you ? "

Captain Larsen shook his head. " Cannot do that. Not allowed. Plenty of time to go ashore when we get alongside."

After breakfast the captain unburdened himself to Merrion.
" You see now why I never promise passengers too much. The
pilot, he tell me not go into Istambul. You see that ship lie
over there ? "

He pointed to the Asiatic shore. Following the direction
of his finger Merrion made out a vessel lying at a quay,
beyond which was the big building of a railway terminus.
" Haider Pasha," the captain went on. " Railway from there
to Ankara. We go in where that ship is when she come out.
To-morrow morning, perhaps. But you get to Istambul just
the same. Ferry-boat across every half hour."

" That sounds good enough," said Merrion. " Have you
any idea how long we shall stay here ? "

Captain Larsen shrugged his shoulders. " Day and a half.
Two days, perhaps. After we get alongside, that is. And I
tell you something, Mr. Merrion. The pilot, he brought me
letter from the owners. From here we go to Fetiyeh. Load
two thousand tons chrome ore."

" Fetiyeh ? " Merrion repeated. " I never heard of the
place. Where is it ? "

" You come with me, I show you," Captain Larsen replied.
He took Merrion up to the chart-room, where a chart was
spread out, and pointed to a circle he had pencilled. " There
you are. I never been there myself."

The circle enclosed a port marked on the chart, with the
name Fetiyeh printed against it. It lay at the head of a land-
locked bay on the south-western coast of Anatolia, nestling
beneath the foot-hills of the Taurus mountains. As far as one
could tell from the chart, these cut it off from road or railway,
which ran far inland. A remoter spot could hardly be imagined.
" It looks interesting, if not exciting," Merrion remarked. " I
wonder what Mr. Wilberton will make of this."

Mr. Wilberton wasn't making much of lying at anchor at the
mouth of the Bosphorus. He was pacing the boat-deck like a
caged tiger, growling at anyone who ventured to come near
him. It was preposterous that the captain refused to lower a
boat and put him ashore. He was going to write to the
Company about it when he got home. He didn't seem to see
the fascinating prospect of Istambul, which Mrs. Stewart-
Patterson, once more perched on the hatch, was already
sketching assiduously.

Mavis and Mrs. Lavenham were sitting in the shade, and Merrion, having ordered beer, sat down beside them. " I don't mind not being able to go ashore yet," Mrs. Lavenham was saying. " The view from here is perfectly lovely, whichever way one looks. But it will be wonderful to explore that beautiful town."

Merrion smiled. " First impressions are often best, Mrs. Lavenham. In my experience, however picturesque a port may be, it always looks better from the sea than it does from the land. I hope you won't be disappointed."

" How like you, Desmond ! " Mavis exclaimed indignantly. " Trying to damp our enthusiasm. Well, you can stop on board the old ship if you like. Mrs. Lavenham and I are going to poke about Istambul as soon as we get the chance."

Cinevra brought the beer on a tray, which she laid on the deck beside them. Stocks having run low, a fresh supply had been taken on board at Beirut. As Merrion filled the glasses, he noticed that the name on the bottle was a Dutch one. " Well, there may be something in the United Nations idea after all," he remarked. " Here are we, three English people, drinking Dutch beer on a Norwegian ship in Turkish waters. A good omen ? "

" I don't know about omens," Mrs. Lavenham replied, as she took a sip from the glass Merrion handed her. " But it's jolly good beer. So long as this holds out, we shan't have much to grumble at."

That Sunday passed comparatively peacefully. Only comparatively, for Mr. Wilberton, whose frustrated frame of mind made it necessary for him to pick a quarrel with somebody, picked upon Mr. Pulham.

What the argument had been about was not apparent. But Mr. Pulham took himself off to the fore-deck, where he sat in offended isolation.

Early on Monday morning the ship lying at the quay in Haider Pasha harbour passed out. A pilot boarded the *Ballerina* and her anchor was raised. Within half an hour she was made fast to the vacated berth, and unloading began.

At breakfast, Captain Larsen made an announcement. " You not have any Turkish money, and no bank here this side. I give Mr. Merrion two Turkish pounds, and he pay your fares for ferry-boat. You pay him back and he pay me. You find ferry-boat quite close, at pier outside railway station. You go enjoy yourselves. We not sail to-day."

Merrion shepherded the rest to the ferry-boat booking office. All but Mr. Pulham. He wasn't going ashore. Not yet, anyhow. Not with all that crowd, like a bunch of Margate trippers. Merrion bought tickets for himself and his companions, and distributed them. They boarded the ferry-boat, a somewhat antiquated steamer, with room for two or three hundred passengers. However, she was not crowded, and in twenty minutes they had reached the European side at Galata bridge.

Here the party split up. Mr. Bewdley and his uncle, the latter no doubt in search of some nebulous fun. Mrs. Stewart-Patterson and Miss Cassidy, intent upon viewing St. Sophia and the Blue Mosque. The Merrions and Mrs. Lavenham, their first objective being a bank, at which to cash travellers' cheques. All these turned to the left, towards Istambul. Only Mr. Grampound, alone, turned to the right, towards the residential quarter of Galata.

The Merrion party fully obeyed the captain's injunction to enjoy themselves. Having provided themselves with Turkish money, they found their way, as though by instinct, to the bazaar. Here they spent the morning, chaffering for trinkets in shop after shop. Then Merrion discovered an eating-house, which, in spite of the primitive sanitary accommodation, provided excellent food and drink. After lunch they hired a taxi, the driver speaking a strange jargon in which a few English and French words were barely recognisable. Emulating this as best they could, they made him understand what they wanted. He took them to various places of interest, then for a drive round the Wall of Theodosius.

They returned to the Galata bridge, and boarded the waiting ferry-boat, in which they found Mrs. Stewart-Patterson and Miss Cassidy. On reaching the *Ballerina* they saw Mr. Grampound already on board. To Miss Cassidy's polite enquiry as to whether he had had a good time, he replied stiffly that his only reason for going ashore had been to leave his card at the Embassy. Much later Mr. Bewdley and his uncle appeared, the latter loud-voiced and unsteady. He had evidently found means with which to dissipate his boredom.

There was no sign of Mr. Pulham. Noticing that Nina had

served supper single-handed, Merrion had drawn his own
conclusions. And these were confirmed by Mr. Pulham when
he reappeared about ten o'clock. " Did you have an interesting
visit to the town, Mr. Pulham ? " Miss Cassidy asked.

" I didn't go there," Mr. Pulham replied loftily. " I don't
care for these foreign towns, they're all so much alike. I
found a steamer at the pier here which ran a trip up the
Bosphorus, so I went in it. And I took Cinevra with me. I
thought she deserved a treat, after the way she's looked after
us all."

It was not until after supper on Tuesday that the *Ballerina*
left Haider Pasha. Wednesday was spent uneventfully at
sea. Merrion was on deck before breakfast on Thursday, the
first day of October. The weather had not yet broken, and
seemed almost as hot as ever. The *Ballerina* was entering a
wide bay, with mountains on either side. They must be
coming to that place nobody had ever heard of, Merrion
thought. What was the name of it ? Yes, that was it, Fetiyeh.
Right off the map. Mr. Wilberton would find it even worse
than being at sea. Nobody could expect anything exciting
to happen there.

CHAPTER XVI

BY THE TIME that breakfast was over, the *Ballerina* was
navigating a narrow channel between the mainland and one
of the islands strung out across the bay. The channel opened
into an expanse of water three or four miles across, which
looked like an inland lake. Merrion saw a few villages scattered
on the shores, and, to the right, a small town, which might be
Fetiyeh.

The *Ballerina* kept on towards the town, which showed no
sign of life, in spite of repeated screeches from the whistle.
At last she stopped and dropped anchor. But it was a long
time before the watchers on board saw a motor-boat put off
from shore. As it approached the ship they saw that it was
packed with men. It came alongside, and the whole party
trooped up the gangway, and into the captain's cabin.

The pilot was the first to emerge, and he and the captain

mounted the bridge. The rest wandered on to the boat-deck, led by a stout gentleman girded with a sash, who proceeded to introduce the visitors to the assembled passengers. " I, mayor. Him, master of harbour. Him, big man of custom. Him, boss of police. Him, Company man. Him, governor of mine." The lesser crowd of customs officials and police, standing respectfully in the rear seemed unworthy of notice.

Each of the officers named insisted on shaking the hands of the passengers in turn. Merrion guessed that the arrival of a foreign ship, carrying passengers, was an almost unprecedented event in this out of the way port. The ceremony over, a very cursory inspection of passports was made. Merrion went on deck again, to find to his astonishment that the ship was heading, not to Fetiyeh, but in the opposite direction, across the land-locked bay. In a few minutes his destination became apparent. A long and narrow spit of land projected into the bay, and at the top of this was what in the distance seemed to be a low wharf.

Nearer approach revealed this, not as a wharf, in the usual sense of the term, but a dismantled concrete ship. This battered-looking hulk had been grounded at the end of a spit. Her decks and vacant holds had been partially covered with old sleepers and such other odd pieces of wood as had been available. On this, a narrow gauge railway-track had been laid, which, from the improvised wharf, led waveringly inland up the spit. Beside the track was an untidy row of tumble-down houses, from which, as the *Ballerina* approached, emerged a swarm of wide-eyed women and children.

It was past noon by the time the *Ballerina* was somehow made fast to the hulk. The mayor, who with his fellows had retired to the smoking-room for refreshment, reappeared. " You see town. Very fine town. Not afternoon. Too hot, all sleep. Morning, boat come. Good-bye." He collected his retinue, and in procession they all descended the gangway into their waiting motor-boat which immediately set off across the bay towards the now distant Fetiyeh.

At lunch, Captain Larsen was more than usually reticent. The only words he spoke were in reply to the questions fired at him, the familiar ' I can't sigh.' But afterwards, seeing Merrion alone in a corner of the boat-deck, he went up to him. " They ask me how long we stay here," he said irritably.

the exception of Mr. Wilberton, found sufficient amusement in watching the ludicrous process of loading. Perhaps, also, in the contrast between this remote backwater and the busy ports they had hitherto visited. Next morning, Friday, the mayor fulfilled his promise by sending the motor-boat across the bay. All the passengers got into it, and were taken to the landing-stage at Fetiyeh, the journey occupying about half an hour.

They were led to an awning, stretched between a couple of trees at the entrance of the only street of the town. There, surrounded by an interested but perfectly well-behaved audience, they were served with coffee. Mr. Wilberton endeavoured to make the mayor understand that he wanted something stronger. When at last he grasped what he was driving at, the mayor shook his head. " Islam here," he whispered. " Very strict. You like sherbet, no ? "

Mr. Wilberton loudly and forcibly expressed his dislike of sherbet or any other soft drink. When the coffee had been drunk, the mayor insisted upon leading his visitors on a personally conducted tour. " Fine town," he said proudly. " You not see many like." They walked in the intense heat, the whole length of the dusty and ill-paved street, then back by a rough track that formed the sea-front. At last they were allowed to return to the landing-stage, where the motor-boat was waiting to take them back to the *Ballerina*.

" Not quite so bracing as Skegness," Mrs. Lavenham remarked, as Merrion brought her the iced beer. for which they both were craving. " But the mayor meant it kindly, I'm sure. I'm not inclined to go there again."

" Nor I," Merrion agreed. " I'd rather stop on board. There's one at least who's not amused."

Mr. Wilberton was holding forth at the top of his voice. He was going to let the Company know just what he thought about it. What did they mean by bringing him to a place where there was no fun of any sort to be had, not even a drink. And as for this hole, it was like being tied up to a desert island. Unless he had seen it with his own eyes, he wouldn't have believed that such a God-forsaken spot existed.

It was the chief who had the inspiration. Perhaps sitting at the same table as Mr. Wilberton and having to listen to his imprecations, he was driven to it. " I tell you ! " he announced

in the smoking-room after lunch. " We lower motor-lifeboat.
Go off to one of the islands. How that ? "

A chorus of approval greeted this suggestion. Thus encouraged, the chief proceeded to elaborate the idea. " We
have bathe. Then we have, what you call ? Picnic. Take the
girls, they make coffee. What ? "

This, in comparison to sitting on board listening to the
unceasing clank and rattle, was something approaching
romance. The motor lifeboat was lowered, and when, not
without difficulty, the chief had got the engine to start, and
some of the accumulated oil and filth had been baled out, the
passengers, with Cinevra and Nina, got into it. Most were
wearing bathing dresses, covered by a garment of some kind.
Mrs. Stewart-Patterson refused to be parted from her stool,
sketching-block and shooting-stick. The neck of a bottle
protruded from Mr. Wilberton's pocket. Cinevra and Nina
each brought with them a covered basket.

When all were aboard, the lifeboat cast off, and purred away,
the Chief at the helm. He took them first on a wide curve
round the bay. " Not land at town," he said. " Customs not
like that. We explore island by and by. Like Captain Cook,
what ? "

From where the boat was, in the middle of the bay, it could
be seen that there were three islands. The one nearest the town
had a light-house upon it. It was between this and the
mainland that the *Ballerina* had entered. A narrow but deep
channel separated it from the middle island, and a similar
channel separated this from the third, nearest to the spit of
land and the hulk at which the *Ballerina* lay. The channel
between this and the spit was wider and apparently shallower.

The Chief chose this last island on which to land. He skirted
the shore of it until he perceived a small sandy and shelving
beach, which, owing to the shape of the island, happened to
be out of sight of the ship. On to this he ran the bow of the
lifeboat, then, jumping into the water, he helped his passengers
ashore.

Most of them prepared to bathe from the beach. But
Merrion, with his usual curiosity, felt an urge to explore the
island. He strolled away, striking inland from the beach, up a
gentle slope, studded with low trees and brushwood. The area
of the island, he guessed, was somewhere under a square mile,

wild and overgrown. Its surface was irregular, little hollows and shallow depressions. These latter were now completely dry, but their appearance showed that during the rainy season they held water.

The island was at present uninhabited, but round the shore, mainly miniature cliffs, nowhere more than a dozen feet high, dropping perpendicularly into the sea, with here and there a sandy cove, were a few untidy shacks, widely scattered. These, though not quite derelict, were now unoccupied. Merrion guessed they that had been built, or rather knocked together, by the inhabitants of Fetiyeh, seeking refuge from the intolerable heat of summer week-ends.

He was wandering along the shore of the island, where it faced the narrow channel separating it from the next, when he came upon Mr. Grampound. He was sitting on the edge of the cliff, rapt in deep thought. Every now and then he would abstractedly pick up a stone or a piece of fallen twig and throw it into the water at his feet. Merrion wondered idly what he was thinking about.

Merrion's approach roused him, and he turned his head with the expression of a man awakened from a dream. " Ah, Mr. Merrion ! " he exclaimed. " So you are not bathing ? "

" Not yet," Merrion replied. " I'm just having a look round. I may have a swim later."

Mr. Grampound shook his head. " Better not. Haven't you noticed those boys who bathe close by where the ship is lying ? They never go more than a few yards from shore. I shouldn't dream of disagreeing with the chief engineer. The ship's officers must always be supposed to know best. But when he suggested bathing I was extremely dubious. Sharks are by no means uncommon in the Eastern Mediterranean."

Merrion smiled. " We haven't seen any yet. You know this part of the world ? "

" My duties have brought me to the Levant from time to time," Mr. Grampound replied. " And, although you may not have seen sharks in these waters, I have."

There was something conclusive in this remark, and Merrion strolled on. Mr. Grampound was certainly a dark horse. He had spoken of his duties, not his business. That seemed to support the Cyprus agent's suspicion that his affairs were confidential. Whatever they were, he was obviously not pre-

pared to talk about them. Merrion, who had frequently been
in a similar position, fully sympathised with this attitude.

His tour of the island brought him in sight of the cove in
which the lifeboat was grounded, her painter made fast to a
near-by tree. On a slight eminence not far away, Mrs. Stewart-
Patterson sat, her paraphernalia about her. She was sketching
the bay and the surrounding mountains. In a little hollow
Cinevra and Nina were chattering away animately in Norwegian. They had lighted a fire, to replenish which Mr.
Pulham was collecting dry twigs and branches. Mr. Wilberton,
glowering, was sitting apart with a glass, into which he kept
pouring something from the bottle in his pocket. The rest sat
round, watching the kettle, already filled with coffee and tinned
milk, simmering on the fire.

" Where have you been, Mr. Merrion ? " Mrs. Lavenham
asked, as he came up to the spot where she and Mavis were
sitting on the ground. " You ought to have come for a swim.
The water's lovely."

" Better take care," Merrion replied. " I'm told there may
be sharks about."

" Oh, we've heard that before ! " Mavis exclaimed. " They
said there were sharks at Cyprus. I don't believe it."

" Well, there's the man who told me," said Merrion. Mr.
Grampound had appeared, but he did not join them. As usual,
he kept himself away as though to avoid questions. Mr.
Wilberton, on whom his potations seemed to have a mellowing
effect, called out to him. " Come over here, Grampound, old
boy. I'll give you something that'll do you a lot more good
than that damned coffee."

But Grampound merely shook his head. The kettle boiled.
Cinevra and Nina poured out the coffee and carried round the
cups, followed by Mr. Pulham distributing the cakes and
biscuits they had brought with them. " Isn't this a jolly
party ! " Miss Cassidy exclaimed. " I feel as if I was a child
again, back home in Ireland. We used to have picnics just
like this on the shores of the lough."

Everyone agreed that it was a jolly party. Everyone, that
is, with the exception of Mr. Wilberton, who growled something about a Sunday-school treat. The chief, in a melodious
if untrained tenor, struck up a Norwegian song, in which
Cinevra and Nina joined. His example rather unexpectedly

emboldened Mr. Bewdley to break into a popular ballad. Miss
Cassidy allowed herself to be persuaded to a spirited rendering.
of ' The Wearing of the Green.' It was all very companionable.

The time came to pack up and re-embark in the lifeboat.
The sun was setting behind the mountains as they returned to
the *Ballerina*. Loading was finished for the day. Everyone
would have been quite content but for Mr. Wilberton, who,
being more than slightly drunk, made an intolerable nuisance
of himself.

Talking to Merrion after supper, Captain Larsen expressed
himself as at least fairly well satisfied. " They work well all
day. Half of the ore on board already. They work all day
to-morrow, Saturday, but not Sunday. We ought to get away
Monday afternoon."

" You'll be glad to get away, I daresay," Merrion remarked.

Captain Larsen had evidently not been captivated by the
beauty of the mountains and the land-locked bay. He made a
sweeping gesture with his arm. " Glad ? To get to sea again
after this ? I should say. Four day we spend loading two
thousand ton of ore. What the Company say I don't know.
Glad ! "

The shore gang certainly started work early on Saturday
morning. It was barely six o'clock when the Merrions were
awakened by the familiar clanging. Just outside their cabin
scuttle, too, for the ore was being loaded into number 2 hold.
They stood if for a while, then got up in despair.

The noise and the heat, for that morning seemed hotter than
ever, had its effect on all on board. On Mr. Wilberton in
particular, for in addition to the common discomfort, he was
suffering from a heavy hangover. He was like a bear with a
sore head, picking quarrels with all he came across, and cursing
the place, the ship, and everybody connected with her. What
a fool he had been not to leave her when he had the chance !

" How devoutly we all wish he had ! " Mrs. Lavenham
remarked to Merrion. " But he'll have to stay where he is now.
I don't see that he has any chance of getting away from here."

Merrion pointed to a couple of small boats rowing about the
bay, with lines trailing astern. " He might get one of those
fishermen to row him across to the town. But what then ?
The mayor said something about a weekly boat to Ismir or
Smyrna, if you prefer it so. And vessels from the outside

world must call at Fetiyeh sometimes. How else do the folk there get their supplies ? "

The morning passed somehow. At lunch, the chief announced that if they cared to, they might do the same as they had the day before. This was received with acclamation. The lifeboat was again lowered, and the party set out. The picnic was not quite such a success as before. The second time the adventure fell rather flat. The passengers were bored, not only with themselves, but with one another. Besides, the fire didn't seem to burn properly, and the coffee was luke-warm and tasted smoky.

A rather dejected party returned to the ship. It was Mr. Pulham who carried Mrs. Stewart-Patterson's belongings up the gangway. She thanked him, and said she was quite capable of carrying them to her cabin. The rug, the sketching-block, the stool, the box of pencils. " Oh, and my stick, Mr. Pulham ? "

" Haven't you got it, Mrs. Stewart-Patterson ? " Mr. Pulham replied. " I haven't seen it."

" Then you must have left in in the boat ! " she exclaimed. " Oh, do please look for it, somebody."

CHAPTER XVII

By this time the davit-falls had been hooked to the lifeboat, and it was being hauled up, two of the crew in it to fend it off the ship's side. The chief, hearing Mrs. Stewart-Patterson's cry of distress, called out in Norwegian to them to look for the stick. When the boat was swung into its cradles, they searched it thoroughly, without result. " You must have leave it on island, Mrs. Patterson," said the chief.

That was the only possible explanation. When she was being helped in or out of the boat, she entrusted her belongings to the others. She couldn't remember who it was she had handed her precious stick to. Mrs. Stewart-Patterson was not only inconsolable, but resentful. She valued that stick more than anything she possessed. It was the last thing her husband had given her before he died. She was quite sure someone had hidden it in order to distress her.

So to Mr. Wilberton's sound and fury were added Mrs. Stewart-Patterson's lamentations. In addition, it was learnt that loading was to continue till ten o'clock. The atmosphere became heavily charged with irritation. Even Miss Cassidy lost her habitual cheerfulness.

The climax came in the smoking-room after supper, when the chief was fiddling with the wireless, trying to find a station which spoke some language he understood. Mrs. Stewart-Patterson approached him. There was obviously nothing to be done about the stick that night, for it was already dark. But they would be going to the island to-morrow, wouldn't they ? She must find her stick, at any cost.

The chief was most sympathetic, but shook his head. There were many reasons why the lifeboat could not be lowered again. On Sundays the crew were off duty. The captain had said they were using petrol which would have to be accounted for. In any case, the chief explained, he could not go. He had matters to attend to in the engine-room before they sailed on Monday. At this, Mrs. Stewart-Patterson incontinently burst into tears.

She did not appear at breakfast next morning. Miss Cassidy went to her cabin and came back to report. " The poor soul has made herself quite ill. She says she feels so poorly that she doesn't feel she can get up and see us laughing at her. She says we're all in a conspiracy to prevent her finding her old stick. And if it isn't found, she simply doesn't know what she'll do."

" I feel extremely sorry for her," said Mr. Grampound primly. " The stick may not be worth much, but no doubt she values it for sentimental reasons. It must be somewhere on the island, I suppose. I wish there was some means of getting across and looking for it."

Merrion pointed through the scuttle. Sunday seemed to have brought out more fishermen than usual, for there were half a dozen small boats scouring the bay. " I daresay, for a matter of a few piastres, one of those chaps would consent to act as ferryman," Merrion remarked.

" An excellent idea, Mr. Merrion ! " Mr. Pulham exclaimed. " I feel we ought to act upon it."

" I quite agree," said Mr. Grampound. " This is what I suggest. After lunch we will hail one of the fishermen, and make him understand what we want. If he agrees, some of us ought to go and search the island. Men only, I think. Those boats look filthy and smell disgustingly. I don't think the ladies would like to get into one of them. I am quite ready to go, for one."

Merrion and Mr. Pulham said they would go with him. Mr. Wilberton laughed derisively. " Going to waste your time looking for an old woman's twopenny-halfpenny stick ? All right, I'll come too. Any excuse is good enough to get away from this damned ship."

A little later Merrion, sitting on deck, saw a small steamer enter the bay and steam towards the landing stage at the town. He drew Mrs. Lavenham's attention to this. " Just as I thought. There is some communication between Fetiyeh and civilisation. No doubt that steamer is bringing stores, and perhaps a passenger or two as well. But I don't suppose she calls very frequently."

" Oh, for mercy's sake tell Mr. Wilberton ! " Mrs. Lavenham replied. " He's always ranting about wanting to get away from this ship. And if we have much more of him, we shall all go crazy."

Merrion laughed. " I shouldn't care to suggest it. He'd probably take it as a mortal insult. Besides, I haven't the remotest idea where that steamer came from, or where she may be bound for next."

The problem of getting in touch with the fishermen solved itself. After lunch one of the boats came alongside the *Ballerina*, and the occupant, a grinning young Turk, made gestures appropriate to lighting and smoking an imaginary cigarette. " It's cigarettes he wants," Mr. Pulham explained. " I got a box from the steward yesterday. I'll go and fetch them."

He returned with the cigarettes, and descended the gangway, followed by the other four men. Upon being given a whole box of cigarettes, the fisherman exhibited transports of delight. Much to Mr. Pulham's embarrassment, he seized his hand and raised it to his lips. Mr. Pulham replied by going through the motions of rowing, then jabbing vigorously with his finger towards the island. The fisherman nodded and grinned even more widely than before, pointing downwards into the boat invitingly.

They accepted this, and crowded into the little craft. Mr. Grampound's misgivings proved correct. The boat was ankle-deep in fish offal, and stank to high heaven under the burning sun. The fisherman bent to his oars and, guided by Mr. Pulham's pointing finger, landed them at the familiar cove. Mr. Pulham pointed to the sand on which the boat had grounded. " You stop here. No go away, savvy ? "

The fisherman nodded and grinned. By way of showing his comprehension he curled himself up in the stern of the boat as though preparing for siesta. " I hope he does understand," said Mr. Grampound. " I shouldn't like to be marooned here indefinitely. The most obvious place to look for the stick is where the fire was lighted yesterday."

They made their way to the spot, looking about them as they went. But in spite of all their searching the missing shooting-stick was not to be found. " I saw Mrs. Stewart-Patterson wandering about the island yesterday, looking for a good place to sketch from," said Mr. Grampound. " She may have left it anywhere. The best thing we can do is to separate and cover the island till we get to the other side."

They scattered, and moved slowly off, soon losing sight of

one another among the brushwood. Even Mr. Wilberton
raised no objection. His heart was obviously not in the search,
but he seemed to have made up his mind that the island was
not more depressing than the ship. Merrion, who had seen the
neck of a bottle again protruding from his pocket, imagined
that he would not get very far before sitting down to enjoy
a pull.

Merrion walked slowly on, following more or less ill-defined
tracks through the undergrowth. He reasoned that if Mrs.
Stewart-Patterson had dropped her stick on the island, it
would have been on one of those. Indomitable old lady as she
was, she would hardly have tried to force her way through the
tangled brushwood. Mr. Grampound had remarked that he
had seen her wandering about, looking for a suitable spot from
which to sketch. Presumably she would have chosen an
eminence for that purpose. Whenever he came to rising ground
he stopped and looked round thoroughly.

As he went on he became conscious of a queer and rather
satisfying feeling of being utterly alone. When he came to
think of it, never for an instant in the last few weeks had he
been more than a few feet away from some other human being.
Now he could play with the illusion of being by himself on a
deserted, though not a desert island. His companions were
lost among the trees and undergrowth on either side of him.
He could not even hear their footsteps.

At length he came to the further side of the island at a
point where the trees overhung a low, almost perpendicular
cliff. The next island in the chain was only a few hundred
yards away, across the still water. The cliff fell vertically into
the sea, and, looking down, he could see the bottom, over
which a shoal of tiny fish darted backwards and forwards.
Pretty deep, ten or twelve feet, he estimated.

From where he stood he could see the town of Fetiyeh in
the distance, straggling along the water-front. The steamer
was still lying at the landing-stage, and he could see her
derricks moving. The fact that cargo was being worked on
Sunday suggested that she was due away again without unnecessary delay. He wondered idly where she might be bound
for. Some other little port along the coast probably.

He had lighted a cigarette. It was pleasant standing there
in complete solitude, under the shade of the trees. In the bay

the fishermen, some near, some far, were rowing languidly about. Not a very profitable occupation. Watching them, Merrion could not see that they ever caught anything.

Suddenly he remembered his purpose on the island. Not to indulge in solitary meditation, but to find Mrs. Stewart-Patterson's lost shooting-stick. Half regretfully he turned away and plunged inland once more. Not of course by the way he had come, for that would be to cover the same ground twice. He found a meandering track which led from one of the tumble-down shacks. He wondered that none of these were occupied on such a hot Sunday. Then he realised that the arrival of the steamer was such a momentous event as to keep all the inhabitants in the town.

He sauntered slowly back, looking about him keenly, as before. Eventually he made his way back to the cove. Looking at his watch, he saw that he had been absent more than an hour. The boat was still drawn up on the sand, with the fisherman curled up in the stern, now genuinely asleep. Of the rest of the party there was no sign.

Merrion sat down in the shade and lighted another cigarette. He didn't care how long he stayed there. It was a relief to be out of the range of Mr. Wilberton's blustering for a little while longer. Perhaps a quarter of an hour elapsed before he heard slow footsteps. Mr. Grampound came in sight, looking steadfastly on the ground, and empty-handed. Merrion hailed him. "No luck, Mr. Grampound? I've had none either."

Mr. Grampound looked up and shook his head. "No luck, Mr. Merrion. I've been thinking that we're on a wild-goose chase. How do we know that Mrs. Stewart-Patterson left her stick on the island? She may have dropped it in the water when she was getting in or out of the lifeboat. It would sink of course. It's more than heavy enough, with that metal folding seat. I'm truly sorry for her, but if that's the case, we shall never find it."

Merrion had no comment to make, and they relapsed into silence. But, in a few minutes they were startled by a wild whoop at no great distance. Mr. Pulham burst out of the undergrowth, brandishing the long-lost shooting-stick above his head. "I've found it!" he yelled. "Just back there. Stood upright in the ground. Looked just like one of those young saplings, with the top broken off. Didn't see what it was, till I nearly fell over it."

" Well done ! " Mr. Grampound exclaimed. " Mrs. Stewart-Patterson will be most grateful to you, I'm sure. Stick in the ground ! I never thought of that. I was looking for something lying on the ground. We might all have passed close by it without noticing it. You have sharp eyes, Mr. Pulham."

" You are hereby awarded the prize," said Merrion. " The grateful thanks of the distressed lady. Well, as soon as the other two turn up, we can return in triumph, bearing our spoils with us, the Argonauts with the Golden Fleece."

Mr. Pulham was immensely pleased with himself. He kept rambling on about his wonderful discovery. Looked just like thousands of other stems growing on the island. Might have passed it a dozen times and not noticed the difference. Just a matter of luck that it happened to catch his eye. And so on and so forth.

But as time passed, his urge to restore the stick to its owner and receive her thanks prevailed. " It's time we were getting back to the ship. Where can those other two have got to ? "

Merrion smiled. " I expect they're taking it easy somewhere."

" And keeping us kicking our heels," Mr. Pulham replied indignantly. " I'll see if I can call them." Carrying the precious stick he climbed to the summit of a near-by hillock, and bawled " Mr. Wilberton ! Mr. Bewdley ! The stick's been found ! "

" They aren't likely to hear him, if they're at the other side of the island," Merrion remarked.

" That's true," Mr. Grampound agreed. " Don't you think we should go and look for them ? "

Merrion shook his head. " No, I don't. While we were looking for them they might come back by a different way. Then they might start out to look for us, and so we should go on interminably. We'd better stop where we are. They're bound to turn up before long."

Mr. Pulham rejoined them, hoarse with his shouting. " I say, this is an infernal nuisance ! It'll be getting dark before long. How would it be if we went back to the ship and sent the boat over to wait for them ? "

" I don't quite like the idea," Mr. Grampound replied

doubtfully. "It would be very difficult to make the fisherman understand what we wanted him to do. I feel we oughtn't to desert them."

But, after they had waited some time longer, the fisherman took a hand. The sun had set, and distant objects were already becoming indistinct in the short twilight. He made significant gestures towards the mainland, then put his shoulder to the bow of the boat, as though to push it off. "It's pretty clear that he's had enough of it," Merrion remarked. "He'll go off without us unless we restrain him by force. And I don't suppose any of us feel inclined to do that."

It seemed that Merrion was right. Seeing that they made no move, the fisherman pushed the boat off, took up his oars and rowed a few yards from shore. Then he stopped, with an expression which indicated as clearly as if he had spoken, "Are you coming or aren't you?"

There was nothing for it, and they walked on to the sand. The fisherman grinned, and brought the boat within their reach. They scrambled into it, and the fisherman, hardly waiting for them to do so, rowed away like a man possessed. "We must somehow make him understand that he'll have to go back and wait for the others," said Mr. Grampound.

But they were given no chance to do that. They reached the *Ballerina's* gangway, and got out. Merrion was the last. He had one foot still in the boat when it shot away from under him. He only saved himself by grabbing at the hand-rope. He turned, with an angry word. But the fisherman was rowing away with redoubled energy. Not towards the island, but to the town of Fetiyeh, whose lights could be seen glimmering across the bay.

CHAPTER XVIII

MERRION FELT that he ought to tell the captain what had happened. He found him in his cabin, and was bidden come in. Captain Larsen listened to the story with a smile of amusement. " Mr. Wilberton, he got drunk ? " he asked, with his usual insight.

" I shouldn't be surprised," Merrion replied. " What I imagine may have happened is this. Mr. Wilberton settled himself down somewhere and drank himself off to sleep. Mr. Bewdley found him, and either couldn't wake him—if he did, Mr. Wilberton refused to be disturbed. And Mr. Bewdley felt he couldn't very well leave his uncle alone."

Captain Larsen shrugged his shoulders. " It not do Mr. Wilberton harm to spend night where he is. Teach him good manners, perhaps. We see, Mr. Merrion, ship not sail till afternoon to-morrow."

But Captain Larsen was not so callous as he chose to appear. Merrion's theory was probably correct. If so, when Mr. Wilberton recovered from his debauch, and he and Mr. Bewdley found they were marooned, they would probably make their way to the point of the island nearest to the ship, and shout. They should be heard on a still night, over little more than a mile of water.

In addition to her four lifeboats the *Ballerina* carried a small pram. Captain Larsen gave orders for this to be lowered and made fast alongside the gangway. Then he posted a watchman on the bridge with orders that if he heard shouting from the island, he was to put off in the pram and fetch the shouters on board. Captain Larsen felt that no more could be expected of him.

By the time that Merrion reached the smoking-room he found that everybody had heard the news. Mr. Pulham could be trusted for that. He, as the finder of the stick, was the hero of the ship. He had bashfully declined to take it to Mrs. Stewart-Patterson himself. He wouldn't dream of intruding into a lady's cabin. In the end Miss Cassidy had taken it to her. It had acted as a magic talisman to cure her indisposition. She had announced her intention of getting up and thanking Mr. Pulham personally.

As for Mr. Wilberton's plight, it created general amusement and satisfaction. Mrs. Lavenham voiced the common opinion. " It serves him jolly well right. He's made himself intolerable, these last few days. Of course I'm sorry for Mr. Bewdley. But if one indulges in the luxury of an uncle like that one must expect to bear the consequences."

The evening passed by with no sign from the truant passengers. Merrion felt a trifle guilty. Perhaps they oughtn't to have left the island when they did. On the other hand, if they hadn't, the fisherman would have marooned the lot of them. He wouldn't have waited a moment longer. No doubt he had been eager to join the festivities occasioned by the visit of the steamer.

Merrion went up on to the bridge. He found that the watchman posted there spoke good English. He was a young dental student from Oslo, who had signed on as ordinary seaman for the voyage, as so many Norwegians did, by way of taking a pleasant holiday. He assured Merrion that he had heard no sign from the island. The night was perfectly still and clear. A shout could have been heard for a long way across the water. Even a match struck on the island would have been visible.

While they watched a sound did come to them. Not a shout, but the distant hooting of a steamer's whistle. One of the lights visible in the direction of Fetiyeh seemed to detach itself from the rest. Another, green, showed below it, and both moved slowly towards the open sea. The steamer which had arrived at Fetiyeh that morning had taken her departure.

Merrion turned in, but was up again at dawn. He went on to the bridge. The dental student had been relieved and the man who had taken his place had very little English. However, he made Merrion understand that he had seen or heard nothing. The island was now clearly visible but exhibited no sign of life.

Breakfast time came, with no further development. Captain Larsen showed signs of concern, tempered with profound annoyance. " We lower lifeboat," he announced curtly. " First Officer, he take search-party. Anybody like to go, he can."

The three male passengers volunteered. The lifeboat set out, with a dozen or more men in her, and landed them at the cove. Under the first officer's direction they all spread out to quarter the island, with instructions to be back within the hour. Each man had been equipped with a whistle and very soon the island resounded with discordant shrieks, which would have roused, if not the dead, at least the dead drunk. Between them, they must have covered nearly every square yard. But, when at the end of the hour they had all re-assembled, none of them had seen a vestige of the missing passengers.

They returned to the ship, and the first officer reported their ill-success to the captain. The latter beckoned Merrion into his cabin. " I not understand this at all, Mr. Merrion," he said. " What you think ? "

" They aren't on the island," Merrion replied. " And they can't have been spirited away from it against their will. Since the Turks have become Westernised, genii are quite out of date. We got one of the fishermen to take us across. There were plenty of those chaps about yesterday. They may have hailed another, and got him to land them at Fetiyeh."

" What they do that for ? " Captain Larsen asked incredulously.

" Well, you'll have formed your own opinion about Mr. Wilberton," Merrion replied. " He's a man of an exceedingly passionate nature, liable to fly off at a tangent at any moment. For the last few days he's been cursing himself for not leaving this ship before. Now yesterday a steamer called at Fetiyeh. We all saw her. I have no doubt that Mr. Wilberton saw her as clearly as any of us."

Merrion's meaning was clear enough. " What ! " Captain Larsen exclaimed. " Gone so ? He did not tell anyone ? And how his baggage, his money, his passport ? "

" I'll take those question in order, Captain," Merrion replied. " He wasn't sufficiently fond of any of us to feel impelled to say good-bye. Such belongings as he has on board he can collect when the ship gets back to London. Since there was no question of bathing, we were all more or less fully dressed when we went to the island yesterday. Both Mr. Wilberton and Mr. Bewdley may have had their money and their passports in their pockets."

" I tell steward to look in their cabins," said Captain Larsen. " Then we see. But Mr. Bewdley he not behave like that."

" Mr. Bewdley feels responsible for his uncle," Merrion replied. " What ever wild idea Mr. Wilberton may have suddenly taken into his head, Mr. Bewdley would never have let him go off alone. The only time he left him, in Alexandria, Mr. Wilberton got himself into trouble, which might have been more serious than it was."

Captain Larsen thought this over for a while. " The agent, he come aboard before we sail, we speak to him together, you and me. But this I tell you, Mr. Merrion. I not wait for those two, no, not five minute. As soon as loading finish, we sail. We waste too much time here already."

The agent came in the motor-boat from Fetiyeh just before noon. On his arrival Captain Larsen called Merrion into his cabin. The agent had no Norwegian and only sufficient English to enable him and the captain to transact the ship's business in that language. It would not run to the discussion of the possible doings of Mr. Wilberton and his nephew. However, he spoke French fluently and Merrion was able to act as interpreter.

The captain's questions concerned the steamer. The agent replied that she hailed from Ismir, and traded between there and neighbouring ports, Fetiyeh among them. Perhaps every three weeks, perhaps not for a month. It depended on what cargo offered. Oh, yes, she carried passengers. The agent had often travelled by her. She had left Fetiyeh at ten o'clock the previous evening. The agent had not been on the landing stage when she sailed.

Nothing to prevent the captain's two passengers from sailing in her, if they had passport and money for their tickets. Her next port of call would be Rhodes. She would have got there early this morning. Good place, Rhodes, plenty of enjoyment. " A Rodi on s'amuse," was the expression he used. Oh, yes, one could fly from Rhodes to Athens, and from there of course to London.

Merrion left the captain and the agent to their business. The latter left the ship just before she sailed at two o'clock. Merrion leaned on the rail as the *Ballerina*, leaving the land-locked bay, passed between the mainland and the island lighthouse. Although the rhythm of the engine was much the same as ever, the ship seemed to be travelling faster than when she came in, Merrion thought. He, always curious about such matters, wondered. A favourable tide could not account for it, for there were no perceptible tides in this part of the Mediterranean. Then an incident which had made no impression him at the time occurred to him.

That first visit to the island, when he had come upon Mr. Grampound idly throwing whatever came to his hand into the water. Merrion remembered noticing that such of these as would float had drifted fairly rapidly seawards. That was the reason for the ship's increase of speed over the ground. Not tides, but currents, of which there were many in the Mediterranean. As, for instance, those flowing through the Straits of Messina and the Dardanelles. There was obviously a current flowing out of the bay of Fetiyeh. Fed, probably, by many small streams flowing down from the surrounding mountains.

By supper time the town of Rhodes was clearly visible, as the *Ballerina* passed through the channel between it and the mainland. Merrion, remembering the agent's words, and the leer which accompanied them, wondered whether Mr. Wilberton was amusing himself on shore there. Or had he already found a plane to fly him on the first stage of his homeward journey. He would have to stop off at Athens. Perhaps he would call on Mrs. Mallory. She at least might be glad to see him again.

Captain Larsen was not in the least concerned about what Mr. Wilberton and his nephew might or might not do. His only interest was that two of his passengers had left the ship, and were not in the least likely to make any attempt to rejoin her. The steward reported that he had searched both cabins and had found no money, passports or other documents in either. This seemed conclusive. The captain sent a wireless message to the head office of the Company in Oslo, reporting vacancies in as few words as possible. This was necessary in case they should receive applications for homeward passengers from any future port of call.

Captain Larsen announced at supper, " We go back now to Kalimata. Pick up drums, full this time, for London. May get orders there, I cannot say. If not, to Algiers for fuel. Sure to get orders there. Perhaps go to some Spanish port. We shall see."

" Algiers, Captain ? " Mr. Grampound remarked. " That will be most convenient for me. I shall be able to call upon the French authorities there, among whom I have many friends."

Captain Larsen shook his head. " You not have much time, Mr. Grampound. Only stay there three or four hour. We go to oil wharf, long way from town. You have to take boat across harbour to get there."

" I daresay I shall find time," Mr. Grampound said easily. " I'll see when we get there."

Mr. Grampound's remark strengthened Merrion's idea that he was concerned with confidential matters, possibly on the fringes of diplomacy. Well, that was his affair, and nobody else's.

Late in the afternoon of the next day, Tuesday, the *Ballerina* arrived once more at Kalimata. The little agent-cum-consul was waiting on the quay, capering and waving his gigantic satchel. He leapt on board and shook hands with everyone he could find. He was delighted to see his kind friends, but broken-hearted that they were to stay so short a time. The cargo was all ready, only two hundred and fifty drums. It would take only two or three hours to get them aboard. And then, alas, good-bye.

When the *Ballerina* left at nine o'clock, the agent was on the verge of tears, in spite of the fact that his satchel was bulging with whisky and cigarettes from the ship's stores. Captain Larsen explained to Merrion. " Company pay. If they don't get something, they delay ship. What you say ? Blackmail ? Same every port you go, out here. No, he bring no order. We go Algiers straight."

Relieved of the presence of Mr. Wilberton the atmosphere had undergone a subtle change. Everyone seemed more at their ease, and more inclined for one another's companionship. The seven remaining passengers became a happy family party, to which Mr. Pulham, who displayed less irritating fussiness was admitted. Mrs. Stewart-Patterson, who felt under a great obligation, re-adopted him as her willing page-boy. Even Mr. Grampound came out of his shell. Hitherto he had rarely been seen, except at meal times. Now he was constantly on deck, and, in the evenings, he and Miss Cassidy played double-demon together in the smoking-room.

Mr. Wilberton and his nephew rapidly became a memory. Stories were exchanged about them, or rather about Mr. Wilberton, since Mr. Bewdley had always been less colourful than his uncle. In retrospect, his behaviour could be regarded with amusement, shorn of the irritation it had caused at the time. Everyone agreed that as a fellow-passenger he had been impossible. " It's all very well to laugh at his antics now," said Mrs. Lavenham, " but there's no getting away from the fact that we're precious lucky to be rid of him."

Algiers was reached early on the following Saturday morning. The *Ballerina* tied up at a depressing-looking wharf, devoted entirely to oil-tanks, from which the city beckoned invitingly across the wide harbour. At breakfast Captain Larsen laid down the law. " Agent here with boat. He says take anyone ashore and bring them back. But only two hours, you not find it worth while. As soon as we finish taking in oil, we sail. Not wait for anyone. What I tell him ? "

" I'd like to go, Captain," Mr. Grampound replied. " I feel very strongly that I ought to go."

" You go if you like, Mr. Grampound," said Captain Larsen. " But you hear what I say. If you don't come back with agent, and I sail without you, Company not responsible."

Mr. Grampound smiled. " I shouldn't expect them to be. I shan't miss the boat. Or, if I do, I'm quite sure the French authorities will get me home somehow."

Nobody else wanted to go. The Merrions had no wish to revisit a town they both knew under such hurried conditions. There had been a moderate sea during the night and Mrs. Lavenham confessed that she did not feel up to it. Miss Cassidy said that she daren't. She always missed Irish trains at home, and they were always late. What chance had she of catching a ship that might sail punctually ? Mrs. Stewart-Patterson expressed her intention of staying on board and sketching the town from the ship's deck. Mr. Pulham was perfectly frank about having spent all his money.

By the time they came on deck again, an unfamiliar sight greeted them. An Algerian merchant, corpulent and perspiring, had come on board and spread out his wares on number four hatch. Trashy though these might be, there was no question of their not being colourful. " He's undone his corded bales, all right," Merrion remarked. " But instead of shy and dark Iberians, his customers are keen blond Norsemen. Just look at them ! "

The crew, and especially the stewardesses, were clamouring round the hatch, bargaining for mats, scarves and trinkets. The Algerian, and his two villainous-looking assistants, who between them probably had a smattering of a dozen languages, spoke to them in one they seemed to understand. The ladies of the party could not be restrained from joining the throng.

The time passed rapidly enough. The chief, who had been narrowly watching the taking in of the oil, reported to the captain. The officers bundled the merchant and his wares off the ship. The agent came across the harbour in his boat. He hadn't seen anything of the passenger he had taken ashore. There were plenty of boats he could hire to bring him back. Hadn't the captain better hold on for a bit. Half an hour, say ?

" Not five minute ! " Captain Larsen exclaimed. " I tell him I not wait. What you think, Mister ? Tanks all full, papers in order. I sail now."

The agent shrugged his shoulders, shook hands with the captain, and left the ship. The pilot was already on the bridge. A defiant blast from the whistle, as though to notify the errant Mr. Grampound that he had missed the ship. Orders to cast off. Then the sight of a motor-boat speeding across the harbour towards the *Ballerina*.

Captain Larsen paused with his hand on the telegraph. His passenger had run it pretty close. But, as the boat neared the ship, he saw that Mr. Grampound was not in it. Only the man at the helm, frantically waving something. One of the crew flung a rope ladder over the side, climbed down it, and took this from the boatman. It was a letter, addressed to Captain Larsen.

When they were clear of the port, the captain descended from the bridge. Merrion was on the boat-deck, and Captain Larsen summoned him into his cabin. " Read this, Mr. Merrion," he said, handing him the letter.

It was on a sheet of paper headed ' Grand Hotel d'Afrique,' and had been written in haste. ' Dear Captain Larsen, I find that my duties will detain me here over to-morrow, and I therefore shall not have the pleasure of continuing my voyage with you. Alternative arrangements for my return home have already been made. I will not say good-bye, for I shall meet the *Ballerina* on her arrival in London. With regrets, yours sincerely, Stephen Grampound.'

" Well, what you think ? " Captain Larsen asked, as Merrion handed him back the letter. " He hush-hush man, so Cyprus agent say. Said he was going to see the French authorities, eh ? "

" I thought all along that he was a confidential agent of some kind," Merrion replied. "At least he had the decency to let you know he was leaving the ship, which is more than the other two did."

Captain Larsen shrugged his shoulders. " Passengers not like ship, perhaps. Why they come, then ? Never mind, they pay fares before, and that all Company care. They get no money back. This, I tell you, Mr. Merrion. Agent, he bring orders. We go to Spain now, Valencia. Load up all oranges we can take. That good, for cargo hard to find. Then not call anywhere again. Straight to London."

Valencia was reached during Sunday night, but the *Ballerina* did not berth till after breakfast on Monday morning. Mr. Grampound was hardly missed. He had not been one of the original members of the party and for the greater part of his time on board his fellow-passengers had not seen much of him.

Captain Larsen made one of his announcements. " You all go to police station with passports. Taxi come take you there. This port, not town. Town two, three mile away. You take tram or taxi. How long we stop, I cannot say. Two day, perhaps. But you come back to ship. I not want to lose all passengers."

A call at a Spanish port not having been anticipated, only two of the passengers had provided themselves with travellers' cheques available in that country. Mrs. Lavenham and Miss Cassidy. They most generously undertook to lend the rest sufficient pesetos to enable them to see something of Valencia. The party split up into two groups, Mrs. Lavenham and the Merrions ; Miss Cassidy, Mrs. Stewart-Patterson and Mr. Pulham.

They all managed to enjoy themselves immensely. The *Ballerina* sailed after lunch on Wednesday. She passed through the Straits of Gibraltar on the following evening, bidding farewell to the Mediterranean.

As they forged northwards through the Atlantic, the passengers began to experience that end-of-the-voyage regret, the antithesis of nostalgia. Of course every one welcomed the prospect of being at home again. Home comforts, friends, contact with their own particular world again. Emerging into a North Atlantic autumn, the *Ballerina* revealed herself for what she was, an honest freighter. You couldn't, for instance light a nice cosy fire and sit by it.

All this, yes. But just the same, that indefinable regret beneath it. It had been a good time, at sea and on shore. A minute slice of life which could never be recaptured. In spite of friction, the passengers had, on the whole, got on jolly well together, and in some cases, close friendships had almost insensibly been made. Who could tell, when they parted in the dock at London, whether any of them would meet again?

Six days from leaving Valencia, on the grey morning of Tuesday, 20th October, the *Ballerina* slowed down off Gravesend. Leaving Mavis to finish packing in the cabin, Merrion came on deck to watch the change of pilots. As the pilot-boat came alongside, he saw in it a tall figure in a heavy overcoat and grey felt hat. Evidently a landsman—this man followed the pilot up the ladder with some difficulty. Not until he reached the deck did Merrion recognise him. His old friend Inspector Arnold, of Scotland Yard.

CHAPTER XIX

MERRION, AMAZED at this unexpected appearance, hurried to meet him. But his amazement was quenched by Arnold's matter of fact greeting. " So here you are. I knew you would be on board, for I've seen the passenger list. I want to talk to you. Where ? "

Merrion smiled. " It's not easy to find a secluded spot on a ship like this. Come along to the after end of the boat-deck. There won't be anybody there now."

They went there, and Arnold began. " I've been on a job at a place called Hembury. Ever heard of it ? "

" Yes, and quite recently," Merrion replied. " We had a passenger of the name of Bewdley. He told me that he was on the board of a firm of millers there."

" That's quite right," said Arnold. " What took me to the place was a murder. I'll tell you all about that some other time. We'll begin with something else. About a fortnight ago the captain of this ship informed his owners in Norway that two of the passengers had left, at some place no one had ever heard of. The owners passed this on to their London agents, who, in duty bound, notified the immigration authorities. They, in turn, informed us at the Yard. That's why I'm here."

" Your information is quite correct," Merrion replied. " The two passengers left us suddenly, without telling anyone they were going, while the ship was in the port of Fetiyeh, in Anatolia. They were Mr. Bewdley, whom I mentioned a moment ago, and his uncle, Mr. Wilberton."

Arnold nodded. " I know their names. Are you quite sure that they were on this ship on 17th September ? "

" Quite sure," Merrion replied. " I'll have to look up my diary before I can tell you where the ship was on that particular day. But the pair of them didn't leave her till Sunday, the fourth of this month."

" Very well," said Arnold. " The chap who was murdered at or near Hembury was an estate agent of the name of Rufus Jones. Ever heard of him ? "

Merrion shook his head. "Not to my knowledge. Who murdered him?"

"The local super has a pretty good idea about that," Arnold replied. "Now look here. On the day after Jones was murdered, a man, who announced himself as Jasper Wilberton, Mr. Bewdley's uncle, came to Jones's office. He was expected there, for they had had a letter from him a couple of days before. He came to try to find a house in Hembury. Eh?"

"Wait a minute," said Merrion thoughtfully. "Mr. Bewdley told me that he'd been trying to find a house in Hembury for his uncle, but so far he hadn't succeeded. Has he got two uncles?"

"No, only one," Arnold replied. "I'll tell you. The names of the two passengers who had left this ship struck me as remarkably familiar. I'd heard about Mr. Bewdley and his uncle when I was at Hembury on the murder case. I was told by the immigration authorities that they had sailed together on this ship on 4th September. How then could Mr. Wilberton have been in Hembury on the 17th?"

"An Irishman once remarked that nobody could be in two places at once, barring he was a bird," said Merrion. "And if Mr. Wilberton is a bird, he's a most unpleasant one. A carrion crow, or something of that kind."

"You don't like him?" Arnold asked. "Tell me why."

Merrion gave him a vivid but accurate account of Mr. Wilberton's behaviour. "He was, in fact, impossible," he concluded.

"That's exactly what they thought of the Mr. Wilberton who went to Hembury," said Arnold. "I told you that this man had written a letter saying that he was coming. It was from an address in Birmingham. I wasn't interested in him at first, for he didn't turn up at Hembury till the day after Jones was murdered. But when I heard that a Mr. Wilberton had been on board this ship, it seemed to me rather queer. Wilberton isn't a very common name. Besides, the name of the other passenger who had left was Bewdley. Follow me?"

"Every step of the way," Merrion replied. "You made enquiries?"

"I went to the address from which the letter had been written," said Arnold. "There I found an elderly lady, Mrs.

Mary Somerton. She told me that she kept house for her brother, Mr. Jasper Wilberton. He was not at home, for he had gone for a cruise in a ship called the *Ballerina*, with his nephew, Mr. Horace Bewdley, who lived at Hembury. I asked her if she had any other brothers, and she told me that Jasper was the only surviving one. She had had a sister, the mother of Horace Bewdley, but she was dead too. Jasper, she told me, was a childless widower."

That rather odd remark of Mr. Bewdley's occurred to Merrion. " You haven't traced all the family. There is, or was, a skeleton lurking in the background somewhere. However, that's beside the point. You're bound to meet the truants before long. They left all their baggage on board, and they'll be waiting to collect it when we get into dock."

Arnold shook his head. " I don't think so. The immigration people told me only yesterday that neither of them had re-entered the country yet. Well, I'd better get along and see if the captain can add anything to what you've told me."

He left Merrion wondering. There could not be two such people as Mr. Wilberton.   At all events, it was devoutly to be hoped not. And it was rather odd that neither he nor his nephew had got back to England yet. What could they be up to ? Anything, in the case of Mr. Wilberton. But surely his nephew would not be content to hang about indefinitely. It struck Merrion that it was only a guess, though a very plausible one, that they had left Fetiyeh by the coasting steamer.

Soon after lunch, the *Ballerina* entered the East India Dock, and tied up at Canary Wharf. The Customs and Immigration officers came on board, and the various formalities of disembarkation were gone through. The usual farewells followed. Promises to write, and to meet again at some indefinite time. But the only person on the quay to meet the ship was Mrs. Stewart-Patterson's son, who lived in London. She had told everyone that she was going to stay with him for a few days before returning to Edinburgh. The son came on board, and began to carry his mother's voluminous belongings to the large car he had wisely brought with him.

Arnold sought out Merrion. " I've been talking to the captain. He's a hard nut to crack. He seems to have only one answer to any question you ask him, "I cannot say." But he showed me a note from a Mr. Grampound who left the ship at Algiers. He said he'd meet the ship when she docked in London. Is he here? "

" I haven't seen him," Merrion replied. " Do you know anything about him? He seemed a bit of a mystery man."

Arnold shook his head. " Never heard the name before. I asked the captain how long he expected to stay here, but, as usual, he couldn't say. It depended on how long it takes them to unload. As soon as they've finished, he's going on to some place near Oslo to discharge chromium ore. I shall have a man standing by the ship till she sails. What are your plans? "

" We shall spend the night in our rooms in town," Merrion replied. " From there we shall ring up Newport to bring the car, and we shall drive home to-morrow. You'd better come and have a spot of dinner with us this evening."

" I'd very much like to," said Arnold. " I want to tell you about that Hembury affair. It's one of those cases where there's precious little doubt who did it, but there's no proof. Meanwhile, I've rung up the Yard to send a car here to fetch me. I'll take you and Mrs. Merrion to your rooms with the greatest pleasure."

As taxis were not easy to come by at the East India Dock, the offer was most welcome. The police car turned up, and the Merrions with their baggage were somehow packed into it. They were driven to their rooms, which were always kept ready for immediate occupation. Mavis went out to do the necessary shopping, leaving her husband to ring up Newport. When he had done that he lapsed into a profoundly thoughtful mood, which lasted until Arnold's arrival, soon after seven o'clock. " Well, what news? " Merrion asked as he poured his guest out a drink. " Have you made the acquaintance of the unspeakable Mr. Wilberton? "

" Not yet," Arnold replied. " None of your three fellow-passengers have turned up so far. Even the chap who told the captain in his note that he would meet the ship hasn't arrived. The agents tell me that she'll probably sail to-morrow evening. If they haven't turned up by then I shall have their belongings taken to the Yard. That'll give me a chance of seeing them when they come to claim them."

They had a meal which, in spite of the lavishness of her shopping and cooking, Mavis described as supper. Afterwards, she tactfully left the two men to talk while she cleared away and washed up. Arnold, who had brought his note-book with him, gave Merrion a detailed account of the Rufus Jones case. "That's how matters stood when I first thought I'd like to talk to you about it. I rang up High Eldersham Hall, and Newport told me that you were on a cruise, and that he didn't know when you'd be back."

"He knows now," said Merrion. "Anything fresh since then?"

"Just this," Arnold replied significantly. "In spite of search, enquiry, advertisement and all the rest, no will of Rufus Jones's can be found. It looks very much as though young White will scoop the lot."

"Motive as well as opportunity," Merrion remarked. "But where does Mr. Wilberton come into it?"

"He doesn't," said Arnold. "If he was on that ship of yours, he can't have written that letter, or have been in Hembury on 17th September."

"He wasn't," said Merrion. "I've glanced at my diary. On 17th September the *Ballerina* was at sea. Mr. Wilberton spent most of the day in his cabin, suffering from a hang-over consequent upon his being hocussed in Alexandria. You're sure about your facts?"

"Absolutely," Arnold replied. "Somebody who called himself Jasper Wilberton and, from what you tell me of the genuine article, played the part extremely well, arrived at Hembury that afternoon. Several people saw him, and were impressed by the extraordinary unpleasantness of his be-haviour. Who was he, and what was his game?"

"You don't connect him with the murder?" Merrion asked.

Arnold shook his head. "As I've told you, the doctors gave a pretty elastic limit for the time of death. But they won't stretch it to cover Thursday afternoon. And this man, whoever he was, didn't reach Hembury before then. Besides, that clock in the car tells us within a little while when Jones was mur-dered. If this chap had murdered Jones on Wednesday afternoon, he wouldn't be very likely to show up in Hembury next day. And to throw his weight about as he did."

Merrion poked the fire. "I find it a bit chilly after the temperature we had in the Mediterranean. You speak of a telegram received at Jones's office that Wednesday. Have you got it with you?"

"No," Arnold replied. "But I copied it into my note-book." He flicked over the leaves. "Here you are. Handed in at Baleminster 1.25 p.m. 16th September. 'Estates, Hembury. Detained here over to-morrow, apologise Wilberton, pay him special attention, Jones.'"

"Who sent that telegram?" Merrion asked.

"Jones himself," Arnold replied. "He had to take his client back to Baleminster. In any case, he wouldn't have hung about Cherry Trees all day."

"We don't seem able to get away from Mr. Wilberton, do we?" Merrion remarked. "You told me Captain Larsen showed you the note he got from Mr. Grampound in Algiers. He showed it to me, but I don't remember the exact wording. Have you got it?"

"No, but I copied it," Arnold replied, again flicking over the leaves of his note-book. "This is it: 'Dear Captain Larsen, I find that my duties will detain me here over to-morrow, and I shall therefore——'"

"That'll do," Merrion interrupted him. "Don't you see anything queer?"

"I can't say that I do," Arnold replied. "The captain told me he believed this Mr. Grampound to be a political agent of some kind. He, Grampound, said he was going to see the authorities in Algiers. They may have told him something which made it necessary for him to stay there for a day or two."

"Longer than that, apparently," said Merrion drily. "Since he hasn't turned up yet to claim his baggage. But that's not what I meant. Doesn't the similarity between the phrasing of the telegram and that of the letter strike you? 'Detained here over to-morrow.' 'My duties will detain me here over to-morrow.' It's rather a peculiar method of expression, and vague at that. 'Detained here till to-morrow,' or 'for a day or two' would surely be more natural. Don't you think so?"

"What in the world are you driving at now?" Arnold demanded.

"It's a matter that demands a certain amount of imagination," Merrion replied. "I find the coincidence so remarkable that I'm tempted to wonder whether the telegram and the letter were both sent by the same person."

"Don't be so ridiculous!" Arnold exclaimed. "Jones sent

the telegram. He can't have sent the letter, for he was dead and buried by that time. Even your imagination can't jump over impossibilities."

Merrion smiled. " It isn't trying to. I'll admit that Jones can't have written the letter. But I know of no physical reason why Grampound should not have sent the telegram."

" From that ship of yours ? " Arnold asked sarcastically.

" The telegram was sent on 16th September," Merrion replied. " Grampound was not on board the *Ballerina* on that date. He did not join her until she was lying at Limasol, on the 22nd. It is believed that he had flown to Cyprus, and had been there only a few days. I believe it to be a fact that he had booked his passage in the *Ballerina* some weeks previously, in London."

Arnold knocked out his pipe and refilled it. " Very well," he said. " This man Grampound may have been in Baleminster on the 16th. But what's the link between him and Jones ? "

" That I can't tell you," Merrion replied. " I've been asking myself rather a different question. What is the link between him and Mr. Wilberton. Let's clear the ground a bit first. There can be no doubt that of the two, Mr. Wilberton of the *Ballerina* was the genuine article. Mrs. Somerton told you that her brother was on board the ship. A pretender could not have imposed on Mr. Bewdley. And of his honesty I haven't the slightest doubt. He is as sincere as anyone I have ever met.

" Yet from what you tell me, the impersonation was perfect. The Hembury Wilberton behaved exactly as his original would have. And his knowledge of detail was amazing. To cite only one example, that Mr. Bewdley had been trying to find a house in Hembury for his uncle. You can think up several more for yourself. Only someone with a profound inside knowledge could have played the part."

" That's true enough," Arnold agreed. " But who was that somebody ? "

Merrion shook his head. " Mr. Bewdley may be able to answer that question. I can't. As I said a moment ago, this is a case which requires the exercise of imagination. By which I mean that we've got to imagine the explanation of the merest trifles. One evening on board I had a conversation with

Mr. Bewdley, who may himself have been suffering from imagination. The expression he used was that he was haunted by a resemblance. Long ago, he had known a boy, or a young man, whom he allowed me to gather was a member of his family. That young man had in some way disgraced himself, and Mr. Bewdley had lost touch with him, to such an extent that he did not know whether he was alive or dead. But if he was alive, he might have grown into a man not dissimilar to Mr. Grampound."

"What in the world has Mr. Bewdley's imagination to do with the murder of Jones?" Arnold asked.

Merrion made no immediate reply. He sat staring into the fire, inhaling his cigarette, as though to draw inspiration from it. "To me, the murder of Jones is only a side-issue, he said at last. "I'm far more interested in what has become of Mr. Bewdley and his uncle."

"I don't see why you should worry over that," Arnold replied. "The captain told me that Mr. Wilberton had got fed up with the cruise. He and his nephew left the ship at that outlandish place with the intention of making their way home, probably by air."

"They haven't got home yet," Merrion remarked. "So that's what the captain said to you. It's what we all thought at the time. The fact is that we were so glad to get rid of Mr. Wilberton that we didn't trouble our heads more about what had happened to him. The simplest explanation was that he had seen the coasting steamer lying at Fetiyeh, and had gone off on it. Colour was given to this by the fact that their money and passports were not to be found in their cabins. Having accepted this explanation, we didn't think any more about the matter. I certainly didn't, until to-day."

"And now your imagination is seeking another explanation, I take it," said Arnold.

"I'm not sure it hasn't already found it," Merrion replied. "No I'm not going to tell you now. I rather think I shall stay here for a day or two, and let Newport drive Mavis home to-morrow. She'll be glad of the chance to get the place straight before I join her. Then I shall be at hand in case you want me."

"I shall of course be overjoyed," said Arnold drily. "But am I likely to want you?"

"Possibly," Merrion replied. "As a source of information, to fill in the details of any picture you may draw for yourself. You say you're going to impound the baggage of the three missing passengers?"

Arnold nodded. "If they don't claim it personally before the ship sails, yes."

"You'd better run through it," Merrion suggested. "Not that you're likely to find anything very illuminating. I don't suppose for a moment that any of it will be claimed. Meanwhile, it might pay you to consult your records, going back say twenty to twenty-five years, and see if they contain any mention of the name of Wilberton, Bewdley or Somerton. I don't somehow think you'll find the name Grampound."

Arnold laughed. "I'll have that done. The black sheep of the family that Mr. Bewdley told you about?"

"That's about it," Merrion replied tranquilly. "And there's one other thing you might do. One of the passengers on the *Ballerina*, Mrs. Stewart-Patterson, is staying in London for a day or two with her son. You'll find her address in the telephone book no doubt. Go and see her, and ask her to lend you her shooting-stick for a day or two."

"Her shooting-stick!" Arnold exclaimed. "What on earth for?"

"Just to humour me," Merrion replied. "She's rather a formidable old lady, and she'll probably refuse to part with it, but you'll have to persuade her somehow. When you've got it, take it to the Yard, and get one of your microscopical experts to go over it. Thoroughly, mind. The hinges of the folding seat, and all that sort of thing."

Arnold shrugged his shoulders. "I suppose you know what you're driving at. Many thanks for your entertainment. I'll get along now. And if and when I've anything to tell you, I'll come back."

CHAPTER XX

NEXT MORNING Newport arrived with the car. As Merrion had
expected, Mavis raised no objection to going home alone. It
would give her a chance of getting the house in running order
again before her husband's return. Newport had very thoughtfully brought with him all the correspondence which had
accumulated during their absence. Merrion's share of this
kept him fully occupied for the rest of the day.

He went out to dinner, and shortly after his return the bell
rang. Guessing who his visitor might be, he opened the door,
to find Arnold standing outside. " Come along in," he said.
" I can offer you a drink. You look as if you could do with
one."

Arnold certainly did. His face was that of a weary and
sorely puzzled man. He sank into a chair, and finished at a
draught the glass of beer Merrion poured out for him. " That's
better ! " he exclaimed. " I've been at it all day, and I'm
utterly fagged out. Fill in the details of the picture, you said.
You'll have to do more than that. I can't make head or tail of
it."

" That appears to be the object of the modern artist,"
Merrion replied. " He'll plant an eye in the sole of his sitter's
foot, as likely as not. Light your pipe and tell me what it's all
about."

Arnold lighted his pipe, and puffed at it for a few minutes
in silence. " I don't know where to begin," he said at last.
" The best thing is to tell you everything separately, without
regard to the order in which they happened. The *Ballerina*
sailed at four o'clock this afternoon. None of the three missing
passengers had turned up by then. Just before she sailed, their
baggage had been stowed into a police car, and taken to the
Yard."

" Just a minute," Merrion interposed. " It wasn't already
packed, I suppose. Who packed it ? "

" The cabins had been left as they were, locked, of course,"
Arnold replied. " The man I left in charge, helped by the

steward, did the packing, if you can call it that. They just
bundled everything in each cabin into the suit-cases they
found in that cabin, and labelled them with the occupant's
name.

"I had a look through them. Neither Mr. Wilberton nor
Mr. Bewdley's contained cheques or money of any kind. Both
were full of clothing of all sorts. Mr. Wilberton's had nothing
else. But in Mr. Bewdley's were two note-books, one full, the
other about half way full of pencilled notes. I glanced at them,
but they meant very little to me. The sort of notes a chap
might make if he were going to make a speech."

"Not exactly a speech," said Merrion. "Notes of things
Mr. Bewdley had thought of on the voyage and meant to
discuss with his fellow-directors. And Mr. Grampound's?"

"He had two suit-cases," Arnold replied. "One of these
was empty, and my man stuffed it with what was lying about
the cabin, clothes and so forth. The other, a smaller one, was
locked. I broke it open and found some currency—not a lot.
A pound and a few shillings of Cyprus money, and some
foreign notes, which seem to be Turkish and Lebanese. Besides these, dozens of newspapers in languages I can't read,
with marks in blue pencil against some of the paragraphs.
I've sent them to the Foreign Office, and asked them to let
me have an opinion about them."

"You couldn't have done better," said Merrion. "It'll be
interesting to have that opinion. It's just dimly possible,
though I don't think it's very likely, that the Foreign Office
knows more about Mr. Grampound than we do. Meanwhile,
I gather that your day has been more eventful than that?"

"It has," Arnold replied. "I set one of our chaps, I think
you know him, to search the records for any of the names you
gave me. He started twenty years ago and worked backwards.
At last he came across the name Somerton, and looked up the
particulars. George Somerton, aged twenty-two, convicted
of obtaining money by false pretences, and sentenced to a term
of imprisonment."

"That sounds interesting," said Merrion. "George might
be the son of your Mrs. Somerton. In which case he would be
Mr. Bewdley's cousin. What had he been up to?"

"The home-work racket," Arnold replied. "It's an old
dodge, and hasn't by any means been worked to death yet.

George, in the name of some high-sounding and entirely fictitious company, sent out circulars to women all over the country. They could earn good money by hand-hemming materials to be supplied by the company. All they had to do was to send two pounds, as a guarantee of good faith, and to secure a sample of the material, which they were to return duly hemmed. If the work was not up to the standard the company required, their money would be returned. Plausible enough. So much so, that young George gathered in a pot of money before he was caught out."

Merrion nodded. "I've heard of that dodge before. A most despicable form of fraud, in my opinion."

"That's very much what the judge said in passing sentence, I expect," Arnold replied. "It's just the sort of thing judges do say. But now listen to this. The fraud was exposed by a young fellow. I expect a girl friend of his got one of the circulars and showed it to him. He made investigations on his own account, and discovered that no such company existed. Then he turned the whole thing over to the police. And the name of that young fellow was Rufus Jones, described as the son of an auctioneer in Hembury."

"Ah!" said Merrion. "However long one may bide one's time revenge is still sweet. Is that it?"

Arnold countered the question with another. "What does your Mr. Grampound look like?"

"There's nothing very striking about him," Merrion replied. "Fairly tall, thin, skinny and angular. In the middle or late forties, I should imagine. A rather square shaped head, with pinched features and sparse fair hair. He wore tinted glasses, but nearly everybody wears sun-glasses of some kind in that climate. He wasn't made up in any way, for I saw him under the shower on board, wearing nothing but a pair of bathing-drawers, and he looked just the same. It would be difficult to maintain any sort of disguise under those circumstances."

Arnold shook his head. "It won't do. I've told you about the shopkeeper who saw the client in Jones's car. Thin and pinched, he described him. Looked as if he was feeling the cold, was the expression he used. But your description and his might apply to hundreds of people. It wasn't the client who murdered Jones."

"How can you be so sure of that?" Merrion asked. "You

tell me that this client wasn't the man he made himself out to be, and that you haven't been able to trace him."

" Haven't I made it clear enough ? " Arnold replied. " Jones took the client to Cherry Trees before noon on Wednesday. The stopped clock shows that he wasn't murdered till six o'clock that afternoon, or thereabouts. Perhaps your imagination can find some explanation of what the pair of them were up to all the afternoon."

" I'll spare it the trouble," Merrion replied. " Quite frankly, I'm not so convinced as you seem to be by the evidence of the clock. How do you know that it was showing the right time, or even going, that day ? The clock in my car is driven off the battery, and isn't a very accurate timekeeper. I have to set it every time I go out. Jones may not have taken the trouble to do that, preferring to rely upon a watch he carried."

Merrion threw the end of his cigarette into the fire, and then went on. " Nor am I greatly impressed by your theory of the scrap in the car. If there had been so violent a struggle in it as to cause all that damage, the strugglers must surely have sustained some damage themselves. You should have found spots of blood, bits of skin, or other vestiges of humanity. Did you ? Did you or Kingston see any damage about young White when you first saw him ? "

" No, we didn't," Arnold admitted. " But how else could the damage have been caused ? "

Merrion smiled. " We needn't indulge in a guessing-game just yet. Let's get back to the false Wilberton, who seems to have faded out of the picture. What's your explanation of him ? "

" I don't know who he was, or what his game can have been," Arnold replied. " But he wasn't the murderer. Try to keep your imagination down to earth, instead of flying about among the clouds. You seem to think that Jones was murdered on Wednesday morning. I still hold it was in the afternoon. In any case, it was before Thursday afternoon, and the man who posed as Mr. Wilberton didn't turn up till then. And there's this, which seems to me even more conclusive. Can even you imagine a murderer, after the crime, turning up in the neighbourhood and making himself so unpleasantly conspicuous ? "

" Not anyone in Hembury, with the exception of course of

Mr. Bewdley, has ever seen the genuine Mr. Wilberton ? " Merrion asked.

" Apparently not," Arnold replied. " But what's that got to do with it ? "

" It was only a thought in passing," said Merrion. " But don't you see, if that's the case, impersonation would have been ridiculously easy. The impersonator need have borne little outward resemblance to his original. The assumption of his characteristic manner and behaviour would be enough. Add to this the letter, announcing Mr. Wilberton's intended visit. He would be expected."

" I can't make it out ! " Arnold exclaimed. " The fact that the fellow was an impostor was bound to come out as soon as Mr. Bewdley got home."

" When Mr. Bewdley got home," Merrion repeated thoughtfully. " I confessed just now that, having accepted a plausible theory of what had happened to Mr. Bewdley and his uncle, I didn't trouble to go any further. You might say that I closed my mind to any possible alternative. It's a very common frame of mind, and one that you share now. You and your friend the superintendent have convinced yourselves that that young couple murdered Jones between them. That being so, you're not inclined to seek any further. But let me remind you that sticking to a fixed idea is a sign of mental laziness."

" Thanks very much," said Arnold. " I'll pass your kind words on to Kingston next time I see him. I'm sure he'll appreciate them. But tell me now. Can you convince me now that the Whites didn't murder Jones ? "

Merrion smiled. " Not yet. You see, you take such a terrible lot of convincing. Let me hear the rest of your day's adventures. Did you call on my friend Mrs. Stewart-Patterson ? "

" Did I not ! " Arnold exclaimed. " My word, that old lady is a terror ! I called this morning, when I thought she'd be at home. She was, and when I sent in my card she graciously consented to see me. When I asked her if I might see her shooting-stick, she flew at me. Did I suspect her of having stolen it ? She could prove that it had been in her possession for ten years and more."

Merrion laughed. " I can picture the scene. Not a very hopeful beginning. What next ? "

" I assured her that I never for a moment imagined that she had stolen it. All I wanted was to borrow it for a day or two. That made matters worse. Certainly not, she had never heard such impudence. She had lost the stick for a whole day while she was abroad, and it was only through the kindness of Mr. somebody who had gone to great trouble to find it, that she had ever got it back. She wasn't going to part with it a second time, not on any account.

" Then the son chimed in. He seems a sensible chap, but very much under his mother's thumb. He pointed out to her that if the police asked to borrow the stick they must have some very good reason for this request. If she persisted in her refusal, she might lay herself open to some unpleasantness. They might get an order from a magistrate authorising them to take the stick, whether she consented or not.

" At last she allowed herself to be persuaded, with a very bad grace. She wrote out a receipt, and made me sign it ! ' Received of Mrs. Helen Stewart-Patterson, one shooting-stick in good condition.' The stick was in the room, and the son picked it up and gave it to me. I cleared out with it at once, promising to return it personally as soon as possible. I took it straight to the Yard. Handed it over to one of our laboratory people, and told him what you said about it."

He paused, looking intently at Merrion, and then went on accusingly. " Just before I came here, I had a message from them. They have found what they believe to be dried blood and human hairs. How did you know ? "

" I didn't," Merrion replied. " My imagination told me that they might find something of the kind, that's all."

" Do you mean that old woman bashed someone over the head with that stick of hers ? " Arnold asked.

Merrion shook his head. " No, I don't mean that. Though I have no doubt that at times she was sorely tempted."

" Then what do you mean ? " Arnold asked.

" I shall have to explain my mental processes, I suppose," Merrion replied. " I've told you more than once, that I had satisfied myself that Mr. Wilberton and his nephew had boarded the coasting steamer, as a first step towards flying home. You, of all people should know how a guess like that crystallises in one's mind until it becomes a certainty. It wasn't till you told me that neither of them had reached England yet that the crystal disintegrated with the rapidity of an atomic bomb.

" Why hadn't they returned ? Even allowing Mr. Wilberton a day or two's dissipation in Rhodes, if they had flown back, they would have been home days ago. Or again, there was a woman on the ship going out with whom Mr. Wilberton became friendly. She disembarked at the Piraeus, and it occurred to me that Mr. Wilberton might be stopping at Athens for a while to enjoy her company. But it seemed most unlikely that Mr. Bewdley would consent to waste his time like that.

" So I was driven on to another and darkly sinister theory. It was based upon Mr. Bewdley's haunting. That skeleton in his family's cupboard, and its possible resemblance to Mr. Grampound. What if our guess about the coasting steamer had been all wrong ? What if the missing pair had not left the island alive ? "

" What island ? " Arnold demanded. " And what has all this got to do with Mrs. Stewart-Patterson's shooting-stick ?"

" I'll answer the first part of your question," Merrion replied. " One of the chain of islands that stretches across the bay of Fetiyeh. If it has a name, we never learnt it. For want of a better, we called it among ourselves Picnic Island. I think our new friend Mrs. Lavenham was the first to hit upon that name."

" And the second part of my question ? " Arnold asked.

" We shall come to that as I expound my theory," Merrion replied. " But to be perfectly fair, I want to make this quite clear. On a ship like the *Ballerina*, there is practically no escape for the passengers from one another's company. It is no exaggeration to say that one discordant element can drive the rest to the verge of murder. And to describe Mr. Wilberton's behaviour as exasperating would be to use the mildest possible term. Now I'll tell you about Picnic Island, and why we gave it that name."

He described in full detail the two picnics on the island, on the Friday and the Saturday. " I want you to form a mental picture of that island. Uninhabited, at least while we were there, and large and wild enough for one to be able to get away from one's fellows without the slightest difficulty. That was its chief fascination, to me at least. The feeling of spaciousness and isolation after the rather cramped quarters of the *Ballerina*."

He stopped to light a fresh cigarette before he continued. " I'm going to be perfectly frank with you. My theory implicates one of three persons, myself among them. These are the facts, without embellishment.

" On our return from the second picnic, on Saturday, Mrs. Stewart-Patterson missed her shooting-stick, and kicked up a terrible fuss about it. On Sunday, Mr. Grampound suggested that we should organise a party to search Picnic Island for it. With the aid of a box of cigarettes, Mr. Pulham persuaded a fisherman to ferry us over.

" When we got there, at Mr. Grampound's suggestion we spread out to search the island. In doing so, we very soon lost sight of one another. I was the first to return to our base, having been away from it rather more than an hour. Not very long after Mr. Grampound joined me. A few minutes later, Mr. Pulham appeared with the shooting-stick. He told us he had found it not very far from our base, stuck upright in the ground."

Merrion interrupted Arnold's half spoken question. " Let me finish. We waited for the remaining two until the fisherman threatened to abandon us, and we were forced to return. A watch was kept on board the ship that night. On Monday morning a search-party, led by the first officer, landed on Picnic Island. They found no sign whatever of either Mr. Wilberton or Mr. Bewdley. Five men landed on the island, and only three had returned."

" The inference being that one of the three had done in the other two ? " Arnold suggested.

" Exactly," Merrion replied. " And I am one of the three, don't forget that."

" I'm not going to caution you just yet," Arnold said, in a tone of much severity. " Mr. Pulham who found the stick ? "

" Undoubtedly he did find the stick," Merrion replied. " And don't forget the old nursery saying, those who hide can find. The point is this. Did Mrs. Stewart-Patterson leave the stick stuck in the ground where Mr. Pulham found it ? She never walked more than a few paces without it. She would certainly have missed it long before she embarked in the lifeboat. Her impression, for what it was worth, was that she had left it in the boat."

"Well, what's the explanation?" Arnold asked.

"You may care to find one for yourself," Merrion replied. "Mine is this. Mrs. Stewart-Patterson had the stick when she reached the lifeboat. It was something of a job to get her into it, and other people had to hold her belongings. Whoever took the stick, hid it in the bushes a few yards from the boat.

"Next day, the five of us returned to look for it. We separated, and, the point I want to make quite clear, soon lost sight of one another. The hider of the stick retrieved it unobserved. You've seen it for yourself. A formidable weapon enough to knock a man out with, if wielded by a strong arm. And, on the other side of the island there is deep water close in shore and a strong current flowing seaward. When it had served its purpose, it was brought back and stuck in the ground."

"Why not have chucked it into the deep water you speak of?" Arnold asked.

Merrion smiled. "Mr. Grampound remarked to me later that if Mrs. Stewart-Patterson had dropped her stick into the water, getting in or out of the lifeboat, it wouldn't have floated. The water, though deep, is exceptionally clear. If the stick had been seen lying on the bottom of the far side of the island, where Mrs. Stewart-Patterson couldn't possibly have left it, suspicion might have been aroused."

"It boiled down to this," said Arnold. "You believe that Mr. Grampound murdered Mr. Wilberton and Mr. Bewdley?"

"I do," Merrion replied simply. "And I firmly believe that Mr. Grampound's true name is George Somerton, and that Mr. Wilberton was his uncle. The motive? That's up to you to establish. Mr. Wilberton was a rich man, with no children of his own. His only surviving relatives, with the exception of the unmentionable George, were his sister and Mr. Bewdley. The outcast may have felt pretty sore towards those who had abandoned him."

"It seems to me that I had better go and see Mrs. Somerton again," said Arnold.

"That is the last thing you should do," Merrion replied. "It seems practically certain from Mr. Bewdley's remark to me that your George Somerton is her son. She may or may not know anything of his recent history. Whether she does or not, her maternal instinct must be to shield him as far as possible. She is not in the least likely to be helpful to you. On the other hand, if she does know where he is, she may find means of warning him that the police are enquiring about him."

"There's something in that," Arnold agreed. "I suppose he'll have to come back to England some time. I'll get the Immigration people to watch out for him."

Merrion shook his head. "That won't do, either. He'll come back all right and, I expect, pretty soon. But not as Mr. Stephen Grampound. You know as well as I do that there is no insuperable difficulty in anyone having two passports in different names. But here's a suggestion for you. When he does come back, the first thing he'll want to know is whether any fuss is being made over the disappearance of Mr. Wilberton and Mr. Bewdley. Unless I'm very much mistaken, he'll go and see his mother. While I strongly advise you not to interview her yourself, there is no reason why you should not have a watch kept on the house."

CHAPTER XXI

NEXT DAY, Arnold came to see Merrion again. "It's about that shooting-stick," he said. "Our laboratory people have verified the fact that the blood upon it is human. And they find that the hairs are of two sorts, belonging to two different people."

"Very much what I should have expected," Merrion replied. "Mr. Wilberton and Mr. Bewdley. Well, the rest is up to you. I'm going home to-morrow, but if you should want me, I'll come up again at short notice."

Rather more than a week later Merrion received the summons he expected. He and Mavis were having tea at High Eldersham Hall, when Newport entered. "I beg your pardon, sir. There is a gentleman here in a car, and he would like to speak to you." Merrion got up, and as he left the room Newport whispered portentously, "It looks to me very like a police car."

It was, though the driver was not in uniform. "Mr.

Merrion ? " said the man seated in the back. " I don't expect
you remember me, sir. Detective-sergeant Wighton. Mr.
Arnold sent me. He would be very much obliged if you would
come back with me to the Yard at once."

" I'll just tell my wife I'm leaving," Merrion replied. " Then
I'll be with you."

During the drive to London they talked of many things.
The case in the course of which they had met, for instance.
But Arnold's reason for sending for him was not mentioned,
and Merrion asked no questions. In something under three
hours they reached Scotland Yard, and Merrion was shown into
Arnold's room.

" Good man ! " Arnold exclaimed. " I knew you'd come at
once. Sit down, light a cigarette, and listen.

" I took your tip and had the house in Birmingham watched,
14 Blundell Street. It belongs to Mr. Wilberton, and he lived
there with his sister, Mrs. Somerton. This morning a man
answering more or less to your description of Mr. Grampound
went there. A plain-clothes man, representing himself as an
inspector from the local authority followed him, and heard
him address Mrs. Somerton as ' Mother.'

" The plain-clothes man thereupon produced his police
card, and asked the man where he had come from. He replied
that he had flown overnight from Paris to London. This, by
the way, we verified easily enough, which is probably why he
made the statement. The plain-clothes man then asked him to
produce his passport. He did so, without hesitation. And,
would you believe it, the passport was in the name of George
Somerton ! "

Merrion laughed. " Clever of him. Since that was his name,
he was perfectly justified in holding such a passport. He
wouldn't guess that George Somerton had once again fallen
under suspicion. You didn't tell him, I hope ? "

" Not we," Arnold replied. " We do behave intelligently
sometimes, you know. The plain-clothes man told him that
he must accompany him to London, in connection with certain
enquiries which were being made concerning the conveyance
of sterling currency into France. He raised no objection, and
he's here."

" Not too bad," said Merrion. " Of that crime at least he
probably knows himself to be innocent."

Arnold nodded. " He didn't seem in any way perturbed. We've finger-printed him of course, and compared them with the set in our records. The experts say they are those of George Somerton of long ago. So there's no doubt about that side of his identity. The question remains, is he your Mr. Grampound ? He wasn't wearing those tinted glasses you told me about."

" Obviously not," Merrion replied. " They were a characteristic of Stephen Grampound, not of George Somerton."

" Well, we shall see," said Arnold. " This is what I've done. I've arranged an identity parade for eleven o'clock to-morrow morning, and I'm going to ask you to attend it. You'll meet some of your friends again, for we've got to be quite certain in a matter like this. We can't get hold of Captain Larsen, for the *Ballerina* is in Oslo. Anyway, he'd only tell us he couldn't say. Mrs. Stewart-Patterson is in Edinburgh, and Miss Cassidy in County Wexford, it's hardly worth while sending for them. But Mrs. Lavenham and Mr. Pulham have promised to come. Three of you ought to be enough."

" A very pleasant party it will be," Merrion remarked. " Anything else to tell me ? "

" Yes," Arnold replied. " We've had time to make a few discreet enquiries. Mr. Wilberton made a will, early this year, when he retired from business. In it he left all he possessed to his sister, Mrs. Somerton, or, failing her, to his nephew, Horace Bewdley. Mr. Bewdley has made no will, or, if he has, it hasn't been found yet."

" If he hasn't, his property will presumably pass to his aunt," said Merrion. " George Somerton would only have to wait for his mother's death to become a very rich man. Meanwhile, she would no doubt share her inheritance with her son. If she didn't—well, I daresay he would find ways and means."

They talked for a little while longer, then went out to dinner together.

Next morning, Merrion was at Scotland Yard well before the appointed time, and was taken to Arnold's room. He had not been there very long when Mr. Pulham was shown in. " Well, I declare ! " he exclaimed. " Fancy meeting you here, of all places, Mr. Merrion. I haven't been invited to identify you, surely ? "

Merrion thought that not very likely. A minute or two later Mrs. Lavenham appeared, charming as ever. " Hullo ! " she exclaimed. " Am I dreaming, or are we back again on board the *Ballerina* ? You can't know how pleased I am to see you again. Have you brought your wife with you, Mr. Merrion? No ? Oh, I am sorry. I should have loved to meet her. But I was asked to come here to identify somebody. Whom am I expected to identify ? "

" I'd rather not tell you that, Mrs. Lavenham," Arnold replied. " Now that you're all here, I'm going to ask the three of you to come with me ! He led them to a room on the ground floor with a wide window looking out on to a courtyard. In the window, which was glazed with that type of glass which can only be seen through in one direction, was a row of chairs. Arnold seated his visitors there. " In a few minutes, eleven men will walk round that courtyard," he said. " I want you to look at them very carefully. If you recognise any of them, say so and point him out, but do not mention his name till I ask you." They waited expectantly. Punctually, as Big Ben struck eleven, a gate opened, and a file of men entered the courtyard. The leader, who was none other than Wighton, set a course round the edge of the courtyard first away from the window, then reaching the corner, along the wall opposite. As the fifth man turned the corner, Merrion recognised him at once. So apparently did Mrs. Lavenham. " Why, look there ! " she exclaimed. " That fifth man. If he isn't——"

Arnold laid a hand on her arm. " Remember the rules of the game, Mrs. Lavenham," he asid.

" Oh, I'm so sorry," she replied contritely. " But I'm quite sure I know who that is."

" I think I do too," said Mr. Pulham. " But I'm very short-sighted. At that distance I can't be sure."

" They'll pass close by the window in a moment," said Arnold. The file reached the second corner, and turned towards the window, giving the observers a full-face view. Mrs. Lavenham could not restrain herself. " It is, of course it is. I knew it was. Even without the glasses——. Oh, oughtn't I to have said that ? "

At the third corner they turned again, to pass within three or four feet of the window. Mr. Pulham had no further doubt. " That one," he said pointing. " One, two, three, four, five.

I recognise that man. I could swear to him, though I never got to know him really well."

The men filed out through the gateway by which they had entered.

" Now, Mrs. Lavenham," said Arnold.

" The fifth man," she replied. " He's Mr. Grampound, who joined the *Ballerina* at Limassol and missed the ship at Algiers. This is thrilling ! Are you going to show us the rest of the passengers ? "

" I'm afraid not," Arnold replied. " What do you say Mr. Pulham ? "

" I agree with Mrs. Lavenham," Mr. Pulham replied. " Mr. Grampound, without a doubt. A most reserved person. I was never able to make out what his business could be."

" And you, Mr. Merrion ? " Arnold asked.

" The fifth man I knew as Mr. Grampound on board the *Ballerina*," Merrion replied simply.

" Thank you," said Arnold. " I am very obliged to you all for the trouble you have taken in coming here. Your verdict is unanimous. Would you mind staying here for a moment, Mr. Merrion, while I show Mrs. Lavenham and Mr. Pulham the way out ? "

He shepherded the two from the room and after an interval returned. " Mrs. Lavenham is very much annoyed with me for keeping you," he said. " She wanted to fix up a lunch party, the three of you. I told her that I was very sorry, but that I had important matters to discuss with you. So your guess was right."

" It was no more than a guess," Merrion replied modestly. " What happens next ? "

" We go to my room, and Somerton will be brought there," said Arnold. " You'll be glad of a conversation with an old acquaintance, I daresay. But remember this. Although you people could see him, he couldn't see you. He must have guessed he was appearing in an identity parade, but he can have had no idea who was watching him."

They went up to Arnold's room. It was a gloomy day, but the room was well lighted. Arnold arranged one of the lamps so that its beams fell full upon Merrion. " Now we shall see," he said. " I'll leave the conversation mostly to you, to begin with, at all events."

A minute or two later Somerton was brought in. He looked about him, and started violently as his eyes fell upon Merrion. He recovered himself instantly, and sat down in the chair to which Arnold pointed.

"Good morning, Mr. Grampound," said Merrion. "This is rather an unexpected meeting, isn't it?"

"What's that?" Somerton replied. "That's not my name."

"Not now, I daresay," Merrion agreed suavely. "But it was when we had that pleasant trip together on the *Ballerina*. So short a time ago that you can't have forgotten it, surely?"

Somerton remained silent. "You see, Mr. Somerton," said Arnold. "You have laid yourself open to a charge of travelling under a false passport. It is my duty to caution you that anything you say now may subsequently be used in evidence. You understand that?"

Still Somerton said nothing. "Come now, Mr. Grampound, or Somerton if you prefer it. You may just as well tell us the truth. Shall we run through some points in your recent history, with which Mr. Arnold is acquainted?" Merrion asked.

"You can run through what you like," Somerton growled "I'm not particularly interested."

"No?" Merrion replied. "Then let's see if we can't interest you. We'll begin with the middle of last month. Your family, with the exception of your mother, had cast you off. Unknown to her brother and her nephew, she remained in communication with you. You learnt that Mr. Wilberton and Mr. Bewdley had arranged to go for a cruise in the *Ballerina*. You applied to the London agents, and secured a passage on the ship from Cyprus to England.

"In the absence from the country of your uncle and cousin, you saw an opportunity. That of revenging yourself upon the man who, from your point of view, had wrecked your life. You procured, how hardly matters, a sheet of the business-letter paper of Podmores, Ltd., of Manchester. On this you typed a letter, which you signed 'A. W. Podmore,' expressing a wish to view Cherry Trees, Lingmarsh, which you knew to be remotely situated. You wrote a second letter, addressing it from your uncle's house, and signing it with his name, announcing your intention of visiting Hembury. These letters you posted simultaneously."

Somerton's normally pale complexion had become livid, but he spoke no word. Merrion went on. " On the day and at the time appointed, Mr. Rufus Jones met you at Baleminster station and drove you in his car to Cherry Trees. On this occasion you had assumed little or no disguise. The risk of Mr. Jones recognising you after all these years was negligible. But, while in the car, you took the precaution of sitting not beside him, but behind him, to give him as little opportunity as possible of studying your features.

" Arrived at Cherry Trees, Mr. Jones showed you over the premises. He preceded you into the bungalow, and into the inner room. The light there was dim, and he had no warning of what you were about to do. You sprang upon him from behind and clasped your fingers round his throat. Taken utterly unawares, he had no opportunity of defending himself. In a matter of a few seconds, he fell senseless at your feet. Kneeling upon him, you continued the pressure until life was extinct."

Merrion's matter-of-fact tone was that of one telling an old story, its details familiar to his audience. It gave the impression that he must have been an eye-witness of the event he described. Somerton stared at him in speechless horror, but, barely glancing at him, Merrion went on. " Your plan from the first was to exhibit a false motive. You rifled your victim's pockets, including the letter you had written in the name of Podmore, which Jones had brought with him. You locked the bungalow, and placed the keys where they were not likely to be found immediately. Then you drove Mr. Jones's car into the gravel-pit on Potash Farm. Having done so, you proceeded to fabricate evidence as to the time of death. You set the clock on the dashboard to a few minutes to six, and broke the glass, taking care that a fragment of it should jam the hands at that time. But this alone might have aroused suspicion. So you wrecked the front part of the car as thoroughly as you could.

" You then walked on to where the lane ends, and at the stop a little distance away caught a bus to Baleminster. Your first act on arrival was to send a telegram to Mr. Jones's office. It was a clever telegram in one sense, for it contained a reference to Mr. Wilberton's intended visit, of which few people outside the office were likely to be aware. But you used rather a peculiar phrase. It was the repetition of that phrase on another occasion which connected Mr. Grampound with Jones's murder.

" No doubt you took steps to provide yourself with an alibi covering the time at which you had set the clock. But your business at Hembury was not finished. There was that matter of flying to Cyprus to join the *Ballerina*. Would it be safe for you to show up at the airport? That depended upon what, if anything was known of Jones's murderer. You had already decided to go once more to Hembury and find out.

" This time you assumed a disguise, if such it may be called. A few extra layers of clothing and a little padding would simulate Mr. Wilberton's bulk. The loud hectoring voice and the heavy walking-stick would do the rest. In the absence of your cousin nobody in Hembury knew Mr. Wilberton by sight. Having met your uncle, I am bound to admit that your impersonation of him was masterly.

" Your visit to Hembury fully reassured you. It was obvious that nobody there knew that Mr. Jones was dead. When you demanded why he was not at the office to meet you, you were told that he unfortunately had been prevented from being there that day. That was all the information you required.

" So you had nothing to fear. You presented yourself at the airport, with a passport in the name of Stephen Grampound. A false name was necessary, for to board the *Ballerina* as George Somerton would have been to reveal your identity to your uncle and cousin. You allowed it to be inferred that you were on a confidential mission of some kind. To add colour to this you bought newspapers at every port of call, and marked them. Meanwhile, you kept out of everybody's way as much as possible. You did not board the *Ballerina* until an hour or two before she left Limassol.

" From that time you kept yourself very much to yourself, but all the time were watching and waiting for the opportunity to put your plan into operation. It came when we were lying in the port of Fetiyeh. You saw how the picnics so providentially organised by the chief could be turned to your advantage. On the occasion of the first, you reconnoitered the island thoroughly. You may remember that I came upon you sitting on the edge of it absent-mindedly throwing twigs into the water. Your absence of mind was a mask, hiding your wish to discover the set of the current.

" On Saturday the picnic was repeated. When it was time to return to the ship, you took Mrs. Stewart-Patterson's shooting-stick from her while she was being helped into the lifeboat. This you hid among the bushes fringing the shores of the cove. And on Sunday, it was you who suggested that the five men of the party should land once more on the island to look for it.

" On the island we separated, and you slipped back to fetch the stick. Possessed of this effective weapon, you followed your uncle to the further side of the island. Stealing quietly through the brushwood, you came upon him and struck him down while his back was turned. To push his senseless body over the edge of the cliff into deep water was simple. You then tracked your cousin, who you knew could not be far away, and repeated the process with him. The bodies you knew would be carried out to sea, possibly to be devoured by those very sharks concerning which you were so careful to warn me.

" The next move was to clean the shooting-stick as carefully as you could, to return across the island, and to plant the stick in the ground on a conspicuous mound. You hoped it would be found, and luck was with you, for Mr. Pulham did find it. That looked far better than finding it yourself.

" You, like the rest of us, had seen the coasting steamer, and heard Mr. Wilberton's frequently expressed wishes that he could get away from the *Ballerina*. This, as a theory to account for the disappearance of your uncle and cousin, was to be encouraged. But they could not have gone off on the steamer without their passports and money. It was by no means certain that they had taken these with them to the island. That night you searched their cabins until you found them. There can be very little doubt that you destroyed them without delay.

" For the rest, there is not much to say. Your leaving the ship at Algiers did not cause much surprise, for you had told Captain Larsen that if you were unable to return before he sailed, the French authorities would get you home. But it was careless of you to use the same phrase on your note to him as you had on the telegram to Mr. Jones's office."

Merrion came to an end, and glanced at Arnold. "Well, Mr. Somerton, you have been listening, I hope," said Arnold sternly. "Remember my caution. Have you anything to say?"

"I have nothing to say," Somerton replied, in a strained and broken voice. He seemed to have aged miraculously since he had entered the room, and his manner was now that of an old man.

"Very well," said Arnold. "You will be charged in the first place with procuring a passport under a false name." He signed to the attendant constable, who laid a hand on Somerton's shoulder. With difficulty the accused man rose to his feet. Even supported by the constable, he was hardly able to stagger to the door, which closed behind them.

Since in the absence of their bodies, Somerton could not be charged with the murder of his uncle and cousin, Arnold concentrated upon that of Rufus Jones. Wighton, whom he set to work exploring the underworlds of London and other big cities, discovered quite a lot about Somerton. Since his release from prison, many years before, he had drifted about among more or less shady circles, living by his wits and on a small allowance from his mother. He had appeared and disappeared mysteriously, keeping his own counsel.

Wighton's investigations took him to Manchester, and there by devious channels to the office of a man whose business was ostensibly that of a commission agent. This man, who had his own excellent reasons for keeping on good terms with the police, expressed his willingness to give any information he might require. Yes, he knew a man called George Somerton. Very cagey sort of chap. He had never been able to make him out.

"Well, he's got a charge of murder hanging over his head," said Wighton brutally. "Place called Hembury. What do you know about that?"

The man appeared profoundly shocked. "Murder? How dreadful! Do you know, Sergeant, in spite of his quietness and reserve, I always suspected that Somerton might be a dangerous character. But I know nothing about this murder, I assure you. Hembury, did you say?"

" Yes, Hembury," Wighton replied. " Come on, out with it ! "

" I am perfectly ready to tell the truth, Sergeant," the man said virtuously. " I acted in all innocence, of course. I only did it to oblige him. One day about the middle of last month, Somerton came to me in this office. He had with him a sheet of commercial letter paper, with the heading of a firm in the town here, and another plain sheet, on which he had drafted a letter in pencil. He asked me to type the letter on the headed sheet.

" I told him that I couldn't do it there and then, as I was expecting an important client, and that if he'd come back in an hour or so, I would have it ready for him. When he came back, I gave him the letter I had typed and his pencilled draft. But, unknown to him, I had taken a carbon copy. You see, the request was so unusual that I thought it best to keep a copy of the letter, in case enquiries should be made."

Wighton laughed scornfully. " What you mean is that your copy might come in useful as a means of blackmailing Somerton. You've still got it, I suppose ? Let me see it."

The man went to a steel cabinet, unlocked it, and after some seconds, produced a sheet of flimsy paper. It was a carbon copy of a letter, dated 14th September, and addressed to ' H. Jones and Son, Estate Agents, Hembury.' In it, the correspondent expressed his intention of arriving at Baleminster by the 11.10 train on the 14th.

" I'll take this," said Wighton shortly. " I'd recommend you to stick to your story in the witness-box."

Wighton made another discovery, not so important, but none the less significant, this time in London. Just after opening time on the evening of the 16th, Somerton had entered a public house in the East End, where he was well-known. He had stayed there until late, drinking with his friends, whose favourite resort it was. There could be no doubt about the date, for there had been a noisy discussion of the subject. Somerton had maintained that it was the 17th, and had refused to be convinced otherwise. At last, to end the wrangle, the landlord had told him that he'd better step outside and buy an evening paper. He had done so, and returned to admit his error with a very bad grace. He didn't want the adjectival paper. The landlord had better shove it on the shelf behind the bottles. He might want it some day. To humour him, the landlord had done so, and there it had remained.

Arnold laughed when Wighton told him of this. " Merrion said he was pretty sure he'd have an alibi for the time the clock was stopped at. He's a clever rogue, but I think we've got him now."

The trial of George Somerton took place at the Old Bailey. Counsel for the defence did not put his client into the witness-box, thereby saving him from cross-examination as to his actions and whereabouts on the day in question. The evidence against him was purely circumstantial, but it was ably presented. The prosecution suffered from the disadvantage of being unable to allege the motive for the murder. They could not do so without revealing the prisoner's criminal record. In his summing up, the judge impressed upon the jury that they must not allow themselves to be influenced by the fact that no motive had been alleged.

The jury retired, and were absent for some considerable time before they returned. The foreman announced that they unanimously found the prisoner guilty. The judge assumed the black cap, and pronounced sentence of death.

Somerton was completely broken by his awful experience. That very evening he asked for pen and paper, and wrote out a full confession, not only of the murder of Rufus Jones, but of his uncle and cousin as well. In all three cases, his description of events followed Merrion's almost exactly. He resigned himself to paying the full penalty of his crimes.

Superintendent Kingston made a handsome apology to Tom and Betty White. " You can't help knowing what I thought," he said. " Well, I was wrong, and I'm glad to be the first to admit it. I won't attempt to make excuses. You won't bear me any resentment, I hope ? "

They both assured him they would not, and they kept their promise. Not very long after the trial, they gave up their rather poky little flat, and bought The Chestnuts from Mr. Houghley, as more befitting the head of the firm of H. Jones and Son. There Kingston became their frequent visitor. In view of Rufus Jones's intestacy, Number 12 King Street became Tom's property. Mrs. Paston was pensioned off. Mr. Draycott never tired of repeating his account of the gruesome discovery at Cherry Trees, which remained unsold and empty.

Some of the members of the *Ballerina* party remained in touch for a while. Mrs. Stewart-Patterson distributed some of the sketches she had made during the voyage. It was a happy thought of hers to send the Merrions a study of Picnic Island. Mr. Pulham received a view of the old town of Famagusta, and returned the compliment by sending Mrs. Stewart-Patterson a photograph of himself. Mrs. Lavenham was favoured with a sketch of the domes and minarets of Istambul.

Mavis and Mrs. Lavenham kept up a regular correspondence. In one of her letters, Mrs. Lavenham asked whether they couldn't meet again for another cruise next year. Merrion smiled when Mavis showed him the letter. "We're never likely to have another cruise with so sensational a sequel as the last one," he remarked.

THE END